Sort of Normal

Liz Ashlee

Sort of Normal
Copyright © 2019 Liz Ashlee
All rights reserved.

ISBN: (ebook): 978-1-949931-37-2
(print) 978-1-949931-38-9

Inkspell Publishing
207 Moonglow Circle #101
Murrells Inlet, SC 29576

Edited By Yezanira Venecia
Cover art By Najla Qamber

DEDICATION

For Chelsea—my personality twin, my concert counterpart, my gossip companion and my best friend.

LIZ ASHLEE

CHAPTER ONE

Carter

My pseudo-stalker has no concept of the no-shirt, no-shoes, no-service rule.

He grins at me, showing off his wolfishly sharp teeth, as he places a bottled water in front of me so I can ring it up. He produces a wallet and leans against the counter, waiting.

My eyebrows raise as I give a pointed look at the sign that says in *bold, capitalized, underlined* font, "No Shirt, No Shoes, No Service." The sign has progressed in stages from a small, barely-readable reminder on the front door to what feels like a gigantic billboard by the cash register. I'm not sure what else to do but put the phrase in skywriting.

And this customer, Boone Fell, probably has some ambition to star on the reality TV show *Naked and Afraid.* Thank God he hasn't gone so far as to ditch his pants.

Yet.

"I stop here durin' my run, Carter," he says in a thunderous southern drawl I know better than my own voice. "What—do you want me to dehydrate?"

I don't answer him, because what I have to say isn't exactly appropriate. *Yes, I do want you to dehydrate. Preferably in clothes.* Granted, it's not the worst thing I could say, but I know it's enough to make my boss angry. He's never liked me on account of a one-night stand he once had with my mama, which probably went well up until she stole his TV to sell. I'm surprised he even hired me, but from what I've heard, the manager doesn't bother going to him with potential new hires. It's really no use, given how many people start working here and then quit.

"You're getting so crafty with that sign, Carter," Boone says, getting closer to inspect it. "You know, if you end up going to college, you should give some serious thought to a degree in marketing."

I know he's mocking me, but his words still catch me off guard. Somehow, he knows I've been thinking about not going to college.

"C'mon," he says, reading my mind, "I listen to the things I hear about you. I pay attention. I've gotta if I'm gonna keep track of your schedule. You know how hard it is to schedule my daily runs around you?"

I picture my heart with a chain-link fence around it— also barbed wire and electricity—as I level my gaze with his. I've known Boone Fell since I was in diapers, back when I used to live beside him, our trailers practically twins. Growing up, he was sweet, and it felt like he would move heaven or hell for me. For the longest time, he was the only dependable person I knew and maybe even the only person who cared about me more than drugs, alcohol, sex, and all of the other vices known to man. It was easy to love him then. It didn't help that his dimples were disarming yet innocent, that his now short hair was shaggy—which always made his blue eyes play peekaboo—and that he was sort of awkward in a gangly, young boy sense. Now, he's a man who knows how to use those dimples to get what he wants—the same with those eyes—and he's muscular, tall, and moves like a predator stalking its prey.

The problem is, I've known this version of Boone for long enough to recognize I'm his repeat prey; it never fails once he catches me, and he sort of just leaves me dying out in the sun. For Boone, the game he plays with me has always been about the chase. I wish I would've realized that sooner when he had more of me to catch.

"It'll be ninety-nine cents," I tell him in a most even voice. Some days, like today, I just try to ignore him. Other days, I snap back. No matter what I do, though, it wears me out. *He* tires me out.

He digs through his wallet for change. Only Boone would (a) not have a credit card and (b) want to give me the exact change rather than a dollar bill like most people.

"You know, I was wearing shoes. I put them outside the front door, because of our little inside joke here. I was also wearing socks, but I thought, *what the hell*, and decided to make my feet naked—free."

He carefully sets out nine dimes and starts into the pennies, clacking each against the counter. I don't know if he intentionally tries to be annoying and loud, but he's a pro at it.

"It's not an inside joke, Boone. It's a rule."

"She speaks!" he says, looking up at me. "I love your voice and personality, Junebug."

"Boone ..." I bite down on the side of my tongue; I've already said too much. It barely takes anything to egg him on. He's like a toy that you can crank up but can't stop.

When he's finished with his pennies, I feel his gaze roam over me. I can't look at him. Instead, I mess with my ugly blue work shirt. Since he started coming in, I've started resenting this shirt. I've also started paying more attention to my hair and actually doing my makeup. I shouldn't care as much as I do.

"I'm sorry," he says. It might have a lot more power if it weren't the millionth time I've heard those words come from him. He's gotten awfully good at saying them. "I just want to see you and—"

The door jingles and one of the girls I went to school with walks in, looking as if she were disgusted to have to set foot inside of a gas station. Disgust was always her default, and I doubt things have changed in the year since we graduated high school. Her eyes, though, immediately light up when she sees Boone. I'm not sure why. I mean, Boone's attractive and can be sweet and funny when he wants, but I can count on one hand the number of girls I've seen Boone with. I guess he's just an enigma that everyone wants to make theirs.

The cynic in my head screams, "He's not worth it!" The romantic: "He's mine!"

"Hi, Boone," the girl says, wiggling her fingers. She's wearing a pair of yoga pants and a tank top with her black hair pulled back in a messy bun. Anywhere else she might look like she's ready to take a nap, but here she's runway ready.

"Uh, hi?" Boone says. He suddenly goes from playful and annoying to quiet and stoic. He straightens, reaching a full height well above mine, and doesn't bother turning around. "I'm almost done here."

"Oh, you're fine, I haven't gotten what I want yet," she says. I think her name is Lacey or Lara or something L-related. She was one of the popular people but not popular enough to remember. "I just wanted to say hi. Do you remember me? I'm Jenny. We had gym together."

Well, I was way off on that one.

Boone frowns and folds his wallet back up. "I'm sorry, that was a while ago, and my brain's fuzzy when it comes to high school. It's good seeing you, though."

He waves her off, and she walks away, ducking her head down low, her cheeks red.

"You could've been nicer. She was just saying hi," I say softly.

"Yeah, but I come here to talk to you. I even said it was good to see her—all gentleman-like." I start to say his name again, but he holds up a finger. "Please don't, Carter."

"Why?"

"Because I miss you, and I don't wanna hear how you feel about me. I don't need a reminder of how much I've fucked up. I just—" He shakes his head, and his smile starts to return. "I should go. I'm babbling, and it's probably a sure sign of heatstroke or something. Probably close to seein' mirages. I'll see you tomorrow."

"Wear a shirt," I tell him as he backs away.

"I'll wear a shirt when you stop caring."

That's the thing—I'll never stop caring, and he'll never wear a shirt, and this happens every day, and I don't think it's ever going to stop.

#

After my shift, I come home to find my half-sister, Kara, sitting at the kitchen table with her husband, Gabe. They're perfectly at ease in the relaxing, slightly-chaotic dining room Kara's filled with antique furniture and odd decorations. Whereas Kara is reading a book, Gabe has his head laying on the table while he's holding Kara's hand. The two of them are basically the perfect couple, proof soul-mates exist. Kara's been dating Gabe since high school, and when she decided to take custody of me, Gabe wanted to be a part of my life, too. Kara slipped right into the role of sister, mother, and friend, and Gabe into my brother, father, and friend.

Kara spots me first and puts her book down. "Hey, kiddo."

"Hey," I reply, setting my purse on the kitchen counter and then sitting down across from her. Gabe got called in for a shift he wasn't scheduled for this morning, so he looks half-asleep. It's a wonder he didn't go straight to bed.

"How was your day?" Kara asks.

"Uneventful," I say, even though talking to Boone Fell

is anything but boring. I haven't told them about his daily visits; they're not exactly Boone's number one fan. They used to like him, but then things happened, and I told Kara everything because that's what I do, and now they sort of hate him. "It was good, though. What about yours?"

"Same. I finished a copy-editing job, got paid, and now I'm trying to talk Gabe into taking us on a vacation." She's been working as a freelance editor since college because it's what she likes and what she's good at. I think she was surprised people liked her work enough to pay her for it, but Gabe and I never doubted she would be a success.

"You can break him," I tell her with a laugh. "You always do."

"Hey, my weakness for the two of you is a strength. Ask her where she wants to go," Gabe orders, barely lifting his head to give me a wry grin. He's the exact opposite of Boone—clean-cut, dark-haired, well-dressed, prompt. How is it Kara and I are related, but we have completely different tastes in men? Especially when I do not want to want Boone Fell.

"Where do you want to go?"

"I want to go to Alaska!" Kara cheers, holding up her novel. It's clearly a romance, with the man and the woman on the front dressed up like snow bunnies in, no doubt, Alaska.

"I thought you said you wanted to go on a *vacation*," I say. "As in beaches and sun and relaxation."

"They have all of that in Alaska … It's just colder. Besides, we live ten minutes away from a beach."

"Not a vacation beach," Gabe points out. "But if you want to, we can go to Alaska."

"No, I've been talked out of it already. I don't even like the cold. Or snow. Books just make me want to go places," she sighs and sets her face on her palm.

Kara is pretty in a way that puts her on an entirely different level than me. If I didn't inherit our dad's caterpillar eyebrows, I'd wonder if my mom lied to me about who my father was. Kara's long blonde hair is soft and straight without her ever even touching it, her skin is completely clear, and she's got eyes that always seem to be smiling. I'm a curly brunette who has to climb shelves to reach things and who has the definition of back-road curves. I guess while I've always loved her, I've also always resented her for being so perfect. Our dad isn't the best, but he gave her and her mom a foundation for an actual life. All he left my mom was some money for an abortion she didn't go through with because she knew she could get more by blackmailing him.

That worked until I was four, and Dad came clean with Kara's mom, Deirdre. Dad thought it meant he was done with me, but years later, Kara found out about me, got to know me, and adopted me. My mom didn't mind handing over custody, given she didn't have any interest in being a mom.

Suddenly, I have the urge to hug her. This wave of emotion always comes fast and unexpected because I'm just so … thankful for her. If it wasn't for Kara, I would never have escaped the lifestyle my mom and half-brother, Declan, had or the suffocating trailer we lived in. I also wouldn't have found out what a "home" is.

There's no avoiding the guilt of everything. At the end of the day, I escaped and Declan *didn't*. Kara gave him an opportunity to, and he didn't want it, so I left him. Maybe if I would've stayed or tried harder, he'd still be here. Alive.

"Is something wrong, Carter?" Kara asks softly.

Gabe immediately sits up, stands, and heads to the refrigerator. Before I can answer her, a spoon clanks to the table, followed by a pint of chocolate ice cream. I smile up at him feebly, knowing this is his way of showing he's here for me. When I first moved in with them, I always had trouble sleeping, so I would sneak downstairs. Somehow, Gabe would get up, too, and we'd end up eating ice-cream together. Sometimes we talked about why I was up;

sometimes we didn't.

"I'm just—" I look back down at the ice cream and run a finger around the rim. Tears flood my eyes, a natural disaster waiting to happen, as my chest tightens. "It's a year today."

Gabe pulls the chair up next to me and wraps an arm around me. He pulls my head against his chest and kisses it. Kara scoots closer to me and starts rubbing my arm and brushing away my tears.

"I know, sweetie," she whispers. "We didn't want to bring it up and upset you."

"I miss him," I say. My voice is tangled and hoarse against Gabe's chest.

"I know you do," Kara tells me, "because I miss him also, and I know it has to be worse for you. Declan loved you so much, Carter."

At the sound of his name, it becomes hard to breathe, especially hearing it from Kara. *Did I choose her over him?* The thought has ricocheted around in my mind since the day I told him I *wanted* to live with Kara. Up until that point, he thought I was going to live with her because I *had* to.

You're choosing to leave me? he'd asked with bleary eyes. I can remember looking around and seeing all the things I was leaving that weren't him. Like the kitchen we never cooked in but was a walkway many men took back to Tish's bedroom. Or the broken liquor bottles and bags with who knows what in them. Or the couch we slept on that was lumpy, ripped, and sometimes flea-infested. I wanted to leave all of that behind, not him. Maybe he couldn't see that since he was just as tattered and ruined as everything in that room.

Even though Declan wasn't Kara's biological brother, she always left one of the bedrooms empty for him to use. Her only rule was Declan couldn't do drugs while he stayed with us, and he could never do that, so he barely used the room. He mainly visited us in the space between his highs.

"W-Why did it ha-have to be ... why didn't h-he get—" I'm speaking nonsense. Questions I think about almost every night when I see him in my mind, lying on the floor of the trailer, lifeless.

Why did it have to be him?

Why wasn't it my mom? She was the bad mom—the bad person. She never even tried to love me or Declan or anyone other than herself.

Why didn't he ever get clean?

Why wasn't I enough of a reason?

"Shhh," Kara murmurs. "You're starting to panic. Breathe with Gabe."

I fight to align my breathing with Gabe's, listening carefully to his deep, exaggerated inhales and exhales. Eventually, even the pounding rhythm of my heartbeat slows to match his. I focus on the physical to drown out the emotional pain.

"I'm sorry," I say quietly.

"It's okay," Kara assures me.

"Yeah, kid," Gabe agrees.

"I got you all wet, though," I tell him.

He shrugs. "Worthwhile battle scars."

"Especially since they wash out," Kara jokes lightly. "Are you better now?"

"I am," I admit. "I think I needed that."

"It's good to cry sometimes. It's better than bottling everything up."

"I love you," I tell her.

"And we love you, too. Why don't you go up and take a bath or something? Gabe's going to go to bed, and I was thinking I could go get a pizza, and we could rent a movie?"

"Something funny?" I ask.

"Of course," she says.

"Sounds like a good plan," I say.

"What about the ice-cream?" Gabe asks.

"That comes *after* the pizza," Kara tells him. "You're a horrible influence."

"If that's the worst thing Gabe does as my guardian, then I think we'll be fine," I say with a laugh.

I leave them and head up to my room. Kara painted it a deep maroon because that was the color I told her was my favorite when I first moved in. One day I left a white, sanitized room and came home after school to a mature, maroon room with a black, glittery bedspread and a wall full of books. All of the furniture matched and was new, and it's still the most I've gotten to call mine. Before Kara, I never even had my own hairbrush, let alone room.

As I'm grabbing some pajamas, I notice something out on my window sill. My whole body freezes. I haven't seen a flower on there since I lived at the trailer. I know it has to be from *him*, but I don't know how it got there.

I slowly approach the flower, hoping the wind somehow managed to blow it up. But that couldn't have happened, because this is a perfectly intact yellow lily with a note tied to it.

Whenever he would do something wrong, I always half-expected to find a flower here, but I never did. I thought he forgot about our tradition. There were so many days I just wanted some sort of word from him, even if it wasn't an apology and instead just a simple "Hi," as he'd sometimes do. I never *ever* expected there to be a flower *today*.

I open my window and tentatively grab the flower, careful not to knock it over the edge. My fingers shake as I remove and open the note.

Dear Junebug,

Sometimes it's hard for me to say and do the serious stuff, especially when I'm saying it to you. Growing up how we did, you learned to shut down—not open up. I wanted today to be different because I know what today is, but I just didn't know how to. So, I'm trying to make up for it by writing this. I'm sorry and I'm sorry you lost him. I know today's hard for you. I know how much you must miss him. I miss him, too.

But I also miss you. A year ago today, I also lost you and that's the hardest anniversary I'll ever have to face. Losing the dead is one thing, but the living? I wish I could repair it all. I wish this was like a plumbing problem—something I can solve with a pipe or screw or Draino.

It's not. I know it shouldn't be. I just wish it was.

Yours,

Boone

CHAPTER TWO

Boone

Carter, 9
Boone, 12

I can hear Tish—Carter and Declan's mom—all the way over in my trailer. She's screaming and moaning her head off like she's some sort of sexbot, and I know Carter's in there, listening to it, all alone. I feel sick, and I'm not even there, and Tish ain't my mom. I can't imagine how Carter feels.

I saw Declan leaving earlier with the older guys we've been paling around with, and I wanted to go, too, but I knew my dad would be stumbling home drunk and would need help getting to bed. The last thing we need is another run-in with the cops, where he's howling in the front yard and cursing up a storm. Funny how we get in trouble for that, but the noise levels coming from Tish's are perfectly acceptable in the eyes of the law.

There have been a few cops parked in front of her house, and I doubt they've been there to write citations. No doubt she trades sex for a blind eye.

I push my English homework away because I wasn't planning on doing that anyway. It's time to save Carter.

13

One of the guys Declan left with told me we're too old to be hanging around with her, but I could give a damn. Even if she's still a kid, Carter's my best friend. Sometimes, I think she cares more about me than Declan does.

I'm halfway to her trailer when I notice our cop-calling neighbor's flower bed is freshly planted with flowers. I look around, checking for her, and sneak over. I pluck a wad of them and then head back into my trailer. I find twine to tie them with, then a piece of notebook paper.

"Pretty flowers for a pretty Junebug," I write on the paper. Carter likes this sort of thing—I realized that when I made her a birthday card because I couldn't afford to buy her one.

I walk back over to her trailer and set them on a small window sill. I see Carter inside, sitting on the couch she sleeps on, with her knees pulled up to her chest, staring at her toes.

I knock on the window, but she doesn't hear me over Tish. I hate that woman. When Carter looks up, she immediately grins as though she were not existing in hell. She runs over to the window and opens it.

"Brought ya a present," I tell her with a grin.

"Flowers?" she asks, giggling. "From Miss Blanchard's yard?"

"Wrote you a note and everything."

She unfolds it, and her lips move as she reads it. When she looks at me, her eyes are wide, and she's in awe. For a second, I wonder if anyone's ever told her she's pretty. Someone has to have, right? I remember sweet-talking girls at her age and trying to get them to kiss me.

"Thank you, Boone," she says.

"You're welcome." All of a sudden, her mom's yelling gets exceptionally shrill. I'm not sure if she's having sex as much as she's getting murdered. "Say, why don't we go to the park or somethin'?"

Carter winces, looking in the direction of her mom's bedroom. Her eyebrows pull together, and she starts to nibble on her lip. "Declan told me I'm not supposed to leave the house."

Sometimes I hate Declan, too. Sure, he's a good friend to me, but he's not always a good brother to Carter. I can't believe he would leave her here in this situation.

"What? You don't trust me? I brought you flowers. Does Declan do that?"

She laughs and shakes her head. "He's my brother."

"So what am I that makes it okay?"

"A boy."

I'm not sure if it's because she just called me a boy or if it's because she's suddenly acting shy, but I feel my face heat.

"Then what do boys and girls do? They go out on dates. C'mon, Junebug, let's date."

#

My old man is sitting in front of our trailer in a battered lawn chair, reading his Bible. He's always been in this cycle where he's a God-fearing, sober man for a time, then a blasphemous drunk.

The religion was okay at first—it was nice to depend on. It gave me closure about my ma's death I'd never had because the Bible always knew the cure to the bad stuff. Heaven and angels and God's love and all of that. But every time he'd lose religion, find alcohol, lose alcohol, and find religion again, it seemed like he was more and more devout. Obsessed, even. Now he usually preaches about hell and how there's a special place for me in it. How sweet that the devil would specifically think of me.

As I walk toward him, I can't help but look over at Tish's trailer. She still lives there. Well, when she actually comes home, that is. The grass is all grown up, the siding is green, and the walls and roof are caving in. She's gotta be fucking area planning, 'cause there's no way in hell the place is within code.

I never thought the day would come when our trailer would look like something out of one of those home design catalogs. All we do is mow our grass.

"Son," my dad says, holding up his Bible, "I'd like for us to have a reading together tonight."

"Can't Dad—I've got to be up early tomorrow." Since

15

my dad's been collecting disability since he was in a—you guessed it—drunk driving accident, I've been the one working. I basically do odd jobs around town because they pay better than any other job I can find. Tomorrow morning, I'm doing some work on the local dentist's plumbing, and I want to get there early before they need running water. I like being able to make my own schedule, which gives me time to swing by to see Carter and take technical classes, so I know more about different repairs.

"All right," he says, but he's got the same look on his face he always gets when I refuse to drink or pray with him. It's a mixture of pissed off and resentful. His dry lips are in a tight line, a contrast against his scraggly gray beard. The scar beside his lips from the time he fell face-first against a metal trashcan, is quivering angrily. "Don stopped by. Needs rent."

Damn, if I don't want to slap my knee and start laughing. My dad has never cared about rent, and we both know Don would never tell Dad about it being due. Don knows to tell me because I'm the one who'll get the money together. My dad's not capable of dealing with money. If anything, he's about due to slip back into his ways, so this might just be him looking for money to buy alcohol.

"I'll take care of it," I lie. "You just keep reading that."

I sound like *I'm* the father here. I'm good at charming people, and I like to think it's my default, that I'm not faking it, but with my dad, it's as though the life'd been sucked out of me.

"I really wish you'd read it with me," he says, as I walk past him and on into the trailer. "Your mother would love to hear from you."

I flinch at his words and the sound of the door crashing closed. I hate when he says shit like that. He acts as though through God, he were able to speak to my mom. I never knew her, but if she's in heaven, I doubt she'd be okay with the beatings he used to give me or the quantity of alcohol he drinks. My dad's lying when he says he's speaking to her—he's just using it as an excuse to exorcise his demons so he can have room for more.

If he's taught me anything about love, it's that you can love hard and deep, but at the end of the day, you ruin the ones you love.

I don't know why I put that flower on Carter's windowsill. I just had all these damn thoughts swirling around my head, and I had to get them out somehow. Sure, playing dirty by doing something we used to do when we were kids. I just wanted her to actually hear me instead of the dumb-ass joker I always seem to slip into around her. This was the only way for that to happen.

It was damn hard getting the flower up to her, too. I had to act like some sort of a goddamn burglar, and I wouldn't have survived if I got caught. Thanks to the soured past between Carter and I, Kara hates me, and the last time I saw Gabe, he threatened to cut off my balls if I came near Carter again. He's a doctor, so I should believe him, but I'm an idiot, which explains why I didn't care.

I mean, if I were smart, I wouldn't have climbed a rotting trellis adorned with thorny weeds. It was scratchy and difficult, but it was worth getting the letter to her.

The only problem is that we have to go somewhere from here, and I have no idea where in hell that'll take us.

#

I finish up with the pipes in the dentist's office and check the time on my phone. Shit, if I don't get out of here soon, I'm going to miss seeing Carter. Visiting her has been a part of my routine, and I won't let today be any different, especially after giving her the note.

I wipe at my forehead with a towel and throw my tools into my toolbox haphazardly. I usually fit seeing her into my running schedule, but today I really am going to need water. It's hot as hell, and racing against the clock to replace these leaking pipes isn't helping. Doesn't help either that these damn things are so old that the rust is rusty. Note to self—don't rinse when it's my time in the chair. The water is not safe.

On my way out, I stop by the reception desk to pick up my check. It's one I've been looking forward to because these people (a) actually pay me and (b) pay me well.

I drive, probably breaking a dozen different laws, to the gas station Carter works at. If an officer were to pull me over and ask me why I'm speeding, I doubt telling him I'm going to go see a girl would get me very far.

Thankfully, I don't get pulled over, but I still don't make it there until ten minutes after her shift has ended. I throw my truck in park, pray to the tune of whatever my dad believes in, and jog inside. Maybe she'll be here. The person after her might be running late. She could just now be leaving. Maybe …

My whole body feels as though it had fallen ten feet under at the sight of a young guy sitting behind the cash register, fiddling with a rubber band. He looks up at me, annoyed. "You need help or something?" he asks.

"Yeah," I mutter and turn to leave. "I need a lot of help."

My dad has always said we Fells fit our last name because we've already fallen and are *still* falling. I remember coming home with a test I failed and needed to redo for extra credit, and he told me drunkenly, "Get used to it, kid. No matter how hard we try, we fail, and then we give up."

We give up.

I don't want to give up on Carter, but I'm worried I will. I have in the past just because of simple bumps in the road, and I was lucky enough to be able to repair it all. She's done letting me repair anything, and I'm not sure I'll have the willpower to keep trying. The other thing my dad has told me is that I'm destined to end up like him. He's told me Carter will leave me forever, I'll be a mess, I'll drink, I'll find God, I'll drink some more, find God, and so on, until I finally meet my maker. I might as well reserve a spot in hell now.

"Damn." I run my hand down my face. I've been at this all this time, and I can't give up on her now. I shouldn't be afraid of her leaving me or me pushing her away—all that's already happened. There's nowhere else to fall. I can only move up from here.

"I got your note."

I go completely still at the sound of her voice. It's always been husky with a bit of snark, something that's attracted me to her more than anything, but she's also got this sweetness mixed in with it all. She's always been an enigma to me—a new puzzle to solve every time I see her. When she was younger, I gravitated to her because I wanted to protect her, and when I got older, it was because she intrigued me. She's not like any other girl out there.

She arches one of her thick, brown eyebrows, which have the same expressiveness as a mouth. I can tell if she's smiling or frowning or mocking me based on their tilt. Below them, her green eyes are vibrant, emotions moving like trees in a storm. I shouldn't be afraid of a girl three years younger than me, a foot shorter than me, and whom I've always called my best friend—but I'm terrified of her. You know how they talk about butterflies and all that shit? Well, I've got a bunch of hornets slamming around in my stomach, buzzing and going mad.

Most guys I've known have tried to make it their personal mission to sleep with every pretty girl they pass. I've never been one to do that. I've dated here and there, but I don't have a track record on me. I've seen my dad come off of too many alcohol-fueled one-night stands to know fucking doesn't fix anything.

I wrestle with all the self-control I've got and smirk at her. It's too damn hard for me to be serious around her, because if I am, then I worry I'll spill my guts. I want to tell her everything and purge my soul and *fight* for her. *She* is my version of going to church.

"Never climbed an ivory tower for a pretty girl before," I tell her. "Guess that makes you special."

She stares at me, her red lips pressed into a thin line. She's leaning against her blue VW bug, and I don't know how I missed her when I went running in. I probably looked panicked and out of my mind.

The bug used to be in a neighbor's yard, and Carter always loved it. I bought it for her when she was fourteen for five hundred dollars. It took me years to save up the money while paying bills. Lord knows how many lawns I mowed, how much golf equipment I caddied for rich people, or the amount of food I made at hamburger joints—all the odd jobs in between. Feeling bone-tired and broke was worth getting to see the smile on her face when I delivered the car. I've never felt higher. We started working on it together, and Gabe would help out, too. I guess they finished it without me.

All that work and I can't help thinking my dad was right—maybe I'll just end up alone. Maybe I'm not meant to love or be loved. She pushes off the car and walks around to the driver door. "You should know you can't miss something you never wanted."

"Carter I—" *I've always wanted you.*

The words don't come out becomes she's already in her car and high tailing it out of here.

I stare at the place where she had been standing and try to figure out what just happened. Then all of a sudden it clicks: she waited for me. She knew I'd be by, and she hung out until I got here. She might've been proving a point, but it's the first time she's gone out of her way to do anything involving me for a long time.

She waited *for me.*

#

Carter, 10
Boone, 13

20

There's a stupid stuffed pig I can't seem to win, no matter how hard I try. I can't even try to say the cups are glued or something because I'm missing by a mile. Total user error. I even managed to hit the guy manning the stall.

Carter's eyes lit up when she saw the pig—she's going through a phase, which is weird since most girls are into penguins and cats. I promised her I'd win it, but I lost all my money, and the stupid pig is still hanging from the top of the tent, mocking me.

"Dude, you're taking this breakup harder than I expected. So what if she's dating Brad Sanders? He's a hack," Declan mutters beside me. We're hidden under an alcove while Carter uses the restroom, and Declan's taking the opportunity to smoke some weed.

I didn't even realize my ex-girlfriend, Hailey Harnett, is with Brad—at the stall we were just at—who's trying to win her something. She's clapping and cheering and holding onto him as she was doing with me at school a week ago. We dated for a month. She was my first, and now we're done. The way Declan talks about dating girls makes it sound as though it were the secret key to life— well, other than pot.

It's sad when you're more excited to go broke winning a carnival game for a ten-year-old than you are about girls.

"Yeah, shit, man, I am. That was love. Serious love," I say, cupping my hand over my heart. He nods, obviously serious. In his state, I guess he doesn't understand sarcasm. Truth is, the only person I've ever loved and want to let myself love is Carter. She deserves someone to love her like a brother, a warrior, a best friend, a companion, and I can do that better than anyone else I know. Other than her, there aren't many other people in my life worth loving. Besides, I'm worried that if I do end up falling in-love with someone, I'll end up like my dad—wrecked and alone.

"Well, here, this'll help." He passes me his joint, and I take it. I've gotten high before, but I've always tried to stay sober around Carter. I see the way she looks at Declan when he's going all space cadet on us. It disappoints her. But right now, I'm high-strung and grumpy, and there's no way she's having a good time. This was supposed to be a treat for her—her first county fair ever.

It pisses me off this should even be considered a treat. She deserves better than this.

"Sure," I say and take a hit.

Everything shifts toward relaxation, like my body's liquid, floating on a cloud. It allows me to feel mellow for the first time all night. Normally, I've got happy on tap, but I'm having a hard time pretending today.

It's probably a mixture of not winning the pig and the fact that Carter still stood up on her tip-toes and hugged me anyway, as if I did win it. Then there's also the fact my dad's been nowhere to be found for the last few days and isn't even at any of his local haunts. I know he'll show up eventually—he always does—but I'm worried one of these days someone's going to take notice I'm living alone. The last thing I want is Child Protective Services getting involved.

Something tickles my hand, and I laugh.

"Boone?" Carter asks, lacing her fingers through mine. She always holds my hand when we're out in public since Declan refuses to hold hers. He thinks it's weird. I don't mind because I'm terrified I'll lose her, even if she's old enough to keep up. We once lost her in the middle of the mall, and I had nightmares about it for months. We ended up finding her in the middle of a clothes rack, but the whole thing scarred me. I'll never forget the sweaty palms, the racing heart, the fear that I'd lost the one person who mattered most to me.

She gives me a weird look as I shove the joint back at Declan. She drops her hand from mine and looks away, wrapping her arms around her middle. It's the same look she always gives Declan whenever he's this way. Her eyebrows are pulled close together, and her lips are pursed, which makes her look more like an adult than a kid. She's disappointed in me, and I'll probably feel like shit about it later, but right now I'm too high to care.

"How 'bout we go ride that?" Declan asks, pointing in the direction of a spaceship-looking ride. "You'll like it, Carter. The momentum pushes you up the wall. Spins really fast."

Carter shrugs like she doesn't care, but she still eyes the ride warily as we get in line.

Declan smacks my arm, and I glare at him. He's motioning toward Hailey, who's in front of us, without Brad, and is giving me a *lonely look. "I can take care of Carter. She's grown, anyway," he tells me. "Stop starin' at Hailey and go talk to her."*

He shoves me forward, and I stumble away from Carter and Declan. I glance back at them and see Declan is trying to talk to Carter while she's just staring at her shoes. I'm really going to regret this later.

"Hey, Boone," Hailey giggles.

"Hi, Hailey."

"You know, Brad thinks you're jealous because you've been staring at us."

I was looking at the damn pig. "Brad's a hack," I say, repeating Declan's words.

She giggles again, and I immediately remember why our great love didn't last. That laugh of hers is too much. She's all around too much. Brad should be jealous of me, since I'm single.

"Where is he?" I ask.

"He doesn't like the rides that spin. It's okay. I have you."

The doors open up, letting people leave and more go in. I follow behind Hailey up the stairs and into the ride. Once we're leaning against the wall, I look for Carter and Declan. They're almost directly across from me, and Carter doesn't look happy at all.

I don't know if it's the pot or maybe I already feel guilty, but I think I'm going to be sick. The lights go out except for the DJ's booth, like this is a club, not a carnival ride. Hailey gropes my hand, and before I can try to get off of the ride, it starts spinning.

Across the ride, I hear Declan cackling like an idiot and cursing like a sailor. Beside me, Hailey is screaming and giggling, grabbing at my hand. Then, all of a sudden, it's as though my ears hone in on Carter, because I hear her shriek and then start crying. She made that same noise when she broke her arm a few years ago.

"Stop the ride!" I yell.

No one hears me, and it's as though I were living in purgatory as the momentum pushes me up the wall. I'm definitely going to be sick. This isn't as when I've gotten high before—it's not taking the edge off. It's making everything worse. I should be over there with Carter because Declan can't take care of her. It's not that he doesn't know how to; it's just he can't.

When the ride stops, my heart is pounding in my ears, and all my meals from the last decade force their way up. I push it all down and stumble blindly toward the direction Carter was in. I can still hear her crying, saying Declan's name and mine.

Then the lights come on, and I realize why she's hysterical.

There's a clump of her hair stuck in the slat from where the board moved up the wall and blood is dripping down her forehead.

Declan stands beside her, staring dumbly, as I put my hand on the gaping cut on her head to stop the bleeding. She winces, but I press harder.

My dad falls a lot and hits his head, and the doctors always tell me head wounds bleed a lot. You'd have thought that would've prepared me for this, but it didn't. I'm scared out of my mind.

How can I be her protector or her brother if I can barely keep something like this from happening? She was my responsibility tonight because Declan wasn't—is never—equipped to take care of her the way I can. But what if I can't? What if I'm just meant to be my dad—empty and exhausted and alone?

But the thing is, Carter is the one pure, untainted thing in my life, and I can't let her go. I just have to be better—work to be as good as she is.

CHAPTER THREE

Carter

I grip the steering wheel, begging my lungs to start working regularly again as I drive. I have no idea why I just did that.

I must be losing my mind. I have to be. Boone Fell has broken my heart numerous times. He doesn't even deserve a millisecond of my time, and I just gave it to him like it was nothing!

During my shift today, I kept looking for him. I *wanted* him to come. I was up all last night preparing what I would say when I saw him.

You should know you can't miss something you never wanted.

Then he didn't show up, and I was actually disappointed. For two reasons: one, because I wanted to say that and, two, because he wasn't showing up. *Again.* Since I was about fifteen, he's always had this pattern where he's there for me or does something spectacular and then disappears. Every single time, I let it destroy me. I go through phases of wondering what's wrong with me and what's wrong with him, of hating him and blaming him, wanting to talk to him and fix him, and finally, wanting to give up, put a shield up around my heart where Boone is involved, and move on.

I'm basically a hamster on a wheel, and I can't escape.

Even while I was waiting, I never expected him to show up. More than that, I didn't expect him to look wild—so much so that he didn't even notice me. It was like he had one goal in mind, which was finding me. In fact, seeing him like that put me in a phase where I wanted to talk to him and fix him, so my only defense was to deliver my line and leave.

I have no idea where I'm driving to, until I turn into the cemetery, heading straight for Declan's grave. When I get to the area where he's buried, I pull off to the side of the one-lane road. I send a quick text to Kara, letting her know I'm visiting Declan.

My heart drops when I see her response.

Kara: *Okay. Take your time. Tell him hi. Don't forget Dad and my mom are coming over for dinner.*

Dad and Kara's mom, Deirdre, come over on the first Tuesday of every month. After Kara adopted me, she stopped talking to her family, other than to send my dad bills. Deirdre eventually reached out, and the Tuesday dinners were established. I don't think anyone likes them, but we suffer through them anyway.

I reply I'll be home soon, then walk down a line of graves to Declan's. The funeral home he's in doesn't allow anything except for flat-to-the-ground grave markers. In a way, this made my selection easier. Other than his name, date of birth and death, there wasn't anything else I would want to put on it. No activity emblems or favorite lyrics or memorable sayings.

When we were younger, Declan liked a lot of things, but eventually he only wanted, needed, and lived for one thing: drugs. Not exactly an appropriate hobby for a headstone.

I hated him for so long because of the drugs. I wanted him to love me with the same ferocity he craved them. I don't think that he had the capacity to, so instead, I loved him enough for the both of us.

"Hey," I say and check for goose poop before I sit down. I put my hand on his name. Every time I come to see him—which is about twice a week—I do this, and there's a little imprint of my hand now. "I'm not sure why I came here. I mean, normally I go to Kara ... but here's the deal: your best friend, Boone— he sucks. I really wish I knew what the deal is behind all of this. Is there a reason why he's in my life and we keep doing this? Or is it all just ... nothing?"

I go quiet for a second, waiting for a breeze or a bird or any type of sign from him—even something I can pretend is a sign—but there's nothing out of the ordinary.

I close my eyes, letting a breath out through my nose, feeling my emotions from yesterday bubble up. "But if I start talking about reasons and God's plan, then that means that it was in His plan for you to die. And you're your only reason, Declan. You and your stupid addiction. Why did watching Tish and all of her boyfriends waste their lives away keep me on the straight and narrow, but you ... you *left* me? You told me I left you, but you left me."

When I open my eyes and still feel nothing, I pull my hand away from the grave and drop it to my lap. "Why did you have to leave me?"

#

By the time I make it back home, my eyes are dry and my face is puffy. I meant to leave the cemetery sooner, but I ended up laying with Declan for the longest time—watching the clouds.

My dad and Deirdre's Porsche is in the driveway, parked where I normally park my bug. I sigh as I pull up to the curb across from the driveway and get out.

The house is completely silent, other than the sound of

bluegrass music playing in the kitchen. Kara's not particularly fond of it, but she always plays it when Dad comes over because he *hates* it.

"Great, you're home," Gabe says, making me jump. "Whoops, sorry to scare you."

I turn to face him. He's standing beside the door in a nice button-down shirt and khakis, a beer in his hand. His hair is wild because he tends to run his hand through it when he gets nervous.

I stand on my toes and reach out to fix it. "I'm sorry I'm late."

He shrugs. "I can't blame you when I wish I was."

"Is it that bad?" I fall back on my heels.

"It's just quiet as all-get-out. These people can say whole sentences without moving their mouths. I'll never get over how easily Kara assimilates."

I can't help but agree. My fun-loving, happy-go-lucky sister becomes an angry, glaring, cat on the prowl around our father. "I'll go get changed."

"I'm going to pretend I'm still in the process of grabbing this," he says, motioning toward the beer.

He disappears back in the direction he appeared from, which is en route to the garage, where we keep the refrigerator with all of the beer. Gabe never drinks, except for these Tuesday nights.

I quickly head up to my room and change into something more fitting for dinner with my father and step-mother—a simple cream dress. I throw my tangled brown hair up into a mess of a bun, fix my eye makeup, and then make a face at myself because my eyebrows look exceptionally bushy.

However, on Tuesday nights, there's nothing better than that, because the man who cannot deny me (other than for the several years he actually did deny I was his daughter) has the same bushy brown eyebrows. His genetics were kind enough to bestow upon me such a *lovely* feature that no amount of waxing or plucking can fix.

I can't help myself from looking out at the windowsill. There's nothing. He got the message—well, the metaphorical one. I don't know why, but my heart stalls out for a second. I should be happy there's nothing. It means I won't have to deal with him trying to come back into my life anymore. But at the same time, I'm disappointed because I always hope he'll prove me wrong.

Downstairs, Kara is setting the table. She gives me a wide, almost manic, grin as she puts a bowl of salad down with a clank.

"Hey, Carter," she says.

I smile back, trying to be bright and happy. I like to think I'm doing it for Kara, but really, I want my dad to realize he's missing out on a great daughter. The plucky, sort of grumpy, quick-witted me isn't exactly the type of person you wish you had in your life. I'm sort of an acquired taste and, when you only see someone once a month, you're probably never going to get around to any sort of acquiring—so I pep myself up.

My dad—the devil himself—Ray Cash, is sitting at the head of the table where Gabe usually sits. He's in a suit and tie, looking more like he's at a mob-themed dinner party than a dinner with his daughters. His hair is slicked back to hide his bald spot, and he's wearing a gold watch, gold-chained necklace, and gold rings. I've always wondered what types of dealerships he owns—if he really *only* sells cars. I mean, if he's dealing drugs, then that would make sense how he met my mom.

Probably the second biggest hint Ray is my father (and that my mom didn't like me from the very beginning) is that she ran with Cash part, naming me June Carter—as in June Carter Cash, singer, songwriter, and wife to the Man in Black, Lukeny Cash. Only, thanks to my dad's request for "no scandal," I went by my mom's last name: Hart. So, instead of June Carter Cash, I'm June Carter Hart, which is weird.

It makes me feel like the knock off.

The consolation prize.

Deirdre doesn't look anything like a mob boss's wife. She's wearing a pale blue dress that makes her eyes seem extra bright and kind, and her hair is pulled back in a ponytail that's just as perky as Kara's. She's too good for my dad, especially since he's cheated on her at least once. Heck, even *Tish* was too good for him.

She stands up from her chair and walks toward me, her arms open. I'm not sure why she's always been so nice to me, other than the fact that I'm Kara's family. She should despise the product of her husband's affair.

"You look pretty, Carter," she says as she squeezes me tight. "Kara said you were visiting your brother. I thought about you yesterday with it being a year and all. How are you holding up?"

I stare at her, trying to reign in my emotions. I thought I was all out of them after visiting Declan, but I guess I was wrong.

My dad didn't come to the funeral because he was working, but Deirdre did. She and Gabe took turns holding the hand that Kara wasn't. The three of them stepped into the role Tish should've been in. Instead, she went off on a bender and didn't come back.

"I've been better, thank you," I tell her. For some reason, I don't see a flash of Declan as I usually do; instead, I see that stupid note from Boone.

"You poor thing," she says.

"Ice-cream makes it better," Gabe says, materializing in the kitchen. He kisses Kara on the cheek, which probably means he's been gone this entire time. Going to find a beer can be a very involved task when you're trying to avoid your in-laws.

"*After* dinner," Kara emphasizes.

Gabe only shrugs.

"You're a doctor, Gabe," she reminds him. "This stuff is supposed to be important to you."

Gabe shrugs again and takes a seat at the table as far

away from my father as possible. I sit down across from him, leaving the spot beside me for Kara. For the rest of the night, my dad probably won't acknowledge me, unless there's something he can criticize me over. As it is, he's staring down at his phone with those eyebrows drawn together.

Kara makes quick work of putting a plate full of pasta in front of each of us then sits down. We eat in silence until Deirdre sets her fork down and looks at me.

"Have you made a decision about school yet?" she asks.

She means it as a conversation starter, but she's unknowingly opening a can of worms. I glance helplessly at Kara, hoping she'll know what to say. She's staring right back at me, looking just as lost.

Kara's always been really supportive of me in everything I do, so when I told her I wanted to wait a year before starting college, she was okay with it. I don't want to waste valuable time and money when I have no idea what I want to do. I mean, I don't even know if I want to go to college. We were planning to just keep it to ourselves, because Dad is not going to be happy about this, but now we don't have a choice.

"Carter is going to take a semester or two off," Kara says slowly, turning her attention to Deirdre and *only* Deirdre. "She needs time to figure her future out."

"Figure her future out?" Dad's voice is eerily quiet at the other end of the table. Lethal. "I've been putting money away for her to attend college. *More* than enough. It's not there for her to waste."

"I'm not wasting it," I say automatically, heat rising in my cheeks. "I haven't even touched it."

Kara puts her hand on my knee and turns her gaze toward our dad. She's close to going into her mama-bear mode. "That money is in her savings account for her to do whatever she wants with, Dad. She can go to college or become a clown for all I care. It's there so she can be comfortable and follow her dreams."

There's something else, and it goes unsaid—how because of my dad, I wasn't comfortable for a long time, and I didn't even have dreams. But my dad doesn't care about any of it. He'll do anything to keep any subject about his illegitimate daughter quiet.

"She better not become a clown," he grumbles.

You don't want me following in your footsteps? My dad's the biggest fool I've ever met. He might be rich, but there's nothing else to him. That's his defining attribute, other than maybe his eyebrows.

Deirdre is red, clearly embarrassed about starting the squabble. Gabe takes a swig from his beer and points between Kara and me. "Sorry to tell you, Deirdre and Ray, but we're going to have to reschedule for next month. Thinking about vacationing in Alaska. Carter's going to learn to tame bears while we're there. Practice for the circus, you know?"

He winks at me, and I try to hold back a snort. Beside me, Kara doesn't even bother being subtle; she laughs.

#

"Well, that went smoothly," Kara says as she shuts the front door, not even bothering to wave to Dad and Deirdre as they drive away.

"Should I change the figurative sign to say, 'Zero Days Without Disaster'?" I ask.

"Of all the topics in the world that Mom could bring up, she went there—college. Not, "How's your summer going? Are you enjoying life post-graduation? Can you press the bread, please?"

"She did ask that last one. You just couldn't hear it over Dad demanding to see my bank statements."

She throws her hands up, momentarily speechless as she gears up to continue. "The nerve of that man. Giving you money is the *least* he could do."

"I know. Geez. It's not like he gave me life or

anything." I reach out and squeeze Kara's arm. "I don't need him. I never have. I have you and Gabe, and that's all I need."

"If it wasn't for him, you'd have had us sooner." She sighs and kisses my cheek. "Why don't you go upstairs? I'll clean—work off my aggravation. Where'd Gabe disappear to?"

"He went to Narnia to get another beer."

This time there's a note on the windowsill when I go upstairs. If there's ever a time when we'd all be distracted and not see him, it's when Dad's here. Still, it's weird to think while the mental chaos was happening downstairs, he was doing this. As if it were peace creeping around in a storm.

Dear Junebug,
I've always wanted you. I just didn't know how to have you.
Love,
Boone

CHAPTER FOUR

Boone

Carter, 11
Boone, 14
Declan, 14

"Dude, are you listening to me?" Declan asks. He's been going on about something or other for the past hour and is just noticing I'm not listening. He's been hitting the pot hard, even though we're watching Carter and are in public. I took a hit during the day, when we were skipping class, but I didn't want to go any further for fear Carter would run out in front of a car or something else equally terrifying—for instance, getting her hair ripped out of her head.

I promised her I'd take her to the park today since it's a nice day. I wanted the two of us to walk around and talk, but then Declan decided to come along, and now all he wants to do is sit on a bench. He's on his back, watching the clouds, and I'm busy watching Carter.

One of the kids she has class is on the playground, too. He and Carter are talking intently on the swings. I should be happy to see her this way, especially with someone her own age, but I'm also jealous. I like being the one to draw her out of the shell. But some kid being *able to do the same thing makes her feel less like my Carter and more like she's growing away from me.*

Carter glances up at me, and her grin widens. At least I can get a bigger smile out of her without even having to say anything. Ha, kid.

"Boone."

"What?" *I snap, looking over at Declan.*

"Are. You. Listening. To. Me?"

"No, I'm not."

"Stop staring at my little sister. That kid's not going to do anything to her when we're here. Hell, his mom's here, too. There's no such thing as game when your mom's around."

"How are you okay with this?"

He doesn't answer me.

"I'm going to go over."

"Fine. Whatever."

I roll my eyes and stand up. He's always at an extreme when it comes to Carter—either the best brother or the worst. Last week, he was out in their front yard trying to help her do cartwheels, and he couldn't seem to get enough of her, but now he can't be bothered.

The boy straightens when he sees me walking toward them, and I feel more like an adult than someone only a few years older. Carter claps as if me joining them was the greatest thing.

"Boone, this is Tyler," *she says.*

I don't say anything, and Tyler doesn't either. Clearly, neither of us is happy with the other one being here.

Carter lets out a breath through her front teeth. "Okay. Well, I was just telling Tyler about how I'm getting to meet my sister next week."

Ever since she got a letter in the mail addressed to her from a Kara Cash, Carter's been buzzing with excitement. I think it'll be good for her to have a female figure in her life, since Tish isn't all that great.

"Have you talked to her more?" *I ask.*

"On the phone," *she says.* "She's really nice, and she wants to take me out for ice-cream. I asked her if you could come, but she said maybe next time."

It makes me feel as though I had the whole world in my hands to hear her say she wanted me to come with her to meet Kara. Not Declan, and not this random dude, Tyler. Me.

"That sounds good with me. What sort of ice-cream are you gonna get?"

"I don't know. I like chocolate, but she said she likes hot fudge brownie sundaes. What do you like?"

"I like milkshakes," Tyler answers.

Clearly, she wasn't asking him because she waits for me expectantly. "I like chocolate, too."

Eventually, Tyler's mom calls him over, and he stares at Carter awkwardly before leaving. I can only hope I saved them both from him trying something.

Carter looks ahead at Declan, who's still lying back. I can hear him whistling a tune all the way over here. "I feel bad," she whispers.

"Why's that?"

"Because I'm afraid Declan's mad at me."

I turn to face her in the swing. I immediately reach out and pull her toward me by using the chain, then link my feet with hers. "What are you talkin' about?"

"I have a sister now, and I'm going to be spending time with her instead of Declan."

I rear back. She's worried about Declan's feelings when he can't be bothered right now? I shake my head and try to keep a handle on myself. She shouldn't feel this way about something good happening to her.

"Hey, don't think that way. Declan loves you, and he should be happy you're going to have another person in your life. What's makin' you think this?"

"He gets quiet when I talk about Kara."

"He shouldn't. He should be happy for you. Maybe he just wants a sister, too."

"He already has one," she reminds me in that dry way of hers.

I chuckle. "Okay, an older one then."

"I'll share Kara if he likes."

"You know it doesn't work that way."

"I wish it could. I don't know why I get Kara and he doesn't."

37

She licks her lips and swallows. "I'm worried about him, Boone."

I reach out and take her hands in mine. "You shouldn't be."

"He—he's like Mama. I know what you two do, and I know he does it without you," she whispers in a rush. "I wish you wouldn't."

"I—" I start to tell her I won't, but then I think about how good it feels to be high. It's not as good as when I'm with Carter, and it doesn't make me feel as light, but it's the closest thing I've got to it. I can't be with her twenty-four seven to take away everything that's bad, so sometimes I need to get high. With my dad always drunk, and the bills and the pressure to keep everything together—I need an outlet. "I'll try."

"Declan won't, because Mama doesn't."

"What about me? My dad doesn't try."

"Yeah, but you're strong. Declan ..." She trails off, and the faraway look in her eyes makes her look older than she is. The girl who was swinging on the swing set and laughing just a few minutes ago now looks like she's living a nightmare. "He's not."

#

One of my only friends who's always been on the straight and narrow, Jason Grant, meets up with me at the local bar in town. There's nowhere else for two guys to meet up and shoot the shit. If there were, we'd probably hightail it there. As the son of an alcoholic, I hate anything having to do with liquor. It's not the taste or the way it makes me feel—it's the look of it. I can picture my dad guzzling it all down, ramping up with each bottle or can. My stomach's in knots just thinking about it.

Jason's reason is he's got two younger kids, and he's trying to set a good example. I can get behind that. All it takes is one really bad experience to ruin a kid.

The waitress side-eyes us as she sets down our sodas. I take a long drink of it and let out an exaggerated sigh. "Damn, this is just what I needed."

Jason holds up his drink. "I know what you mean, man. I've been on edge all day waiting for this."

The waitress makes a noncommittal noise and scurries away. That'll teach her for judging us when we're just trying to do right.

"So, I've got a proposal," Jason begins.

I set my drink down and raise an eyebrow. "It's a little soon, isn't it? I mean, you haven't even seen me at my worst yet."

"Yeah, pretty sure I have." Jason was one of those kids most people ignored when we were in school. He was quiet and kept to himself—and was smart, too. I got to know him in shop class. By then, I'd realized I didn't want to stay on the same road to destruction as Declan. I was in dire need of a good influence. "I know you've been doing stuff around town for people, and I have, too. I was thinking that we should try our hand at it. We can split the jobs, get more customers, make more money."

"Here, you made it sound like you wanted to go to Vegas for a quickie." I let out a low whistle and lean back in my chair, crossing my arms. "How long have you been thinking about this?"

"A while now," he explains. "The wife just got promoted at work, and it leaves some wiggle room for me to make this happen. Plus, I can watch the kids more if I work for myself rather than a boss."

I mull it over for a second. I've thought about starting something up like this before, but it's a little stupid when you're your only employee and boss. It's just been easier to pretend I'm only doing side jobs and that this isn't my sole income. At least if I make a business out of it, I can start charging at a fixed rate and maybe won't get the sob stories, as the ones who claim they can't pay me, yet they've got a new car out in the drive.

I don't even need to think about it. "I'm in."

"Really?"

"I'm as serious as a stick of dynamite."

He taps the rim of his glass. "See, that means you could be pullin' my leg. It's hard to tell when you're really serious and when you're fake-serious."

"Didn't know that was a thing."

"With you, it is."

"Yeah, you've got me there." I think Carter's probably said something to me of the same effect. I'm just so goddamn persistent I tend to forget to take constructive criticism to heart.

Eventually, Jason and I come up with some semantics, moving on to our second sodas, which earns us another confused look from our waitress. That's not going to mean a big tip for her.

After a while, we talk about his wife and two daughters—who are cute, but handfuls, something he's not afraid to admit. He ends up telling me a story about finger painting with one of them, which puts a huge grin on his face. I mean, I don't really know much about fatherhood outside of what I've seen in movies and read in books. That doesn't mean I don't want it. No, I want the whole shebang—the kids, the wife, the home, everything. I want the ideal. I want to grin that big about finger painting.

"I've been talking to Carter," I blurt out.

His smile immediately disappears. He leans forward, putting his elbows on the table. He was there for me when I started going toward the point of no return with Carter—a place where I couldn't talk to Declan about anything. He was too high out of his mind to give a shit. I could've told him anything and he would've just stared at me or laughed his ass off, even if it was about me being in love with his kid sister.

"All right, define 'talking.' Did you forget to put an *s* at the beginning?"

I grit my teeth. "I'm not *stalking* her."

"You go see her every day. Last week, Marie said she passed you on your way to 'talk' to her."

Maybe it's not so good having a friend with a wife. "Yeah, well, I've gotta buy food to eat."

"From a gas station. Right."

"Fine, I've been writing her notes because it was somethin' we used to do. Well, it got her to talk to me. Granted, it wasn't the best conversation of my life, but it's more than I've gotten out of her so far."

"You're obsessed, man."

"It's Carter," I tell him. "It's hard not to be."

"She hates you."

"Trust me, I know that. I think everybody in the goddamn world knows it, too."

He stares at me, long and stern. "If you get a restrainin' order put against you, it better not affect the business."

"You're an asshole," I mutter, trying to hold back a laugh.

"And you're a good punching bag. Listen, we've talked about her before, so I'm gonna give you the same advice I always do—you got to clean up your act or else we're just gonna keep havin' this conversation."

This time, I do start laughing. What he said isn't even the least bit funny, but if I don't laugh, I'll punch something or buy a drink that isn't soda. I've been doing the same dance with Carter for years, and I've never learned anything. I try to do good by her, but I'm too weak to do the best thing for her, which is to walk away.

Maybe it's time to start trying to deserve her, since I obviously can't be the bigger man and leave for good.

#

Gabe and Kara's cars aren't in the driveway, so I figure I'm okay to sneak into their backyard to deliver my next note. Lord knows the last thing I want is Gabe fucking Matthews to catch me sneaking up to Carter's room. Gabe's damn good to Carter, but you don't wanna be on his bad side. The last time I hurt her pretty bad, he showed up at my trailer and read me the right act. Words, in my opinion, are more terrifying than fists. I'm used to fists.

I'm lucky Kara installed a trellis at the back of the

house, which acts sort of like a ladder that leads up to Carter's room. I would've had to get creative if it wasn't there—probably would have had to figure out how to stealthily move and hide a real ladder. The only downside is the flowers growing up the trellis cut my hands up, which hurts like hell. Afterward, it's worth it, but that doesn't mean I'm not cursing my whole way up.

I stuff the note in my back pocket, carefully put the stems of the flowers in my other pocket, and then start climbing.

My hands are already raw from doing this twice and then using them to work, so I just clench my teeth when the stinging starts. It's not just the flowers, either; it's the splintered wood.

When I make it up to the top, there's somebody waiting for me. I immediately jolt back, feeling the trellis move with me. "Shit."

Carter is sitting right there, window open. She lunges forward and takes hold of my shirt, pulling me back to the wall instead of letting me fall backward. Well, that's *definitely* progress.

"Are you okay?" she asks, looking me over. Her gaze lands on my hands, still gripping the trellis, which has splatters of blood from cut skin.

"Better than ever, now," I answer. What is pain, really? Mind over matter and all that shit.

Her eyebrows pull together. "You could hurt yourself doing this."

"I've done worse."

She snorts, and it's cynical. Clearly, she agrees.

"Well, pretend you didn't see me leave my stuff here."

Using one hand, I wrestle the note and the flowers out and then carefully set them together on the windowsill. Carter doesn't hesitate to pick them both up and read the note. I wish I weren't here for this. I don't want to see her face when she reads what I sat for the longest time agonizing over. When I finally wrote them, I understood

42

how my dad finds the words in the Bible so holy.

Dear Junebug,
I wish I would've done things differently. I should've tried harder to deserve you and your love.
Boone

She stares at the note for too long. She's not reading it anymore; her eyes aren't moving. They're fixed. She's told me off a hundred times and told me to get away from her, but she's never told me to go away forever. I've always worried the time would come when she'd do that. It always seemed like it was right there, hanging between us, lying in wait.

I shift to head back down because I'm afraid this is going to be the time she tells me to hit the road. Maybe I've finally gone too far. God, I hope not.

"Wait," she says, looking up at me with wide, surprised eyes. "Come in."

"Really?"

"Do it before I change my mind."

That sounds more like she's pardoning me from my execution. Like she's about to say, "You'll keep your head, but if the direction of the wind changes, I might change my mind." Still, I can't see anyone ever disagreeing with their pardon. If you've got the chance *not* to be executed, then you're gonna take up the offer and go for it. That's my reasoning, at least.

Hell, who am I kidding? I don't need any reasoning. I'm in no position to reason.

I climb up the rest of the way, but I already know it's going to be a struggle to fit in through the window. All those years ago, I was wrong to leave flowers on the windowsill. I should have used the damn doorstep. That's easy. You can fit a guy my height in through most doors, no problem.

Carter doesn't help me, and I don't blame her. I'm

lucky she doesn't have her phone out videotaping this. She has her arms crossed, and she looks bored. But then again, sometimes her bored face is also her irritated face.

I use the inside of the wall to push myself up and inside, nearly cracking my head open in the process. I tumble to the hardwood floor with a large, obnoxious bang. It's a damn lucky thing Kara and Gabe are gone. My arms flail, and I grab onto the curtain, trying to right myself, which isn't a good idea, because I hear something pop. Luckily, it's in my shoulder—I didn't break Carter's room.

I somehow manage to sprawl out on my back, staring up at her ceiling. "A cat I am not," I say with a winded laugh.

Carter snorts again. "I don't think I could handle nine lives of you."

"Too hot to handle," I grin. If I could see her, I'm sure she'd be rolling her eyes. "Listen, I'm not like, questioning you or anything, because I'm pretty damn happy right now, bruises aside, but why'd you let me in?"

"Because I forgot once you invite vampires in, they can come in anytime they like."

She delivers the line so blandly that I can't hold in a laugh. "I'm no vampire, Carter. A lot of things—but no vampire. I'd never come in without your permission."

"I know," she says. "I think."

"So, real reason now?"

Her straight face falters, and she looks away from me, in the direction of a bookshelf, which has pictures on it. I'm surprised to see there's a lot with me in them. Even if I was a sucky guy toward the end of our friendship, I wasn't so bad before that; I guess if she's going to hold onto memories, it's better to keep these with her.

My favorite one is sitting front and center. She's probably about twelve in it, and I've got her hanging over my shoulder, and instead of freaking out, she actually posed for Declan to take the picture. It was with a cell phone I decided I needed to buy, even though I couldn't afford to actually use it. Most of the pictures of us are from later ages, when Kara came into the picture because she actually had the money and the heart to print them. There's another one on a lower shelf of me, Carter, and Declan, taken during one of the rare times he spent time with us after he started hitting the heroin hard. He clearly looks drugged out of his mind; he's gaunt, and he doesn't have the huge grin as Carter and I are sporting. We were too happy he was there to notice how shitty he looked, acted, and felt. We're all laying on a trampoline Kara bought and Kara's the one taking the picture. Even though she's got some years on us, she would always hang out with us. Sometimes I thought it was because she felt the need to supervise Carter when she was with us, but other times I think she just wanted to spend as much time with Carter as she could.

"Kara and Gabe are the only people who have shown up and stayed," Carter says softly.

I open my mouth to tell her I wish I could have; only those words won't change our history.

"I wish that would be enough to make me believe in people, but it's not. Not when no one else has been able to do it—my mom, my dad, Declan ... you. I've never been able to tell anyone to go away permanently. My dad came over yesterday, and I wanted to do it so badly." She swallows and looks up at me. "These notes? Is that you trying to be here, or is it you just leading me on again?"

My throat feels dry. "I want to be here."

"Then I'll give you a chance to prove to me you'll stay this time. But if you hurt me again or leave, I'm done with you. Forever." She holds up the note, her hands shaking. I want to reach out and hold them still—hold her—but I know doing so would ruin my chances of ever even being able to look at her again. "I'm tired of feeling like I'm not good enough."

Fire lights up inside of me. "You *are* good enough,

45

Carter. For everything. Too good ..."

"Am I?" she asks, her eyebrows drawing tight. "I don't feel like it." She starts shaking her head, and I can sense she's about to change the subject. I don't exactly deserve this conversation or the reason why we're having it. I have a feeling it has something to do with her dad's visit yesterday. "Tomorrow, I'll have Gabe drive me into work. You can walk me home."

She's testing me. She's purposefully not asking me if I have the time to do it or if I can make it. This is my first obstacle—move around my schedule and show up for her. I'll put my whole life on hold for her if I need to.

CHAPTER FIVE

Carter

Carter, 11
Boone, 14
Kara, 18

Boone holds my hand as a cherry-colored car pulls down our road and parks. It's expensive and out of place in our trailer park. Most people who live here drive battered trucks and cars or walk everywhere.

I didn't get any sleep last night; I was too nervous about meeting my sister today—excited, too. Luckily, Boone came over this morning as he promised. Declan made the same promise, but I don't think he even came home last night. Boone said Declan isn't mad at me, but I think he is. Why else wouldn't he be here?

"What if she doesn't like me?" I ask.

Boone looks down at me. He drops my hand and puts an arm around my shoulders. He's a lot taller than me, so he has to bend down to plant a kiss on top of my head. He does that a lot, and I hate it because Declan does it, too. It means he looks at me like a little sister. That hurts, especially when I've crushed on Boone Fell for as long as I've known what a crush was.

"She'll love you just as much as I do," he tells me. "It's hard not to."

My cheeks get hot; they always do when Boone tells me he loves me. No matter how he sees me, I'll never look at him like a brother. He's more than that—he's my best friend.

I hear Kara's car door open. I wonder if she'll look like me. What does our dad look like? Do I look like him?

"You're okay," Boone whispers. "This is good."

The second I see Kara, I know he's right. She's smiling at me like she doesn't see anything else. She's tall, wearing a sundress that's way prettier than anything I own, since I usually have to wear Declan's old clothes. Kara doesn't look like me at all, but it doesn't matter, because she already feels like a sister.

"Hi, Carter," she says when she's closer. "I'm Kara."

I stare up at her in amazement. She looks as if she wanted to be here with me—as if she liked me. Without thinking, I detach myself from Boone and take a step forward, then wrap my arms around her waist.

She doesn't hug me back. Maybe she's not a fan of hugging? I let go of her quickly and start to turn back to Boone. But then she kneels down and holds open her arms so she can hug me at my own level.

"It's so wonderful to meet you," she says into my shoulder. "I'm so, so sorry this didn't happen sooner."

"It's okay," I say back.

"We have now, don't we?" She sounds positive and sure, which makes me feel the same way. When she pulls back, her eyes are watery. "I've always wanted a sister."

"Me, too," I tell her. "Brothers sort of stink."

She laughs and releases me to talk to Boone. "Are you Declan?"

Boone goes stiff. "No, I'm Boone—the neighbor."

"Oh, Boone," Kara practically sings his name. Boone's my absolute favorite subject, so I talk about him way too much. "I've heard a lot about you."

Boone breaks out in a grin, loosening up. "Yeah. Carter's a little obsessed with me."

"Am not," I mumble.

48

He nudges my shoulder with his hand. "I'm obsessed with her, too."

"That's good. I'm glad you both have someone." Kara stands and looks around. "I was hoping I could meet Declan."

"He's ..." I start but trail off.

"Maybe he'll be here when y'all get back," Boone says, winking at me. "He's notorious for running off at the worst times."

Kara doesn't look like she believes him. "Do you know what time I should have her back by?"

Her question stumps both of us. Tish doesn't really care when Declan and I get home, or if we come home at all. I spent an entire night with Boone in the woods because he wanted to take me camping, and Tish didn't notice.

"Uh, dark?" Boone asks, looking down at me.

"Yeah, dark," I say.

"You don't have a curfew?" she asks.

Boone and I shake our heads.

"Okay," Kara says, drawing out the word. "Well, we'll be home before dark then. I guess Tish isn't home, either?"

"She is," I say but quickly regret it when Kara looks at the trailer as if she wanted to go in. For the first time, she must really see where I live because she turns green.

"You don't want to meet her," Boone explains. "It'll ruin your day."

Kara blinks rapidly and latches her hand onto mine. Panic rises as sharp pangs stab in my chest, and my heart stumbles toward a faster beat. What if she takes me away from Boone and Declan? That happened to the boys down the street—one day they were here and the next, they were gone.

Boone kneels down in front of me. "What's wrong, Carter?" He presses another kiss to my face, this time on my cheek.

I choke on a sob, gasping for air. "I-I don't want to get taken away."

"Hey, it's fine." He wraps his arms tightly around me and whispers in my ear, "Not gonna happen, Junebug. You belong here with us, all right?"

I nod against his shoulder. "I belong with you," I say in a barely-

there voice.

"Oh, gosh, Carter," Kara says, kneeling down beside Boone. "I didn't mean to scare you. I'm just ... I didn't expect ..."

"You're okay, Carter. You're going to have fun, and I'll be waiting here for you when you get back," Boone says. "I'll always be here waiting for you."

#

"So, why am I dropping you off again?" Gabe wonders aloud as he pulls up in front of the gas station. He keeps asking me that, and I keep evading.

"Because I want to be more active."

"You once told me you're chronically allergic to activity."

"I am. But I figure maybe I can become immune to it."

"That's not how it works."

"Are you sure? Because I walked from the house to your car and I feel fine. It's a miracle."

"You're too good at that straight-faced thing, Carter," he says, shaking his head.

Luckily he doesn't push any further. The last thing I want is him finding out about Boone. It's going to be a battle when I come clean about our burgeoning rekindled friendship, so I want to make sure Boone's worth it.

I fiddle with the door handle, but then lean over and press a kiss against his cheek. "Thanks, Gabe." I feel horrible for omitting the truth. I've always told him and Kara everything. We've always maintained a relationship in which we don't lie to each other no matter how mortifying or awkward. He'll be so disappointed in me when he finds out, and I'll have no clue how to handle it.

I head into what I hope is going to be a very calm, boring workday like it usually is during the day in this sleepy town. It's the night shifts that are bad. That's when all of Tish's kind come out.

During my shift, I have a total of ten customers—two

people paying in cash for gas, five buying cigarettes, and the rest buying chips, jerky, water, condoms, and all the other items that fall under etcetera. I always like to play a game where I try to guess what people are going to buy when I first see them. Most of the time, I'm right, thanks to most people being repeat customers, like Boone.

The bell rings, and I don't bother looking up at my eleventh customer, until a pack of beef jerky drops to the counter. "I'll take some of them cigs, too," the man says, pointing over my shoulder. I don't like the guy; he looks like some sort of terrifying lumberjack, with a long, shaggy beard, a horrible sunglasses tan, and a flannel shirt.

He doesn't name a brand, so I just reach in the direction he was motioning toward.

"No, not them. They're expensive."

"Which ones do you want?" I ask politely, even though I want to tell him they're *all* expensive.

"The cheap ones."

I scour the shelf for the cheapest pack. When I turn around, I don't miss the fact that this middle-aged man is checking out my backside. A chill runs down my back. I've been leered at before, but there's something about this man that makes me want to lock myself in the back room and call 911. As I set the pack down on the counter, I slyly reach beside the cash register to slide our emergency can of mace closer. We've never gotten robbed, but a lot of us work alone, so we always make sure we have something to use to protect ourselves.

"Are you Tish Hart's kid?" he asks as I'm ringing up the pack.

My whole body suddenly feels as though it were berated with pins and needles. My hand stills around the pack, and I look up at the man, seeing him more clearly than I did before. The sleeves of his flannel shirt are rolled up, revealing scars and open sores. His face is gaunt and broken-out. Most of his teeth are missing, but the ones he does have are decayed.

Meth.

I don't recognize him, but I recognize his type. Declan never got the chance to go beyond heroin, but my mom did. She started meth a while ago, just before she went AWOL. Gabe and Kara have tried to find her because while she was never much of a mom, it's horrible not knowing where she is. She could be dead.

"Yes, I am," I say slowly.

"Hm," he breathes, his gaze unabashedly roaming up and down my body.

"Do you know her?" I ask cautiously.

"'Lot more than knew her, kid," he mutters. "Fucked 'er."

I put the pack down as carefully as I can, sick to my stomach. "You should leave."

"She's got a picture of you. Says you're rich and gonna be her ticket." He's looking at me as if I were his ticket, too.

I drag the mace out into the open and grip it tightly. My mom's said that to me before. Kara had our dad pay her to give up custody. Money was the only way to get my mom to do it, God knows why. Even after getting that money, she tried (and succeeded) to get more through the years.

"You should leave," I say, fighting to keep my voice even. I'm practiced at keeping a straight face around Gabe and Kara, but right now, doing so seems impossible. I focus on ignoring every single terrifying thought as my finger twitches against the button. "Now."

"You really gonna use that thing?"

"Yes."

"Fuck me." He holds up his hands, cackling. "I'm gone then." There's something ominous about the way he says it. I half expect him to add *for now.*

My heart refuses to stop racing, even when the door's closed behind him. The mace feels heavy in my hands. The plastic is digging into my hand, stinging. I almost want to press my thumb into the button and spray the air, just for good measure—ward off any bad spirit he left behind. I'm more used to men like him than I want to be, but that doesn't mean they don't terrify me. Mama used to bring home his kind all the time, and I always did my best to disappear into the background—to hide. I wish I could do that now.

The bell above the door rings again, and I nearly set the mace off. I have no doubt that if I needed to, I'd use this.

"Carter, what's wrong? Is everything okay?"

I recognize Boone's voice before my vision clears and I see him. He's taking up the tainted space where the man was before. I squeeze my eyes tight, trying to wrap my mind around the man being gone. I'm safe now.

"Was it that creep? Did he try something?" Boone demands.

"No—he just—" I stutter out syllables that aren't much of a response.

"Shit, Carter, give me that before you blind me." He covers my shaking hands with his, and he gently pries the mace from me. "You're safe. It's all okay."

I nod and open my eyes. Boone's standing in front of me like some sort of hero. A weird movie reel starts playing in front of my eyes with "Holding Out For a Hero" playing, light shining down on him, and his face offering a safe, strong place to get lost in.

Am I about to have a seizure or something?

"You're worrying me here, Junebug."

"I'm worrying myself," I murmur. I let out a long breath, trying to get my wits about me. It works, and I start to see reality for what it is. There's no music playing, no light and, while Boone looks ready to avenge me, he also looks afraid. I'm not used to a scared Boone. He's wearing a shirt this time, which is probably a good thing, or else I might pass out. There's nothing that makes me feel dizzier than Boone Fell's lick-able abs.

No, scratch that. I'm thinking about Boone in a way I

definitely shouldn't be. *Especially* after what just happened. There's got to be something wrong with me.

"He didn't hurt you?" Boone asks again.

"No, he didn't," I say slowly. "He was just being … crude. He knows my mom."

"I knew there was somethin' shady about him," he mutters, looking over his shoulder. "If I wasn't so worried about you, I'd go after him."

"Don't. Maybe he'll stay away." *I don't think he will.*

"Well, if he doesn't, you call me or Gabe or Kara or 911 or, hell, call the SWAT Team in."

"I'm okay. I have my mace."

Boone laughs but not in his usual relaxed way. "I'm sure you could do a lot of damage with it, too. But we both know a drugged up guy ain't gonna even care about pain."

"It'd be worth a try."

"It would," he agrees.

"I can handle myself, you know. Kara and I took self-defense classes. I only started really freaking out after he left." With my heartbeat slowing down to normal, I can now delineate Savior Boone from the Boone I'm not quite on board with yet. I glance at the clock on my register. I still have twenty more minutes left in my shift. "You're early."

"Yeah, well, I'm trying to impress this girl, so I figure I need to pull out all the stops."

I raise an eyebrow. "You're not supposed to admit you're 'pulling out stops.'"

"Why not? If I don't, how will you know I'm doing it?"

"I will."

"Yeah, but how?"

He's smirking at me, but there's something off about it. I've become an expert when it comes to Boone's smiles, so if there's ever one thing I can be sure about, it's that I know what they mean. But this one is different and new.

"You're trying to distract me, aren't you?" I ask

skeptically.

"Yeah," he says with a shrug. He looks away, the smile gone. "It's something that's always worked for you when you panic. I always hate seeing you scared."

I can't answer him. I'm afraid if I do, I'll give him everything. "You're okay with waiting twenty minutes?"

"Sounds like the perfect amount of time for a nap."

#

He doesn't nap. Instead, he sits on the floor beside the *Home & Garden* stand with a magazine balanced on his left kneecap and his other leg outstretched. His gaze is hidden behind a pair of aviators, but I don't miss how his head moves subtly as he looks between me and the door for my creepy customer.

When the next cashier, Marcus, shows up ten minutes late, Boone straightens and crosses his arms. Even with those sunglasses on, I know he's glaring at Marcus. I'm a little upset he's late, too, but then I see Marcus' red, sweaty face, and I give him a sympathetic smile. He's been working two jobs, trying to afford college, and it's wearing on him.

"Sorry," he says, out of breath.

"It's okay," I say, grabbing my purse and throwing it over my shoulder.

"Yeah, it's not. That guy looks like he's about to pick a fight with me. What is he—your bodyguard?"

I only shrug. I wish it were so simple.

Boone stands near him, and the squeeze in my chest reminds me this is anything but simple. He's looking at me as he used to, back when his eyes would light up and he'd smile widely, showing off his sharp teeth. Actually, I'm not sure if he stopped looking at me that way, or if I stopped noticing.

"You ready?" he asks.

"You didn't have to glare at Marcus, you know," I tell

him, jutting my chin in Marcus' direction once we're out of hearing distance.

Boone crosses his arms. "He was late."

"He's got a lot on his plate."

"We all do, Junebug."

"Okay, then. What if that was me racing in? What if I was working two jobs and going to school, and I was basically rushing from one place to the next, knowing I was definitely going to be late but always worrying *how* late? Would your reaction be different then?"

My voice is rushed and my words are mangled. I'm tired from the day, but I'm also tired because of the way he makes me feel.

"You got me there. It would be different," he admits. He holds open the door for me. As I walk out, he pulls his aviators down his nose to look up at the sun and slides them back in place. "You don't like it when I call you that, do you?"

I dig in my purse for my own sunglasses. "When you call me 'Junebug'?"

"Yeah. They're in the small part there, yeah—shit."

A blush spreads across my cheeks as I quickly shove and hide a tampon beneath my wallet. Hopefully I remember it's there the next time I pay for something.

I glance up at Boone, and I'm surprised to see he's blushing, too. I've *never* seen Boone blush. I'm not sure why this would make him do that, considering he once held me in his arms when I was having bad cramps. He and Declan were actually the ones who sat me down and gave me the period talk. Maybe it's just because things are different now. I'm not a little girl who has to be taught everything—who you have to take a hand and lead.

For once in my life, we're on even ground. "I don't like it," I tell him. "The nickname, I mean."

"You used to."

"I was little. I liked everything you said—including a nickname after an ugly bug. I tried to find one good thing about them, and you know what I found?"

He actually looks curious. "What?"

"They aren't harmful to humans or animals, and that's about it. They kill crops, burrow into the ground, come back out, and die. Oh, and they make good food for small creatures. I'm really glad that I represent that to you."

"I think they're actually beautiful, you know," he tells me as we come to a stop at a crosswalk and wait for the light to change. "They're resilient, and they *always* emerge around the same time. You can put a lot of faith in a Junebug to do what it's gotta do."

I have absolutely no clue how to respond. Instead I stare at the crosswalk sign, willing it to change. I don't feel resilient right now—I feel vulnerable. He said that as though he'd been saving up his response for *years*. The thing is, I never know if that's how it is with him. I can never decipher if what he says is just a line he's feeding me, or if it's a sentence he's been perfecting. He could just be really, really good at persuasion, and he's using it against me.

The entire time, I feel him watching me closely. Regardless of what he says, he's looking for a reaction. He's meaning to warm my heart—to sway my feelings. Definitely a pro-persuader.

The light changes, and I step out into the street.

"I'll keep the nickname to a minimum then, Carter," he says as he catches up to me.

"Thank you," I say back. At about the halfway mark, he clears his throat and scratches the back of his neck. "So, how'd you get Gabe to drive you here? I'd imagine neither of them are happy about us hanging out."

"He doesn't know."

"What?"

"I didn't tell Gabe or Kara." Oh, the guilty feelings. "I lied."

"Why?" he asks.

I'm not sure if he's asking why I lied or why I'm

choosing to be here under the guise of a lie. "I don't know yet, but I'd prefer it if you don't walk me all the way home."

"Got it," he says, clearly disappointed. "Kara still greets you every day?"

"Yeah. She hasn't missed a day."

"That's good. I always liked that she did that. And how on the days when I'd come over, she always had something good for me to eat."

"Kara *always* has something good to eat."

"Yeah, I mean, she always had cookies and brownies or whatever, but she always gave me the healthy stuff, too."

"You totally had a crush on her," I tease. That comes out of nowhere—because it's something I used to always joke about with him. *Joke* might not be the right word, since most of the time I wanted some sort of a reassurance he didn't like her that way. It's hard not to love Kara, but it's equally hard not to be jealous of her, especially when I was younger. It was as if she somehow managed to be everything and have everything I never had. The happiness, the family, the boyfriend—I never wanted to tack Boone onto that list.

Boone grins at me and shakes his head. "That would be just another reason for Gabe to kill me."

"I don't think he really needs a reason."

"Correction: he doesn't *want* one," he says. "He'll just do it—put his medical degree to use and kill me in a way so it doesn't look like murder."

"Gabe would never do that."

"Or would he?" He reaches his hand out to run it along the fence as we walk. I can't help noticing how calloused his hand is, with a galaxy of bruises spreading across his knuckles. I heard he still does work around town, which explains his hands.

"Maybe you should be easier on your hands," I say softly. "They look like they hurt."

He glances down at them as if he were just noticing

how bad they look. He makes a fist and winces before dropping it back to the fence post. "The bruises are worth the money I make."

"So are work gloves," I add.

"Tried those, but they're annoying as hell. Maybe this thing with Jason will take off, and I'll get to spend more time behind a desk. Until then, I've gotta keep on."

"What thing with Jason?" I always liked Jason, because Jason would never be caught doing the things Declan did.

"Ah, yeah, it's nothing much yet. We're just looking to start up our own business."

"That would be great for you."

"Yeah, it would. Right now I'm making enough to move out and have a comfortable life, but I need to make more—and this would get me that. I don't want to have to take Dad with me. I'll pay his way, but he's staying in that trailer."

"Is he still ..." I trail off, trying to remember if he was drinking when Boone and I last talked, or if he was worshiping God. It changed from day to day. "Is he still going to church?"

Boone nods. "More now than ever. He's been sober for a while, but you never know with him. He's not working, so he's got a lot of time on his hands."

I never liked Boone's dad. He easily fell in the same category as my mom's boyfriends—slimy, mean, creepy, rude, and horrible—when he was drinking. The same could be said when he was attending church. But I hated him the most for the way he treated Boone. I grew up with a parent who didn't care, while Boone grew up with one who cared too much.

"None of this is what I wanted to talk about," Boone says, sounding frustrated, as we come to a halt at the intersection for my street.

"What did you want to talk about?"

"You." He takes a step into my space and looks down at me. He brings his hands up as if he were going to touch me, but then he doesn't. If there's one thing overly-flirtatious, charming, talkative Boone is good at, it's putting up barriers. He's the king of keeping you at a distance, even when he's right in front of you. He manages to do it in a way that makes you look as though you were the one putting them up. "I miss you, Carter. So goddamn much. Not having you in my life is hell. I meant it when I said I miss you."

"Boone," I say softly. "I'm not sure I can do this with you."

"I know I don't deserve it."

"It's not that."

"Well, it sort of is."

I can't hold back a smile. He's just so blunt. "It's just, I can't go through losing someone again," I continue.

"What if you don't lose me this time?"

"I think that every time, and I somehow still do."

"This time *is* going to be different. I'm going to prove I'm not leaving again."

"It's not really something you can prove." I bite my tongue as I carefully construct my words. "There's always someday. *Today* you might not leave, but *someday* you could. I haven't been able to trust in the *always* sense."

"Let me give you that, then."

"I don't know if you can."

"I can, and I will."

"Why now? Why not any of the other times?"

He sighs and steps away, turning his back on me. He links his hands at the back of his head and kicks at a rock. "Because I've never had *always* either, and it's about time the both of us do. It's time I learn to stick around."

"So I'm just something to practice with?"

"No, you're more. You're my …" He trails off, and whatever his answer was going to be, I'll never get to know it. "You have to let me in."

"Boone, it's *you* who needs to let *me* in."

"Okay. I will."

I close my eyes. "It's not that easy."

"When it comes to you, it's effortless. I just never let it happen." He turns to face me and looks as if he were about to drop to his knees and plead with me. "Let me walk you home again tomorrow?"

I can't say no. I never can. Maybe he needs to work on letting me in, and I need to work on pushing him out. "Okay."

#

Somehow, Boone climbs up and places another note and flower before I even make it up to my room. Normally, I might get changed and promptly flop onto my bed until the smell of food revives me, but the call of the letter is too strong. I go straight there instead.

Carter,
I never crushed on Kara. It was always you. Always.
Boone

CHAPTER SIX

Boone

Carter, 13
Boone, 16
Declan, 16

I don't have to see the ripped pages of the Bible or the shattered, empty beer bottles to know my dad's going to be a raging mess. All I needed to see was the date written on the whiteboard at school. Oddly enough, it was written in red, some sort of a fucked-up symbol for the worst day of the year to be William Fell's kid.

My dad is lying on his back in the middle of the destruction, staring up at the ceiling. He's got a pocket knife in his hand that he keeps flipping open and closed. I'm glad it's just a pocket knife this year.

When I was only five, I came home from school to find him sitting in the chair, soaked in the booze he'd been drinking, holding a gun to his head. Every year he's gotten less and less drastic, but it's been harder and harder for me to tell him not to go through with his threats. Sometimes, I wonder if he just got on with it, things would be better. Maybe if he just did it, then he'd finally be with my mom, like he always said he wanted. Then I could be done with him. I don't know what would come next, but anything would be a step up from this.

I don't feel like talking. I've tried that before. He only wants to talk about her—which is fine, except he always gets frustrated with me because I don't have anything to say back. There's not much to say about a woman I never had the chance to meet.

I kneel down and snatch the pocket knife away from him. He doesn't even put up a fight. This is just dramatics—a reason to turn to the alcohol.

His head rolls to the side, almost lifelessly. His eyes are bloodshot and glazed—his skin is the color of death. "Coward," he slurs. "I'macoward."

I carefully fold the knife and then slip it into my pocket.

"I can't do it."

Most people would probably call themselves that for the drinking or for trying to kill themselves, and my dad is calling himself a coward because he can't bring himself to end his life. He says it every year like clockwork.

In an entire day, he manages to go through those damn steps of grief. The part about acceptance excluded, of course. I know from experience he's about to go through his anger phase. I've learned to run for that one, because he always comes after me with something. At first it was just a belt, then his fists, and now he comes after me with blunt objects. My dad can be rough, and he's knocked me around a time or two, but never worse than on this day. This day stopped being about my mom's death, and it started being about what my dad's going to do.

He blames me for her death. She was diagnosed with cancer when she was pregnant with me, and given the choice between saving herself or saving me, she chose to let me live. She didn't have any treatment, and by the time I was born, nothing could be done. She died so I could live. It pisses me off because she must've been a good woman; she had to have been to make that decision.

Dad sits up suddenly, and the fire in his eyes tells me it's time to run. He yells something so colorful his Bible should probably spontaneously combust, and then points at me. "Your fault."

I grit my teeth and look up at the ceiling. Maybe Dad looks up to God because he's looking for answers—maybe I'll find them, too. I do blame myself. But I also know I couldn't help what happened. You don't get to decide who your parents are or what your history is going to be.

There's a knock at the door behind me, and I immediately turn, hoping I'm wrong about who I already know it's gonna be: Carter. She always wants to fix me, and the way I was acting today gave her a reason. I just didn't want to talk to anyone, including her, so I was distant.

She's staring at us from the tear in the screen door. Her eyes are wide, and she looks petrified.

"You should leave," I order her. My voice sounds grainy, as if I took a handful of glass off the floor and swallowed it.

"She will," my dad slurs. "They always do."

"Is he okay?" she asks.

My dad starts to stand, and I know it's about to get nasty. I don't know what he'll do, but he always does something.

"Leave, Carter," I say, using the harshest tone I've ever used with her.

"Boone!"

Before I can do anything, my dad is slamming me to the ground. He's so out of his mind that he goes straight down with me. Glass pierces my skin. My dad falls on top of me, his elbow jamming into my face.

"Fuckin' kid," he snarls, saliva coming out of his mouth. He reeks of alcohol and cigarettes and my mom's perfume.

My whole body feels as if it were in pain, throbbing. He's dead weight, pushing me further into the shards. I know my face has got to be bleeding something terrible because I taste copper. My nose feels like it might even be broken, but I've broken it so many times by now it's hard to tell.

I've learned to deal with him and this and everything else. But Carter seeing it? No. It makes me feel horrible. Like shit. It makes any cut and bruise and potential broken bone seem like child's play

"Needs help!" I hear Carter yell.

Shit.

I shove at my dad's shoulder, who's passed out now. "I'm fine."

"What's the matter?" That's Declan joining our little fucking party.

I drop my arm and squeeze my eyes shut. "Leave me the fuck alone."

"Boone, I—" Carter starts.

"Get outta here."

"I'm sorry, please—"

"Now."

#

I press my hand against the handle of the gas station's door, letting out the longest damn sigh in the history of sighs. If I'm going to do this, I need to do it right. I'm wearing my best clothes, for God's sake. Hell, I'm *actually* wearing clothes. I want Carter to think I'm trying for her, and if that means wearing a shirt with buttons and khaki pants, it's worth it. I mean, it works out because I'll have to look nicer if I'm gonna own a business with Jason.

Win, win, right?

Right. So fucking right.

Pep talk over. I push the door open and walk inside. Carter is standing behind the counter in her usual place, reading a novel. Luckily, she doesn't look spooked as she did yesterday.

I don't know exactly what went down with the two of them, but the look on her face made me want to hunt that guy down. I know Carter can handle herself, but I still hate that she had to. I hate that someone got under her skin and just walked away as if it were nothing. That tells me he'll come back. I wish she would've used that mace on him, taught him a lesson.

She looks up from her book. Her hair is back in a ponytail, stray pieces flying all around her face. I've always liked how she's beautiful without even trying. She doesn't have any makeup on, and she's wearing a uniform that I'd never put my employees in (unless I *wanted* them to hate me) but still makes her look like a dream.

"I'm early," I say as I walk toward her,

"We said we were going to stop pointing out what you're purposefully doing to impress me, remember?" she asks, setting her book down in a way to keep her page marked.

"Today, we're gonna try something."

"I can't leave until I have relief."

"That can be arranged." *Shit*. Not what she wants to hear right now. "Ignore me." The goal is to be less like my usual self and try to flirt with her in a way that'll make her smile, not want to murder me. She hates it when I do this, even if it makes her eyes light up and her face flush. "We don't need to leave to do this."

"Okay," she says slowly.

"I want to start over. We're so caught up in the past that it's holding us back."

"Boone, we can't change the fact we have a past."

"I'm not saying we should. There was a lot of bad, but there was a lot of good, too, right?"

She stares at me.

"Carter, there was good."

She splays her hands on the counter, purposefully not meeting my gaze and watching them instead.

Without thinking, I reach out and run my fingers over the top of one of her hands. Electricity shoots up through my arm. I forgot how life-altering it feels to touch her. It's addicting—the only thing to ever show me how my dad could be so dependent on alcohol or Declan on drugs.

"There was good," she agrees in a whisper.

Relief washes over me. If she can acknowledge that, there's room for us to grow. "All I'm saying is I want to start over with a clean slate. I want to show you I've changed, but that's not gonna happen if you keep comparing me to my worst. I want you to start judging me for how I am now. If I mess up, you can walk away. I *want* you to." I slowly link my fingers with hers. I run my thumb over her knuckles, making her gasp. "I'm ready to start something with you, whatever you'll let me have, but we can't do that if we're going to stay stuck in the past."

"I'm not stuck in the past." She pulls her hand away, leaving mine cold and empty. Lonely. "I remember the past so I can learn from it. I can't make the same mistakes again—not when it hurt so bad."

When *I* hurt her. "Let me learn, too. Please."

Her eyebrows pull down as she worries her lip. She's shutting down on me. Here I've been telling her I'm going to be different—that I'm going to fight for her—and I can't even put up a good case as to why she should give me a final chance, even as just friends. What if I'm just lying to the both of us? Maybe I can't do this. Maybe this'll chalk up to another one of my many failures.

I ball my hands into fists, wanting to grasp at something—anything—her. I can't let this happen. I can't let her go. It's all in or nothing.

"All the things I did—they were never about you, Carter. They should've been, but they weren't. I've always loved you more than anything, but I don't know how to love people. I just self-imploded. I made decisions that were bad because it's what I'm used to doing. ..."

She starts shaking her head, and I trail off. Her eyebrows raise, and she says in a soft, commanding tone, "You know how to love people, Boone. You just don't know how to let anyone love you back."

I deliberately breathe through my nose and unclench my hands. My fingers feel like twigs that'll break with too much force. "How do you always do that?" I ask.

"Do what?"

"You always hit the damn nail on the head when it comes to me."

The bell above the entrance rings, signaling the next shift worker has arrived, and Carter immediately takes a step back, taking off her name badge as she does. At least the next shift is on time today. Very quietly, in a voice I can barely hear or decipher, she says, "It's because I've always loved you, too."

#

Carter's quiet on the walk home, which is fine. I'm just glad she's letting me walk her home after our talk back there. I was convinced it was time to stick a fork in me. It doesn't matter if I'm not done with her—if she's done with me it's over. I'll keep being as persistent as I am until she gives me that final *leave me alone*. Up until now, she's only half meant it, so I haven't listened too closely. When she's serious, though, I'll let her go.

I'll hate it, but I will.

Sometimes, it only feels as a matter of time until then.

Her house is basically at the opposite end town from my trailer. She told me Kara made their dad pay for it, and I was initially surprised Kara didn't choose one of the houses in the historic district of town, which are out-of-this-world expensive, but I think Kara chose right. This house is the sort you only see on television shows when you're growing up—the type where you can't help wondering if they really exist. Picturesque and perfect—what everyone dreams of—just like the family inside. The exterior is as clean as the words spoken inside. The same amount of love is put into the landscape as is given to each other. The inside is just as welcoming as they accustomed to kindness.

Plus, there's more than one bathroom. A step up from the barely-functional one we had in the trailer.

I think when Carter started living with Kara and Gabe, I got something out of it, too. Thanks to them, I know the world's not as dysfunctional as it seems.

Carter's shift today was later, so by the time we get to her street, the sun was setting. I met with Jason early this morning to hammer out some details about our prospective plans. I was surprised to find out he already put in his two weeks' notice at his job. That was the moment when shit got real for me. Granted, I've basically been running my own business for a while, but it's scary when your friend (who has a family to support) gets involved in the venture. There's more to lose.

That's probably why I laid it all out on the line with Carter. It feels like it's now or never. I'm ready to settle down and start a life. I don't know what that entails exactly, but I know it involves Carter. The only problem is I should've started things with her back when I had the chance and not waited until I'd burned every bridge to ash.

"I'm off tomorrow," Carter tells me, sounding unsure.

Damn. I blow out a breath through my teeth, doing my best not to look as disappointed as I feel. The last thing I want is a day apart when we're making so much progress. "All right."

"The hospital is having a cookout, and it's Gabe's year to go."

"You don't have to explain it, Carter. It's okay." I hate the way both of our hands are dangling aimlessly at our sides. All I want to do is reach down and grab hers. When we were younger—even when we got older—I would always hold her hand. It was just something I did. I used to pretend it was to keep her safe, but then I realized how much I liked it, which turned into me noticing I liked Carter, period. It was effortless back then—holding her hand *and* being with her. "The way I see it, I'm doing what I can to see you. I'll work around your schedule to spend time with you. It doesn't need to be the other way around."

"It should, though," she says quietly. "We both need to work at it if we're going to do this."

To say I get hopeful is an understatement. Now I know how puppies feel when they think they've found their owner. "What are you saying, Carter?"

"I'm saying I'll try. Clean slate." She stops beside the stop sign where we'll part ways, and turns to face me. She holds out her hand, which is shaking. "I'm Carter Hart."

My hand is also shaking as I reach out and clasp it. "I'm Boone Fell." She gives me a final nod, smiling a nervous smile, and turns around, walking away. "We're gonna be best friends, Carter Hart, I already know it."

She glances over her shoulder, and I swear her smile looks a notch more real. "We'll see, Boone Fell."

I already know what my note tonight is going to say. I've been pouring my heart out in them, but I want this one to be the start of something normal. Like what a normal guy would say to a normal girl who's his new friend but who he wants to have more with.

Nice to meet you, beautiful.

CHAPTER SEVEN

Carter

Carter, 13
Kara, 20

"Here, take this and go pay the man," my mom says to me. Her eyes are bloodshot, and her mouth is twisted up like she ate a sour lemon. I always wondered if she was pretty before the drugs. We don't have any pictures, so I have no way of knowing.

Her hair is bright pink; she only ever has the money to spend on beauty products and drugs. That explains why she's wearing dark blue eyeshadow and red lipstick. She also has on short shorts—I think some of the girls at my school also have them—and a white tank top, bra-less as usual. Her arms are a mess, with sores open and bleeding. She always itches them when she's waiting for her dealer to deliver the drugs. She used to be able to get by with drinking alcohol during the time between fixes, but it doesn't work anymore.

"Mom—"

She scowls at me, which makes her look monstrous. She hates it when I call her Mom. She prefers I call her Tish, which I hate. She's my mom, and there's nothing worse than calling your mom by her name while everyone else calls their mom, "Mom." When I was little, she wasn't so mean about it, but now that I'm older, she says it shows her age.

She doesn't realize she's already doing that all by herself.

"Tish," I say, nervously. "Kara's going to be here soon."

"Kara's going to be here soon," she mocks. She's never met Kara, thankfully, but she hates her all the same. She hates everybody. Declan and I included. "Well, then answer the door, get me my stuff, and go."

I take the money from her, and she immediately turns and heads back to her room. There's a man in there, and they've been yelling at each other for the last hour about how neither of them has anything on them.

The only thing that makes this easier is if I tell myself she only ordered pizza. She would never do that, but it's better to pretend than face the reality. I open the door, step out, and close it before even looking at the man waiting. I've learned you don't want to be in a small space with my mom's "pizza guys," and you also don't want to give them the opportunity to come inside.

When I look up, I'm met with an annoyed expression. "I got here fast and had ta wait," the dealer mutters around a cigarette. "Money first, kid."

He doesn't even question the fact that I'm a thirteen-year-old girl. I'm just money to him. He carefully counts the wad of cash I give him, then recounts it. Twice.

"This ain't enough," he barks at me. "No money, no product."

I don't want to plead with him, but I know if I don't, Tish will be furious, and she'll take it out on me. "I'm sorry—she can get you the money."

"Ah, that's a 'fuck no,'" he says, spitting out the words around his cigarettes. He holds up an arm and uses it to point backward. "I've heard from other guys about 'er and how she don't pay. I ain't gonna let her con me like she has others." He removes the cigarette and blows out smoke. "'Less you wanta barter for it."

I blanch. Even though he can't be anything more than a few years older than Boone, he looks like he's lived a long, hard life already. He reminds me of Declan in that sense. "What?"

He shrugs. "Worth a try, kid. Tail's tail. You tell your mom to get me more money, and I'll get her her stuff."

"You should leave, or I'm calling the cops," Kara says, her arrival taking me by surprise even though I expected her. I back into the door, wanting to hide. This is the last thing I want her to see. She's supposed to be the good part—the part where drugs aren't an everyday aspect of my life.

"Trust me, honey, you don't wanna do that," the dealer says, slowly turning around to face my sister. She's on the not-mowed, swampy lawn in front of us in one of her pretty sun-dresses, with her hair braided and her toenails painted. "You don't wanna make the whole park an enemy."

"I'm not here to make friends," Kara says evenly.

"That don't mean you can't make enemies," he says back. "Your type would know."

Kara's face starts to turn pink, but she stands her ground. I've never seen her like this before. She's always so upbeat and kind. "You should leave."

"I was going to."

"Then go."

He glances at me. "You tell Tish what I said." He heads toward a junky little car, and I'm glad Kara parked out of the way of it. There's no doubt he'd hit it on purpose.

The second his car roars to life, Kara blindly grabs at my hand and drags me over to her car. She doesn't let me go until I'm in the passenger seat, and then she rounds to the driver's side, gets in, and locks the doors. She grips the steering wheel, her gaze fixed straight ahead. She looks dazed.

"She asked you to buy the drugs for her, didn't she?"

I nod as I answer, "Y-yes."

"Have you done that before?"

I nod again and choke out another, "Yes."

"Can you say, 'no'?"

"No." I have a scar near my ear from the one time I did. Tish was wearing a cheap ring that a boyfriend gave her—she's since hocked it. There were other times, too, but none of them left something that long-lasting. I'm thankful she's nothing like Boone's dad, because he always leaves scars.

Kara squeezes her eyes shut. "Where are Boone and Declan?"

I bite my lip and look out my window. "They're out with friends." It's what I choose to believe, even though Declan mentioned something about a girl, and they're probably getting high. I live in a world of fake pizza and fake trips with friends because my reality makes me feel like I'm suffocating.

"You shouldn't have to live like this," Kara says. When she opens her eyes, tears spill out. "This shouldn't be your life."

#

"You'd think they're doing surgery the way they're staring at that grill," Kara says, pulling her sunglasses down her nose to look at the group of people, Gabe included, who are crowded around it.

"Or that they're monkeys," I say, just in time for one of them to reach out and try moving something, only to give up. I'm pretty sure they've been touching the same knobs for the last hour. If their attempts didn't work the first time, they're not going to work the second time. Or the millionth.

We haven't been able to make the doctors' annual grill-out in years, mostly because Gabe's a low man on the totem pole, since he hasn't been there long. He's always had to cover everyone's shifts. I guess he's finally less green.

"*This*," Kara says emphatically, "is why I do the grilling."

"How much do you want to bet they're going to burn the burgers?" I ask.

Kara laughs. "I'm not going make a bet I know I'll lose. They'll definitely burn them."

She slides her sunglasses back up her nose and shifts around on her towel. We were swimming, until Gabe decided to help grill, now we're sunning, which probably isn't for the best. Our complexion is very anti-sun. It's one of those nice reminders that Kara's my sister—that we share some of the same DNA.

When we're burnt to a crisp, we'll bond. We'll whine together and rub aloe on each other and drive Gabe crazy. *I'm a doctor,* he'll say, *so it's my job to explain the dangers of skin cancer to you.* And he will in *extensive* detail. It's fun and weird and us.

"So, that Dr. Green has a cute son," Kara prompts.

I roll my eyes and adjust the towel I'm using as a pillow. When Gabe introduced us to Dr. Green and his family, Kara had elbowed me not-so-slyly. She's right; Dr. Green's son, Luke, is cute. Even though he's my age, he's playing volleyball with the kids. He's tan, with short brown hair and tawny eyes. His kind, unabashed grin is infectious, something I notice because he directs it toward *me.*

I'm not used to anyone really looking at me, other than to see through me. It felt nice to have this guy actually seem interested in me—he even tried joking with me, although I couldn't hear him over Gabe and Dr. Green's conversation. I was too embarrassed to ask him to say it again, so I just pretended to laugh. Jokes aren't funny the second time around. I'm pretty sure Kara thinks the exchange means we're married.

"I'm going to go for a walk," I tell her, more than ready to escape this topic of conversation.

Kara sighs. "You're right. Maybe he's too perfect."

"If anyone's too perfect, it's Gabe," I say back. I don't belong with perfect. I'm too rough around the edges, thanks to my childhood. What I'm more concerned with is finding someone who's perfect *for* me. I want somebody who's my other side of the coin, which was how I used to always see Boone.

Why am I thinking about him? I don't know why I keep trying to keep him at arm's length, only to let him get closer. It's crazy. I'm crazy. He says he won't hurt me again, but I know he will. I just can't say no to him—I don't want to. He means so much to me, and I guess a girlish part of me will always see him as the average, everyday superhero I love.

"Can I join you?"

I jump and immediately wrap my arms around my middle. Kara talked me into wearing one of her two-piece swimsuits today, which was a little stupid on both of our parts. There's more to me than there is to her, boobage included. She clapped and said I looked beautiful, whereas Gabe glowered, stepping into his dad role.

I glance up at Luke and see he's smiling shyly at me. "Sure," I say.

He falls into step beside me. I notice he's only wearing his swim trunks. At least Luke is shirtless and shoeless in a place where he's allowed to be.

"So, you're Gabe's sister-in-law?" he asks.

I blink at the wording. *Sister-in-law* isn't really what we are to each other. If that were the case, I don't think we'd be as close. "Yeah, but he and my sister have basically raised me."

"That's what my dad said," Luke tells me. "Well, Gabe's a cool guy. He's been letting me shadow him since my dad's more involved in administration."

Gabe literally never mentions work. He loves it but doesn't talk about it, because he already feels like it takes up so much of his life. It might be a little rude to tell Luke he's never mentioned him. "I'm sure Gabe's a blast to shadow."

"Yeah, he is. So, how much do you wanna bet they're going to tell us they only overcooked the burgers to help everyone's cholesterol?"

"They're smart people, yet they have no idea how to work a grill," I say, laughing.

"And here I want to be one of those smart people."

"Well, now you know you need to brush up on your grilling skills," I tell him.

"I'll get right on that. Maybe it'll set me apart."

"It always does. I mean, Gabe almost didn't get the job because of the other guy's Labor Day kabobs. But then they heard Gabe actually went to medical school and they figured that, gee, maybe he deserves it."

"Fair. Guess education is pretty crucial, too."

I hold up my fingers an inch apart. "A little bit. There's wiggle room, of course."

"Of course." He laughs. "You're funny; you know that?"

"I've been told it a time or two." *Just not by anyone other than my immediate family or Boone.*

"You're good at keeping a straight face, too."

"Goals."

He chuckles again, and I hear cheering back at the shelter. "Food's done," he says.

"We'd better get back."

"Yeah."

"Listen, I was wondering if maybe you'd want to do something sometime."

Stupid Boone flashes through my mind, as if our newly-official standing-date where he walks me home was my sole reason for living. Totally ridiculous. I'm allowed to have a life and friends.

I catch myself before the firm "I can't" slips out. "Sounds like fun."

"Really? Good."

Kara will be thrilled at the thought of me hanging out with Luke. I can already hear her squealing.

Luke eats with us, which I don't expect to enjoy as much as I do, and I think he manages to impress Gabe and Kara even more, if that's possible. When we're about to leave, he makes sure to get my number and texts me right away, which has Kara beaming. My cheeks feel as though they were on fire, especially when we get back to the car, and Gabe declares that Luke's "a good kid."

#

"Shit."

I bolt up in bed at the sound of a curse and grope for my lamp's light switch. That was totally Boone's voice. I'd know it anywhere. Was I dreaming that or ...?

"Fuck."

I throw off my covers and run to the window, not bothering to worry about what I'm wearing. Not that I'm scantily dressed as girls are in the movies when an attractive guy comes to their window. Nope, I look like a bag lady in an oversized shirt of Gabe's. I'm wearing booty shorts, but there's no seeing them since the shirt was made for a giant.

I tug on the blinds to pull them up, and as soon as I do, I gasp. Boone is on the other side, looking just as shocked as he did the other day when I caught him. The only difference is this time he's pale, and the note on the windowsill is red, along with the windowsill itself and his arm.

With a lot of force, I manage to open the window. It's as if Gabe knew that this would someday happen, so he put me in the room with the crappy window. "Boone, what are you doing? Are you okay?"

He smirks. "Thought I'd show my everlasting devotion to you by making a blood oath."

"Blood oath? You look like a sacrificial pig." I open the window further and reach out to grab him by his shirt collar. "Get in here."

He bulks. "I prefer sacrificial goat. Goats are awesome."

"Well, pigs are cute, and this is a really weird argument."

"Ain't an argument, and maybe I should be a pig, since I'm pretty damn cute. Am I more awesome or cute—what do you think?"

"Boone ..." I trail off and listen for any signs that Gabe and Kara heard us. Luckily, the house is silent. Gabe sleeps like the dead because he's always tired, and Kara tends to pile pillows on top of her head. If we're quiet, I should be able to help Boone without them finding out he's here. In my room. Again. "Get in here."

He grins. "Yes, ma'am." All of his confidence leaves him as his hands scrape against the riveted sill. He leaves behind a handprint that I'll have to clean up later. He curses again. "Tell Kara it's hard to play Rapunzel and Prince when there's damn thorns everywhere."

"You shouldn't be doing this if it's hurting you."

"Yeah, well, I heard something about how you're supposed to fight for things, and I'd rather fight thorns than Gabe."

He straightens once he's inside my room and opens his hands to look at them. I wince at the sight of one of the thorns sticking out of a cut. I want to tell him this doesn't earn him a medal of valor when it comes to repairing things between us, but in a way, it does. I forgot how much it warms my heart to know he'd go to the ends of the earth for me.

"Sit down, and I'll go get the first aid kit."

He looks around, somehow managing to smirk and look unsure all at the same time. This is unexplored territory for the both of us, and he's not as good at hiding it as he thinks he is. Somehow, his nervousness adds to my confidence.

"The bed's fine," I tell him.

I don't give him time to answer. I go to the bathroom downstairs where Kara keeps a first aid kit. Every time a floorboard creaks, my heart ticks up in tempo. That shouldn't wake them up and, even if it did, I could lie. Easily. They wouldn't suspect anything. But I would hate to do that. I hate leaving details like this out, because I don't do that with them.

After I grab the kit, I head back up to my room. Boone is sitting on my bed, his palms up on his thighs, careful to not drip blood on my bedspread. He's looking around my room, studying it, just as he did the last time. There's something about the image of him on *my* bed that makes my thighs clench.

I always wanted this. Not him bleeding and sneaking around, but I wanted him in my space. There were too many nights where I'd think about having his arms around me—and then asking him to stay with me forever. It would be so easy to talk him into it right now because I think he'd let me do anything I want. All I would need to do is bandage up his hands then kiss him—let hands roam, lose clothes, and pray he means everything he's been saying.

But I can't do that, because I'm not sure if praying will work.

There's a minute where he doesn't realize I've returned, and he squeezes his eyes shut. Without those piercing eyes of his, I can see the unease he always tries to hide. The lines of his face are sharpened, his shoulders are hunched up near his ears, and the muscles in his arms are rippling.

He's the most complex person I've ever met. In one light, he's charismatic and confident, but in the other, he's unsure of himself and watchful of everything. He's not a *liar* or an *actor*, as I sometimes tell myself—he's just trying to evolve as we've always had to. We were literally born into Darwinian families, and who we are now is a product of that—of a fight to survive.

"If we're starting out again, I don't think that this is the way to do it," I say softly.

He jumps, and whatever emotions were there before slip away. "I'm trying to go for memorable here, Junebu—Carter."

"Memorable doesn't mean you have to be stupid," I remind him. "Give me your hands."

"Well, that's forward of you," he says in a mock scoff.

I give him a look, and he grins as he holds out his palms. I set the kit on the bed beside him and rummage around for the tweezers, antiseptic, and large Band-Aids. I'm probably too used to cleaning him up because I used to do it for him all the time. Declan, too. Between bad parenting, parents' bad relationships, fights, and random accidents—it was hard not to play ER doctor. They were always beaten, bruised, or bleeding. Boone doesn't even wince as I pick out the thorns and dab his injuries with the antiseptic.

"Even though I know this isn't exactly fun, I, uh—it's good to see you, Carter." He works his jaw, the movement exaggerated by a layer of thick blond stubble. There's nothing better than standing over the man who's always given you pesky butterflies. "Didn't think going a day away from you would make me miss you this much."

I missed him, too. Not that I'm going to fess up to it.

"How was Gabe's work thing?"

"It was nice. I made a friend." *A male friend.* Not that Boone really needs to know.

He tilts his head and reaches up with his bandaged hand to run his fingers along the edge of my jaw, then down my neck to my collarbone. Goosebumps erupt in the wake of his fingers, and I fight the urge to move into his hands. Into him.

"Did this friend happen to be the sun? You're of the medium-rare type right now," he says with a quiet chuckle.

"We all can't be tan, Mr. God of the Sun," I tease back.

He tucks my hair behind my ear, and his gaze unmistakably flickers to my lips. My breath catches as he closes the space between us, each second audibly ticking by. It's amazing how I never really paid attention to the little analogue clock on my dresser—it doesn't even show the right time—but right now, it's all I can hear. By the tenth click, he's so close I'm sure he's about to kiss me, and I'm about to let him.

Just as his lips are about to brush mine, he skates past them and presses them against my jaw. My heart feels as if it were about to jump out of my chest, giving up on any chance of ever functioning right again.

"Where is this going?" I ask breathlessly.

Another kiss. This one less hesitant. "Somewhere

permanent, I hope. I'm in it for real this time. I want this from you, but I'll take whatever you'll give me."

"I want it, too," I say back. "But you haven't exactly proven that you know what permanent is."

He pulls back. "Carter—"

"What happened between us wasn't just a crush or something, Boone. It was real." Instead of my voice getting louder, it gets quieter. I'm too aware of Gabe and Kara down the hall to do anything but whisper. "Why did you leave me?"

"It was because ..."

I close my eyes and step away from him. Another excuse. *It was because I wanted tonight to be special for you. It was because we were just in the heat of the moment. It was because we're not meant for anything more than this—I'm not made for it or for you.*

"Listen to me, Carter, please?" he asks.

"You're just going to tell me an excuse. You always do," I tell him. "I can't hear it right now. You should go. We'll go through the front door. Quietly."

When I open my eyes, his brows are drawn together. "Let me just—" He holds up his hand, as if the rest of the sentence was written on there. He stands and goes over to my desk to get a pen, then heads back to the windowsill and writes something on the paper he left there. Boone winces as he scrawls down the final words.

Eventually, he neatly folds the paper back up and sets it on the sill. "I can show myself out," he tells me. He leans toward me and presses a kiss against my forehead. "I'll see you tomorrow. Same place."

I hold my breath as I listen for him to walk out the front door. I'll need to lock it later, before everyone gets up. Right now, I'm too concerned with whatever he wrote on that note.

Beautiful,
Sometimes I think about when we were kids—when things were

easy. When you used to look at me like I had the world in my hands. I wish you still looked at me that way. Did I look at you like that? There's no way I couldn't have.

    Boone
    It was because I loved you too much.

#

Carter, 13
Kara, 20

Kara parks in the driveway of a yellow house with white fencing around it. There are white flowers in the front yard with pretty sunflowers peeking out. There's a swing on the porch, making the house look like something on a gas station postcard.

    "Whose house is this?" I ask her. "Is it Gabe's?"

Kara told me that he's been looking at apartments, but I can't imagine Gabe moving straight from his parents' place to a house. He's looking for something manly and industrial, but she said she suspects he'll end up buying something with mostly older people in the community. It would fit him.

    "No," Kara says. "It's mine. Well, ours."

    "I don't understand," I say.

    "How about we go sit on the porch?"

    "Can we do that?"

    "We can do whatever we want," Kara explains. "It's in my name."

She gets out first and waits for me at the front of the car. I take my time meeting her, because I don't understand what she's saying. This house can't be ours—I only get to see Kara a couple of hours a week. And it can't belong to Tish, because she can't afford a real home with a real yard— plus, all these flowers would be dead within a day if it were hers.

I follow Kara to the porch, but I can't bring myself to sit on the swing. It can't be my swing—or even our swing. I sit on the steps instead, and Kara takes the spot behind me. She sets a hand on my knee reassuringly.

"I know this is probably confusing, but we're going to live here—you and me."

"I have a house."

"No, your mom has a trailer," she corrects softly, "and she barely even has that. After seeing you with that man the other day—your mom's dealer—I decided it was time I did something about the way she's been raising you. You deserve better, and I can give that to you. I asked Tish to sign her rights over to me."

"What?"

"It's official as of this morning."

"She wouldn't do that." She's my mom. No matter how horrible they are, moms don't do that, right?

Kara squeezes my knee. "She did. She wasn't going to at first, but I offered her some money and to pay her rent."

My stomach sinks. She would do anything for money, including giving up her daughter.

"This house is still in the same school district, but it's a better place to be. The trailer wasn't a good situation for you. You understand that, right?"

"Yes." I stare down at my toes, which feel like they're baking in the sun. "What about Declan? And—"

"Boone?" Kara asks with a smile. I talk way too much about Boone and my crush on him. Stealthy, I am not. Even he probably knows by now. "Well, this house has four bedrooms. I need one for an office space and, of course, you and I get our own, so that leaves the last one open. We can make it a guest room for Declan, but only for when he's clean. I don't want that in our house, okay?"

I manage a nod. I'll have my own room? And Declan can have one, too?

"And as far as Boone is concerned," she says, singing his name, "he's welcome, too. Anytime."

"Really?"

"Of course." She moves her arm away and leans back so she can put it over my shoulders instead. "You're okay with this? I know I should've talked to you about it first, but I didn't want to get your hopes up ... and I also didn't want to hear you say 'no.' I think this has to happen, even if you don't want it to."

Tears spring to my eyes, and Kara immediately starts to apologize. "No," I tell her, "it's okay. I'm happy. I want to live with you."

CHAPTER EIGHT

Boone

Boone, 18
Declan, 18

I knock on the door to Declan's trailer, then push it open. The place is a dump—well, the whole park is, so I guess it's no different. The once-white walls are now a dingy gray, the laminate floor is dusty and warped, and late at night, you can sometimes hear the mice in the walls. This trailer is a lot like mine, which is why I don't hesitate to stomp in with my muddy shoes.

His room over at Kara's is a lot nicer than this once. But I guess that's because he doesn't stay there often enough to dirty it up. If I had the chance to have a house like that—a life like that—you'd be damn sure I'd be milking it for everything it's worth. I don't get why Declan continues to stay with his fucked-up mother rather than live with Carter. I guess fucked up only knows fucked up.

He's lying on the couch, staring at the ceiling fan. It's only got three of the five blades and one of the three lights. His shirt is untucked and unbuttoned, his pants are undone, and his tie is fisted in his hand. His eyes are glazed over.

"Aren't you supposed to be somewhere?" I ask.

He doesn't move. His head just lops to the side so he can look at me. His gaze fixes on me, but I'm not sure he sees me. "Boone, my man, what're you doin' here?"

"Thought I'd crash here tonight. My piece of shit dad is drunk and rampaging. Needed an out."

He waves an arm and says, "Mi casa es su casa. This grand place is yours for the night."

I walk up beside him, fury burning in my stomach. "Are you fucking stoned?"

"Well, I was fucking," he snorts. "And then I got stoned."

I rub my hand down my face so hard I wouldn't be surprised if I left a bruise. I've been trying to stay clean. Kara drew the line about no drugs in her house, and she's stood stern about it, which I respect her for. She's doing it for Carter's best interest, and I can't blame her for that. I'm not about to piss her off and not get to see Carter. Problem is that in the face of this line in the sand, Declan's chosen to get high more often and see Carter less.

"What about Carter?" I ask.

"I'm on it."

"Like hell you are." I glance over at his clock, unchanged since daylight savings time. "You should've been there fifteen minutes ago. She's waiting for you."

He shrugs.

"You promised her you'd go to this dance with her."

"She doesn't need her big brother taking her to homecoming. They'll make fun of her."

I shake my head and clench my fists. I've always hated how Declan has Carter but doesn't treat her right. When you have someone sweet who loves you unconditionally, you grab hold of them. You never do anything to lose them.

"She wants to spend time with you," I remind him. "She doesn't care what other people think."

Another wave.

"Give me your fucking tie, jackass. Your suit, too."

#

90

Carter lets me walk her home every day for a month—a whole thirty-one days. Well, thirty-two, if you count the walk home we're about to do. Not that I'm counting. All right, fine, I'm counting. Minutes, hours, days, whatever. I'm a fucking sap when it comes to her.

It sort of makes me feel like an addict, whose evolving mantra is something like: thirty-two days without screwing things up. I keep waiting for everything to change—for a day to come when I relapse and she cuts me out, but it hasn't happened, and I hope it doesn't.

I'm trying to prove to her that I can be good for her, just as much as I'm trying to prove it to myself.

"You're being unusually quiet," she says, surprising me. She's been initiating more and more with me lately. At first, she'd just ask me about my day, but now she asks me about my runs or my business with Jason. Her starting conversations is a huge step forward.

"Yeah," I say back. "I, uh, guess I'm just starting to get afraid I'll say or do something wrong. It's easy to blow smoke when you're starting out at something, but now that I'm proving to be awesome at winning you over, it's gettin' scary."

"Well, if it makes you feel better, you're not really that awesome. Just okay."

She talks with a wry smile on her face, her eyebrows pulled high. I try to laugh, but really, it sounds as though I were being punched in the gut. I haven't gotten that expression from her in a long time. I can't even remember the last time she looked at me without a lifetime's worth of bad memories clouding the space between us.

"That makes me feel better, thanks," I tell her. "Room to grow and all that shit ain't a bad thing. I was afraid I'd reached my peak." I motion to the road where we usually part ways and let out a shaky breath. "Hey, you, uh, wanna take a longer route?"

She looks down the street reluctantly, probably envisioning her house. And Kara. And Gabe. She still hasn't told them about me, and I don't blame her. There's no use dragging them into this until she's completely sure. They were like extended family, so betraying Carter meant betraying them.

"How long will it take?" she asks slowly.

"However long you want it to," I say.

"Let me text Kara first," she says softly. She pulls out her phone, and a smile tugs at her lips over whatever she sees there. I crane my neck, wondering what it is in that holy grail of a device that's found a way to make her smile.

Note to self: Get her number later.

I expect the message to be from Gabe or Kara or some friend of hers, and it just might be, except it's a fucking *man's* name. I know I have no room to feel jealous after I've pushed her away. It's just damn hard enough knowing this could be a guy who's just a friend, let alone something more. I used to be that to her—friend and potentially something more. She used to smile at me like this and no one else.

One step forward, two steps back.

Luke: Alright, so my suggestions are completely off. Never met a girl that serious about her burgers. Usually they only like salads and chicken. Wilma's it is. Five tomorrow okay? Maybe Gabe'll let me off early since I'll be hanging out with you :)

She's got a date or something with this Luke guy? Jealous floods my chest like the plume of fire beneath a launching spaceship. *No, I won't be this way with her.* I grit my teeth and try to pretend I didn't just see that. I'm not going to screw this up after thirty-two days over something I don't know about and probably have no room to question.

"You were looking at my phone," she says. "I could feel it."

I run my hand over my chin and down my neck. "Yeah, I was. I'm a curious son of a bitch, huh?"

"More like nosy."

"That, too. You're right."

We head in the direction I want to go—toward the

park where I first realized she meant something more to me than just a friend. I haven't been there in years, because it never felt right to go without her. It's *our* place, and I'm hoping by taking her here, it'll reiterate what I want to happen with us. This is the one place where nothing bad ever happened—only good.

"So, you're not going to ask me about Luke?" she asks.

"You wanted me to read that, didn't you?"

She only stares at me. Evidently silence is both of our answers for evading questions we don't want to answer. I'm too afraid to say something and ruin this. I want to ask her about Luke and if he's competition, or if there's even a competition. She's my endgame, but that doesn't mean I'm hers.

This jealousy thing is a fickle, fickle fucking beast, all the same.

Carter looks up at me, giving me the most unguarded smile yet when she realizes where we're going. It's stupid that this park made us as happy as it did, but we could've easily had less. I spent hours with her here and sometimes Declan, too. It was easy to pretend we were two kids messing around on the jungle gyms, even when I was well into being a teenager. There were a whole bunch of other kids here, too, and I don't know about Carter, but that made me feel normal. As if I was just any other kid playing around.

Luckily, there's no one else but us here today. At this time of day, I'll bet most kids are eating dinner.

Carter immediately heads for the swings. I follow behind her, trying not to enjoy the bounce she gets in her step. She always got that when we were younger, and I'd go home feeling proud of how happy I could make her by bringing her here. Now, though, it's more than just the emotional side of things. There's a whole lot of physical, too, like the way her ass bounces or how her short legs look so incredibly long in her stride. I also love how she glances back over her shoulder every so often, a grin

93

sparkling in her eyes.

If I hadn't made any mistakes, I could've always had moments like these with her. I was wrong to think pushing her away was for the better. *This* is for the better. *This* is what we both need. To be together and be happy.

She turns and sits in the swing's seat. I try to keep my happiness at a less-visible level as I take the seat beside her. I don't want to overwhelm her with how I'm feeling right now.

She kicks off the ground to start swinging and leans back. Her hair is inches from the ground, but she doesn't seem to care. I don't think she ever has. She laughs as the swing suddenly jumps from her movement.

"That sounded like it broke your ass," I say, sitting still.

She tilts her head to see me. "My ass is perfectly fine."

Goddamn, it is. "You broke your arm here, you remember that?"

"Is something like that even possible to forget? God, it hurt so bad," she says.

"You say that, but after you screamed like a banshee, you got all quiet."

She kicks the dirt to slow down. "That's because you looked really scared, and I hated it."

"I was scared," I admit. "Scared out of my mind."

"But you carried me all the way to the doctor."

"Yeah, it's just down the street. It would've been more heroic if I'd carried you to the hospital."

"You were eight."

"That didn't mean I had the right to be dumb. Hospitals fix broken bones, not general practitioners. Might've saved Tish an ambulance trip fee."

"I doubt she paid it. She was bad when it came to medical bills."

"Dad could be, too. He doesn't see the point in paying what's already been fixed. That's why we had bill collectors coming out the ass until I got a handle on things."

It's nice to talk to her about these sorts of things. I

haven't met anyone else who gets it, even if she's removed from the situation. But I don't want to revisit these sorts of subjects with her. If we're leaving our past behind us, then this is the part I definitely want to say good-bye to.

I reach out and grab her chain, and she instantly starts shrieking as the swing starts going all crazy, this way and that.

"Boone Fell!" she yells, her voice swirling right along with her. She starts laughing, and it's contagious. She's always had the best damn laugh around, impossible to ignore. Sort of husky for a girl, but still musical.

The slower her swing spins, the more breathless she gets, until it's at a complete stop and she's doubled over.

"You gonna make it?" I ask.

"I feel dizzy" is all she says.

"That happens when I get involved. Dizzy, sweaty palms, nervous giggling are clear indicators that you've got the Boone Fell Flu."

"Sounds nasty," she says, wrinkling her nose. She does look a little pale, but she's all grins, and there's a lightness to her I haven't gotten to witness in a while. "Maybe we should off patient zero—you."

"No can do, pretty girl."

"Well, it would be the heroic thing to do if you gave your life to the cause."

I reach out again and, instead of spinning her this time, I pull her by chains until our knees are touching. I don't miss the fact that her breathing has suddenly gotten unsteady. Mine has, too.

"You're patient zero. Always have been, always will."

"I can't *catch* your feelings, Boone."

"What's that supposed to mean?" I ask, teasingly.

She licks her lips and holds up her chin indignantly. "Well, you're the one in love. Not me."

"Nope, sorry," I say, leaning in closer to her. I can feel her breath on my cheek and smell the taste of her I've always wished I could forget. It's so all-encompassing that

I want a hit of it. I want to inhale her, taste her, and inject her into my veins. "I've already got this other disease. June Carter Hart Syndrome. Symptoms are heavy heartbeats, stirrings of the body, and rashes."

"Rashes?"

"Well, I've gotta throw something bad in there." *One taste. One kiss. Maybe that's all we need to be reminded of what we have.*

"You didn't throw anything bad in there when it was your disease. Besides, that sounds like I give off an STD or something."

I need her. I've always needed her. Wanted her. If there's one thing I can be sure of, it's that. We've always had perfect chemistry. We can build something on that. "All right then, we both come with a heavy sense of irritability."

"Irritability? That might be—"

My brain short circuits, and I close the distance, cutting off whatever the hell she was about to say. I don't even know what we were talking about, other than that it probably would've been a pretty fun conversation if I was paying attention. It just goes to show how easy it is to joke with her. It's effortless.

The second my lips touch hers, I realize I'm not going to make it another day without kissing her again. I could be on my death bed and this would heal me; I'd jump out of bed and sing and dance and say, "Hallelujah." She's a drug, yeah, but she's a defibrillator and whatever else I need her to be.

She gasps and her lips part, so I pray to God it's some sort of an invitation to get closer to her.

One of my hands moves up the chain, rung by rung, until it's level with her neck. I reach for the back of her head and massage my fingers into that feather-soft, thick hair of hers.

There shouldn't have been a day when I wasn't allowed to do this.

It's me who makes the next sound—a groan that

extends deep down into my straining cock—because I feel her tongue flick against my lips. She wants me, as well. She's starving for this, too. My tongue darts out to meet hers—mingling and reintroducing itself.

I've wanted to do this for so long, and it's kept me up more nights than I can count, and now that it's happening, everything from my head to my cock feels as if were just about to explode. All my nerve endings are just going to decide their time has come and detonate. This would be a good way to die.

I stop kissing her and start traveling my lips down her neck. Her skin even tastes like heaven. I love how warmth spreads beneath my lips. I love the fact that she's arching her neck, that her hands are moving to grip my thighs ...

"Mommy, what are they doing?"

I'm too stoned out of my mind by her to react to the little voice that sounds like it's equally curious and appalled. Carter, though, isn't. She reacts as if she were about to ignite straight into a ball of fire. She pushes away from me, stumbling off the swing. She immediately moves her hand to cover her mouth.

"Oh, no," she whispers, her face turning bright red—almost purple—and looking so embarrassed that I worry we're about to have another playground accident where I have to carry her somewhere. "I'm so sorry—we weren't—"

"Mommy, why was he trying to eat her? Is he a vampire?"

The kid knows what a vampire is, but not what kissing looks like? Kids these days.

"Tommy, be quiet," the little boy's mother hisses. My hazy, Carter-induced fog starts to clear, and I see the mom is older and well-dressed. Not the type who's going to understand what she just walked in on. "You're on a *children's* playground. This is not the time or place to be doing something you should be doing behind closed doors."

"We're so, so sorry," Carter apologizes, backing away. "Things just got out of control."

"I can see that," the woman says, and her eyes tell me she suspects we do this all the time. As if we were nymphomaniacs who fucked like rabbits at kid's playgrounds. "I should call the cops."

"Woah, that's a little out of hand, don't you think? Hell, we were only kissing," I say, standing up.

"Language."

"We'll leave," Carter says softly. "I'm sorry for being inappropriate—I'm not like this, I promise."

"Uh-huh," the woman *tsks*.

"We're gone," I mutter. The woman's acting as though we were doing more than what we were actually doing. We *were* alone until she crept up on us like some sort of creeper. Maybe she goes around trying to catch people doing shit like this. Maybe *she's* the one doing wrong and getting off on it. "C'mon, Carter."

Carter walks briskly ahead of me with her arms around her waist. Shit, this is her shutting down on me. No, she can't do this, not after that kiss.

When we're far away enough from the lady and little Tommy—the future priest I guess he's going to be—Carter whirls around on me, pointing her finger. "We're done."

"What?"

"We're. Done."

"What, no? No." I start to reach out for her but think better of it. I run my hand over my head instead. "You kissed me back."

"And it was a mistake."

"Carter, it might've been that, but it was the best kind of a mistake. Admit it."

She doesn't answer me and instead looks away. "Don't follow me."

"It's gettin' dark."

"Boone."

"Fine," I lie. I still follow her to make sure she gets home safe. If she knows it, she doesn't show it. She just keeps going until she's inside the house.

I walk around her block, wondering where it all went wrong and how I can fix it. The only thing I can think of is to give her a letter. That's what's always made her forgive me. Maybe that'll make things right. It has to.

Carter,
That kiss meant everything to me. Don't let it end this way. Our first kissed was ruined. This one can't be also.
Boone.

But when I climb back up the next day, it's still there.

CHAPTER NINE

Carter

Carter, 15
Boone, 18

"My sister is such a catch," Kara declares. "The boys at the dance are going to go crazy over you."

Hopefully she can't see my blush underneath my makeup. I'm not used to being told I'm pretty. "Nobody is going to look at me twice if my date is my brother." Especially if he's high. God, I hope he's not high. He promised me he'd stay clean tonight. He keeps disappearing deeper and deeper into the life of an addict. Maybe a fun night out will be enough to make him want to try to get sober—I want him to expect more of himself.

The doorbell rings downstairs, and I can't help giggling; I've been looking forward to tonight.

Kara insisted I try on as many formal dresses as we could find, so we spent weeks going around to different stores. Eventually, we both fell in love with a sky blue dress with a knee-length hemline. When I spin, I feel like Sleeping Beauty in the cartoon movie. Kara paid to have my hair done in a pretty, messy bun that's swooped off to the side of my neck. She also made me get my nails done, which was fun *because she got hers done, too.*

"One final touch?" Kara asks, going over to her jewelry box. She opens it and carefully searches for something before turning toward me. In her hand are beautiful diamond earrings in the shapes of flowers. She holds them out to me, smiling. "When I went to my first dance, my mom gave these to me. I wanted to make a tradition out of it when my daughter had her first dance. I want you to have them."

In the middle of reaching toward them, I stop. Daughter? "Kara, you keep them for when you and Gabe have kids."

"I want to give them to you," Kara says, closing the distance between us and dropping them into my palm. "You're my kid."

Flash flood sirens swirl in front of my eyes. What did I do to earn someone like Kara in my life? "Thank you."

"Don't cry," she says, "or else I'll cry."

I squeeze my eyes shut, willing myself not to. I won't ruin my makeup and look like I'm having my mugshot taken instead of going to a dance. After I put the earrings on and manage to strap myself into a pair of heels, Kara links her arm through mine to help me down the stairs, so I don't fall flat on my face.

I think I can hear Gabe talking in the living room to Declan, and I tell myself it has to be a good sign. The last time he came over, he was so strung-out that Gabe had to ask him to leave, which didn't end well. I'm glad it's all been forgotten and they're moving on.

Kara rounds the corner first, and I immediately know something is up. Her shoulders droop slightly, and she looks back at me, her excitement still there, but also nervousness.

I find Boone sitting on the couch, wearing the suit we bought Declan. He immediately stands, gripping a bouquet of violets tightly. There's a note tied by lace to the flowers. He looks absolutely handsome, even if the suit is tight because Declan's thinner and shorter. Boone shaved, which makes him look younger and his hair is brushed to perfection.

My heart should drop because he's here and not Declan, but it doesn't. It soars. Don't get me wrong, I'm disappointed in Declan for not showing up, but there's no better consolation prize than Boone. I've been dreaming of this moment with him since I realized boys could be more than just friends.

His gaze moves in slow pursuit of the way I'm dressed. I don't think I've ever really looked like a woman to him. I've always been too young. Only, right now, I feel mature and beautiful, caressed by the look in his eyes. I've always thought—or maybe pretended—that there were moments here and there, but this is on a whole new level. It's almost as if he likes me as much as I like him.

"You're beautiful, pretty girl," he breathes, coming toward me. The term of endearment leaves me breathless.

"Thank you," I say. My voice sounds far away. "You look very handsome."

"When I have you on my arm, I will be." He closes the distance between us and leans into me. I think maybe he's about to push my hair behind my ear or hug me, but instead his lips find my cheek, barely missing my mouth. He smells like cologne—maybe Gabe's—and his lips are soft against my cheek. He's kissed me like this a thousand times before, but I've never noticed that his kisses heat my skin like a hot spring in the middle of a tundra.

"Oh," I sigh, my body tilting into his.

His free hand moves down my arm as he pulls away and laces our hands. We haven't held hands in a long time. "These are for you," he says in a quiet voice. "I couldn't reach your windowsill."

"Thank you," I repeat, taking them from him. I'm at a loss for words, for breathing. I'm pretty much at a loss for everything. I'm a mess. I carefully maneuver the flowers so I can read the note and not drop his hand. "Your brother shouldn't have stood you up, but I'm glad to be here with you. There's no one else I'd rather be with."

"I want tonight to be special for you," he tells me when I look up. I already know it will be.

#

My high school managed to decorate the dance with paper mâché stars and shimmering centerpieces. I heard someone say that this was all of the leftover decorations from the senior prom last year. Hand-me-down or not, it looks perfect to me.

It felt as though the whole school stopped to look at us when we arrived, since he doesn't come to these things. He ignored them and guided me to the edge of the dance floor, isolating us. Whenever a girl walked over to talk to him or asked him why he's here with me, he put less distance between the two of us to make a point. It's like he's my boyfriend for the night.

We danced to two slow songs already and are on our third. Boone's not a very good dancer, and neither am I, but then slow music comes on, and he wraps his arms around me. I rest my head on his shoulder, and it's like we're gliding on clouds. I want to live in tonight forever.

"You know," Boone says into my ear, so I can hear him over the music, "this is my first dance."

I look at him, biting at my lip. I knew that already. I made it my business to know Boone's dating life. I just always feared he'd take a girl to a dance, they'd laugh over punch, and fall in love to the tune of some eighties song. I only ever wanted that to happen with me, but I just never thought we'd have the chance.

Boone runs his hands up my back then down, dangerously close to my butt. I don't know if he means to, or if I'm just imagining it. He starts to sing, and I shiver. His voice is a raspy, barely-there wind against my skin, and easily one of the best things I've ever experienced. I move closer into him until I can hear his rapid heartbeat and feel it thrumming against my cheek.

When the song finishes, we stay like that. Even when a new fast beat one comes on everyone seems to magically know the dance to. Maybe he doesn't want to leave either? Maybe this is magic for him, too?

"Let's go somewhere quiet," he says, pulling away.

He leaves his arm behind my back as he guides me over to the table where our drinks and purses are. We sat down with his friend, Jason, and his girlfriend, Alex. She broke her foot playing soccer, but they came anyway. I love the way they look at each other—almost as if they were dancing in their imaginations. Jason laughs at something she's saying and leans in to kiss her, then notices us.

"Hey," he says. "Not fans of the Cotton Eye Joe?"

"Don't even know what that is," Boone says with a laugh. "Can you watch our stuff? We're gonna take a walk."

"Definitely," Alex says. "Take your time. We're stuck."

"At least you're stuck with me," Jason says.

"Thanks," Boone tells them both before he leads us away. He moves us through a small crowd on the outer perimeter of the dance floor and through an exit I didn't know existed. I've been in high school for a few months, but I've been avoiding the gym at all costs.

The fall air is chilly against my bare arms, and cold bumps spread out along my arms. Boone looks down at me, then down at himself, and then back at me.

"Don't even think about giving me your jacket," I tell him. *"You'll be cold."*

"That's not my ingenious plan," he says and winks at me. We walk around the back side of the school until we're near the wetlands I've visited for my freshman science class. The grass is a healthy green, the algae are thick, the cattails are reaching for the stars, and the water is completely still in the moonlight.

Boone leans against the shed next to the wetland. I start to lean beside him, but he reaches out and pulls me so my back is against his chest. He wraps the lapels of his jacket as far around me as they'll go and then braces his arms around my middle. He lays his forehead against my shoulder.

"Are you having fun?" he asks. The vibration of his voice is delicious.

"Yes," I say back. I can't talk above a whisper after the dancing, the chilly air, and his close proximity to me. It's all so dreamy, and I don't want to shatter it.

"Even though I'm not Declan?"

"I'm happy it's you here," I admit. It's the most I can say without feeling guilty. Honestly, if I had known Boone would come with me, I'd have asked him instead.

"Me, too," he agrees. He starts moving his thumb in gentle circles above my belly button. It lulls me farther into him. I wonder what it would feel like to be this way with him whenever I wanted—if we could always be like this. *"Getting to spend time with you like this is somethin' to treasure."* I don't know if I just imagine it, but I swear I feel something soft brush against the apex of my neck. His lips? God, just the thought of that being a possibility makes me shiver again. His arms tighten. *"You really look gorgeous tonight, Carter.*

You're the prettiest girl I've ever laid eyes on."

I don't know what to say. All of the air leaves my lungs. He really thinks that? Boone Fell thinks I'm the prettiest girl he's ever seen? How can that be? Boone has his pick of girls, even if he never seems to want to do any picking, so it doesn't make sense for him to think about me like this.

"I've been thinking too much about you for my own good—I always have," he continues. "You mean the most to me. You own me."

I'm not sure what he's saying. I hope he's telling me he has the same feelings for me I have for him, but I don't want to get disappointed if that's not it. Maybe he's talking in "brother" or "friend" terms like he normally does, and I'm too busy reading between the lines.

I turn in his arms, needing to see his face, hoping the answers will be there. They are. He's looking down at me with a soft, intense expression, his eyes glowing in the star light. He looks as he did back at the house—as if he wanted to kiss me.

Please kiss me.

He slips a hand up to my neck as he leans into me. He murmurs unintelligible words, and something like doubt flickers in his eyes before he angles his face to press a soft kiss against my lips. My first kiss.

It's like any kiss he'd put on my head or my cheek, only there's more pressure and it's on my lips. A romantic sort of kiss I can't think through or process. He pulls back slightly, looking for something in my wide-eyed expression.

"Should I have done that?" he asks.

My answer barely comes out. "Yes."

"Should I do it again?"

"Yes."

This time I process too much—everything. Not just his lips and hands and heat, but also the magic of the moment. We're on my high school grounds, but my heart would adamantly say we're floating in the sky, surrounded by glimmering lights.

He kisses me deeper, holding me tighter, but the kiss doesn't go any further. It stays in chaste perfection, which is probably all I can handle. This is as far as I've ever let my dreams go.

#

"I hate him. I hate him. I hate him," I say over and over again as I shove my laundry into the washer. I don't know how many times I've said that or some variation of it. I was keeping count, but at about twenty-nine I gave up. I mean, it's not as though he were worth me counting how many times I've said I hate him if I actually do hate him, right?

"Stupid," I rant, slamming the door shut. "Stupid," I continue, pressing the button, "asshole," I finish, relishing in the loud noises of the washer gearing up. I might have added a pair of my shoes for the added clunk. I can pretend it's Boone's head or something equally liberating.

I cross my arms, and the satisfaction instantly fades away. What was that even supposed to accomplish? I've been avoiding and ignoring all things Boone for six days now, but he's still at the forefront of my thoughts. I can't escape him, no matter how many times I beat up the washing machine or throw clunky shoes in it.

"Gah," I mutter. I should've told Kara about the kiss, only she was too giddy to notice my downer mood. Gabe must have mentioned my plans with Luke, and I didn't have the heart to bring her down. Also, I don't want another lecture about letting my heart get the best of me. I already know how much Boone affects me, and I really don't want to talk about that.

Plus, if I think too much about him, then I think about how wonderful it felt to kiss him. How it made me feel whole and right and how empty I've been since we lost contact. How I hate him and love him, but that stupid, stupid, asshole managed to make the love side win out.

"What did that ever do to you?"

I jump, immediately straightening the tank top I'm wearing because it's not exactly flattering. "Luke? What are

107

you doing here?"

Luke gives me a strange look—as if I should know the answer, which I probably should. We've been texting a lot, only I don't really remember what's been said. Luke's sweet, cute, and smart, but for some reason my mind feels as though it were everywhere else except with him. I *want* to like him. He's the type of guy you meet, fall in love with, and grow old with. He doesn't leave or go back on promises. He's there. *Forever.*

"My parents and I came over for dinner," he answers.

"Oh, gosh, yeah." I remember now. Gabe said they would be coming over because—he claimed—he wanted to pick Luke's dad's brain about administration, but I wouldn't put it past him to have an ulterior motive. I didn't expect them for a while, but I've been purposefully hiding and avoiding all human contact. Time flies when you're miserable. "Sorry."

"It's okay," he says, shrugging. "When I get angry at washing machines I forget things, too. So, why do you hate it, and what makes it an asshole?"

I stare at him blankly. Great, he heard that. "My clothes just didn't get dry."

"That's not the dryer," he points out.

"That must be why."

"Right." He grins, as if I were hilarious or something. I'm not sure what it says that he hasn't noticed I've lost my mind. Maybe he's a smile-through-the-pain type of guy. "Well, Kara asked me to come find you. She has the food ready."

"She's used to dinner parties," I explain. "Our dad and her mom come over a lot." I have no doubt my voice shows just how much of an enjoyable experience that is.

He laughs. "I get that. It's the same with my grandma."

"Glad to know everyone's family is dysfunctional," I say. "Not just us."

We walk to the dining room where everyone's already seated and waiting on us. I feel a little better about the way

I'm dressed when I see everyone else looks just as casual. Well, except for Luke. I've noticed he dresses as if he were always prepared to go to a last-minute business meeting.

It's nice getting to hang out with another family of three. I like the way Luke's parents boast about him and how he's more than happy to gloat about them, too. I haven't gotten a lot of healthy instances of what a family should be, so it's nice to have them as an example. It's also nice having a reminder not all dinner parties have to include a dad that wishes you didn't exist.

#

After we're done eating, Luke's mom and Kara shoo us outside so they can do the dishes. I don't miss the conspiratorial look in their eyes. It seems as though everyone but me had a plan for my life.

I blush and lead Luke out the back door.

"You know, I think we have a fan club," he announces once the door is closed. "And we've only been texting." The blush suddenly turns cold and I feel the color drain from my cheeks. The idea of dating Luke is nice—he's a good fit for me, he has a stable life, Kara and Gabe approve of him. But *actually* dating him? It doesn't feel right.

But maybe that's how dating is supposed to be. You are getting to know another person, maybe even getting to know yourself in the process. Nobody in their right mind goes into that without an ounce of nervousness, right?

Except it should be good nerves. Not that what I feel for Luke is bad, necessarily—just platonic. Then again, that could be exactly what I need. I'm so used to crazy highs and dramatic lows, to messy hearts, and to broken promises that I might not know a healthy way to love and need another person. Luke might be what I need to learn to be normal.

"Hey, Carter?" Luke says. There's something weird in

his voice.

"Yeah? Sorry I'm going all space cadet on you. I'm just—life with washers is hard, you know?" I laugh nervously.

Luke doesn't laugh back. "It's not that. Why's there a guy up there?"

My heart drops.

No.

Of course he'd be out here. He only ever comes when it's dark because he doesn't want Gabe finding him. He's still delivering these notes even though I haven't been reading them. They're piling up on the window; the paper getting ruined and the flowers dying. It's been hard to ignore them, but I have. I've been tempted to read them and pretend I didn't. My fear is if I do that, I'll find something worth reading that'll send me back in his direction. After our kiss, I can't do that again.

"Boone," I yell in a whisper, stomping to the bottom of the trellis, "why're you here?"

He removes the flowers and note from his back pocket and sets them on the windowsill. He glances down at me, grinning. "Hey, pretty girl. You're talkin' to me."

"You shouldn't be here. I told you to leave."

"Yeah, but that was a few days ago, and I figured my restrictions were up. You know, expired."

He expertly climbs down the trellis, knowing where to grab to not hurt his hands. Close to the bottom, he lets go and jumps off, landing on his feet like a cat who's about to catch his prey.

"Who is this guy?" Luke asks me. "Should we call the cops?"

"It'd be worse if you called good ol' Gabe. He's the big guns," Boone says with a deep chuckle.

"Well, if you're not quiet, he's going to come out here anyway," I warn.

Boone just grins at me. I'm sure he thinks this means we're best friends again. I tell him to leave, and he thinks he should stay; I tell him to quiet down, and he thinks it's me saving his life.

He brushes his hand on his dirty, grease-stained jeans and then holds it out to Luke. "Boone Fell. The *it's* to Carter's *complicated*."

CHAPTER TEN

Boone

"Luke," he answers suspiciously. He shakes my hand, definitely sizing me up.

So, this guy—who looks like he's about to go out for a round of golf—is Mr. Burger-Date. Well shit, he's a total catch. He looks like he's the type of guy who will own nice cars for the rest of his life, impress everyone he meets (including Gabe and Kara), and will only stay at exclusive resorts on vacations. His confident, cordial look is going to get him places. Still, I have a feeling he's going to be washed up in a few decades. Balding, fat, going through a midlife crisis, thinking he's still at his best.

Hell, that's where we're all going. It's just better to think about his impending doom than mine.

"We're not complicated because we're nothing," Carter tells me, yelling slightly. She moves her arms to emphasize each word. It's pretty damn cute, if you ask me. Still, the words hurt even if I don't believe them.

"Whatever you say, pretty girl," I tell her. I jut my thumb over my shoulder, toward her window. "I just had to drop by my final note."

She blinks on the word *final* and her mouth opens as if she were going to question it. I was hoping to get this reaction out of her. Once again, she's showing me she's not entirely ready to let me go. She's all talk—when it comes to me really leaving, she falters. She might not be reading these notes, but that doesn't mean that they're not important to her.

I cover my mouth to hide my grin. "After this, I'll go back to the regular ones," I continue.

"What?"

"Oh, yeah, you're not reading them. Well, you see, the last few ones have been part of an anthology—they go together. I'd get to reading them soon, because they're all weathered, and before long, you won't know where the beginning is."

"Anthology?" she repeats.

I can't help but laugh. Sometimes she's on her A-game and the best at dishing shit back, while other times, she's a parrot. "Read 'em to see."

She looks up at her window in a way that has me half-expecting her to parkour her way up there. Then her eyebrows slam down hard and indignance shows up. Most guys wouldn't know how to handle a girl like Carter—who's as stubborn as they come—but I like how she can be challenging. After all these years of knowing her, she keeps me on my toes. That's the type of thing you want to have for the rest of your life—someone who won't let you get away with anything.

"Not going to happen," she tells me.

"Well, that's your decision," I remind her. "They're ready when you want them, just like me."

She narrows her eyes and, yeah, that was probably the wrong thing to say. I haven't exactly been here when *she's* wanted me. I've mostly been here when *I've* wanted her. Time for things to change.

Luke clears his throat. Totally forgot he was here. "Maybe it's time for you to leave."

"Maybe," I agree. "I tend to overstay my welcome."

"Yes," Carter says. "All the time."

"In the eye of the beholder," I answer. I bring my hand up to my forehead and salute them both. "Happy reading."

CHAPTER ELEVEN

Carter

Carter, 15
Boone, 18

My heart is beating like a roadrunner as I walk from Boone's trailer to the woods. There's an old, rotting picnic table there that he and Declan like to hang out on. I was hoping he'd be at his trailer, but his dad answered the door instead, holding his Bible. Between spouting verses, he told me where he thought Boone was.

I haven't seen him since the dance. He kissed me again when he dropped me off, lingering against my lips and leaning into me. It felt like the beginning after an unreasonably long prologue.

Then nothing.

There has to be a reason. The kiss meant far too much for Boone to just ignore, right? Oh God, I hope so. I don't know if I'm ready to hear anything different. As much as I want an answer, I'm not sure I want the truth.

I hear Boone and Declan laughing obnoxiously before I actually see them—meaning they're probably under the influence. What influence, I don't want to know—particularly concerning Declan.

When they come into view, I see that Declan is laying on the top of the table while Boone is sitting on the grass with his back propped up against the bench, facing away from me. Boone is only wearing a pair of sweatpants, whereas Declan is wearing a pair of tight black jeans and a shirt that's so ripped up, it looks as though he was in an accident with scissors.

Declan notices me first. "Hey, it's my sister," he says dreamily. "Sorry I missed your dance."

I've talked to him and listened to his apology. The day after his high wore off, he showed up at our house. He was cranky and difficult and refused to leave unless he could "see" I accepted his apology.

"It's okay, Dec," I say softly.

At the sound of my voice, Boone shoots up off the ground.

Declan's head lolls to the side. "You find an ant in your pants?"

Boone swallows, pale. His eyes are red and distant, but something's in them fighting to gain some control. I should've waited for him to come to me. I didn't think he did this anymore, but I guess he does. He's not in the frame of mind to talk to me about the kiss or about what it means.

"Carter," he starts, "what are you doing here?"

I stare at him. What am I doing here? I don't even know, other than that I needed some sort of a resolution to what's happening between us. I keep thinking about the kiss, and the more I dream, the more his disappearing act hurts.

"I'm here to talk," I finally say. "About what happened at the dance."

"I'm so sorry I missed the dance," Declan apologizes again.

I ignore him. He's too spaced out to hear, care, or remember if I respond.

Boone's gaze flicks over to Declan and never returns to me. "We don't need to talk. Nothin' happened."

My heart stops beating. Nothing happened? But he kissed me, and he made it sound like he wants me, too. "What?"

"Nothin' happened. It was just a kiss. People kiss all the time. It doesn't always mean anything."

"But this did," I argue. "I know it did."

"Carter, you're confusing yourself. Just 'cause it was your first

kiss, doesn't make it special."

"Yes, it does. It does mean something, and it's special because it was with you."

"Fine. It didn't mean anything to me."

Tears fill my eyes, but I blink them away. "No, it did. I know it did."

"It didn't, Carter." His jaw pops, and he crosses his arms. Defensive. "I've kissed enough girls to know when it matters and when it doesn't."

"Why are you doing this?" I ask, frantic. I move closer to him, the bench still between us. I set my hands on the wood, not even bothered by the icky, wet feeling it's gotten from being outside. I don't know how Declan is just lying on it; I guess there's a reason why his clothes are always dirty.

"Because I don't want to hurt you by leading you on."

"You don't want to hurt me by leading me on?" I shake my head. I should've never come here. "You've already done that."

"It's best to give up now, then," he says.

I miss the guy who was tender and joking, who held my hand even though everyone made fun of him for it, whispered kind things into my ear whenever I got hurt, kissed my head every chance he got, who put me first.

He shoves his hands in his pockets and walks off. I wait for him to turn around and say he's joking or ask for it all to be taken back. He doesn't, and I refuse to run after him when I don't know why he's walking away.

I remain standing, and Declan's hand finds my shoulder. "I'm sorry I didn't make the dance."

"I know," I whisper.

"I'm sorry Boone kissed you."

"Me, too."

He lets out a long sigh. "You're too good for this life, you know. You're too good for me and him and everything else we grew up with." Whatever he's on has him thinking retrospectively. "You should use this chance to leave it all behind."

His words hurt just as much as Boone's. "What about you? Dec, I can't leave you behind. I can't lose both you and Boone."

119

"What if you've already lost us?"

"What does that mean?"

He doesn't answer, and I turn to look back at him. He's fallen asleep. The whole world could be falling apart around him—and not just feel like it is—and he wouldn't care. He can just shut down and let everything go.

I think this is the most alone I've ever felt.

#

"You shouldn't read those notes," Luke tells me quietly as his parents say their good-byes. As soon as Boone left, I did my best to pretend like he was never there. I monopolized the conversation so Luke wouldn't have a chance to ask about Boone. Evidently Luke was only biding his time to bring Boone up. I should have guessed—Luke is the type of guy who wants to solve problems. "I don't know what's going on between you two, but it can't be good for you."

I offer a sad smile. "You don't know the situation."

"You're going to read them, aren't you?"

I refuse to make eye contact. "I don't know."

"I hope you don't," Luke murmurs. He kisses me on the cheek and gets into his parents' car. As they pull away, I bring my hand up to my face. Instead of tingles and butterflies, it feels numb. I don't even know what his lips felt like against my skin. Maybe it's because I'm older now, but I used to memorize all of Boone's kisses because they were all significant.

When they're gone, I tell Kara and Gabe goodnight and head up to my room. I close my door and listen to make sure they don't follow me up to talk about Luke. When I hear the TV on, I back away and head for the window. I nearly trip on the shaggy rug. Panic and nervousness bring out the klutz in me.

An *anthology*, he called them.

I carefully unfold each and lay them on my bed in order of how they're stacked, so I know which ones come first. Each paper is more weathered than the next, with some of the letters barely decipherable. I drop down to my knees beside my bed and lean in to read them.

Carter,
That kiss meant everything to me. Don't let it end this way. Our first kissed was ruined. This one can't be also.
Boone.

That one doesn't feel like a part of the anthology, but it still grips at my chest. Our first kiss wasn't ruined. It was perfect. It was the after that was ruined, just like what happened on the swing set.

The next ones are the anthology because they're numbered one through five.

1. I never told you this, but when I was young, I didn't know how my mom died. I was too young to remember her death, so I believed my dad when he told me she left us. When I got older, he told me it was all a lie.

2. I think he waited so long to tell me because he wanted me to remember it. Understand it. He was sober and he didn't have his Bible. I think he wanted his sole focus to be on torturing me.

3. He told me I killed her.

4. I know I couldn't help it, but sometimes I wonder if I hadn't been born, if it'd all be okay, you know? He'd be happy, she'd be happy, you'd be happy. I think the real truth of it all is that my mom chose to die for me, but my dad let me kill him. He may be breathing, but he's cold and in Hell.

5. I'm not telling you this to make you feel sorry for me. I just want you to know I've grown up thinking I was a killer, in more ways than just the murderous one. I didn't want to kill all your hopes and dreams, so I got close to make sure you achieved them and then I'd push you away out of fear I'd ruin it all. I hurt you because I didn't know how to love you.

Tears slip down my cheeks. He was such a sweet person when he was younger. How could his dad make him think he'd killed his own mom? It's not his fault she had cancer or that she'd chosen his life over her own. I always knew his dad was cruel, but I didn't realize it was to this extent. No wonder it seemed like whenever we'd reach a certain point, he'd push me away. He knew how to love me like a friend or a sister, just never how to *love me* love me.

I fall back on my butt and shimmy until I'm sitting up against my bed. I grope behind me for the letter that says, "He told me I killed her."

I remember asking him about his mom when we were younger. I thought it was amazing how I didn't have a dad and he didn't have a mom, as though it somehow made us connected and closer. When I asked, he was really distant and fearful-looking, never answering me. I was too little and maybe too self-absorbed to see his heartbreak.

More tears start to fall the more I look at the letter, so I reach for the final one. My fingers trace over the line about not knowing how to love me. He told me in another letter that he "loved me too much," which makes sense now, too. He didn't know how to love.

Behind me, I hear my bedroom door open. I smack at my face, trying to get rid of the tears. It's like Kara has some sort of a spidey sense for when I'm ugly-crying.

"Yeah?" I ask, trying to keep my voice even.

Please don't come around the bed. Please don't come around the bed.

"What are these?" she asks.

Never mind.

I have no choice but to look at her. The second she

sees me, she drops the paper—the second note—back to the bed and moves to sit by me.

"Why're you crying? What's wrong?"

"It's nothing," I whisper.

"It's something. What are these?"

"They're notes from Boone," I admit. "I've been letting him walk me home, and he's been writing them for a while now."

"Oh, Carter," she says, smiling sympathetically. "I thought you were done with him."

I want to tell her I am, or I will be, but instead, I burst out into more tears. "I'm not. I don't know how to be."

She pulls me into her arms. "I know, sweetie. I know."

She lets me cry until there aren't any tears left and then she just holds me while I sit and think. She rubs my head and tells me it'll be okay, as moms always do in the movies.

"What's wrong with me?" I ask. "I want to like Luke, but …"

"But Luke's not Boone."

"No."

"Sweetie," she says, but doesn't seem to know what to say next. I don't either. She hugs me tight and then lets go. She reaches for the other notes and reads them over in order, then shuffles back to the beginning to read them all again. "It sounds to me like he's serious about you this time around. He's being open and honest." She sets them in her lap. "There are others?"

I hesitate before I nod. The answer to that should be there *were* others. If I were in my right mind when I first received them, I would have burned them or shredded them or let a pack of wild horses trample over them. Obviously, I wasn't and—I'm still not—sane. I've completely lost it. Instead, I put each letter into a plastic bin hidden beneath my bed. The only thing holding me back from being full-on mental is I haven't re-read any of them. Believe me; I've wanted to.

I roll onto my hands and knees and grope beneath my

bed until I find the bin. I pull it out and force myself not to look at Kara. I know I have a problem. I'm just not at the "admitting it" stage.

"Can I look at them?" Kara asks.

"Yeah."

I slide it her way. She spends the next fifteen minutes reading each note thoroughly. She has the look on her face she gets whenever she has a new novel to read—a mixture of excitement and reluctance. It's a pipe dream, though, because Boone and I don't have the type of love story she likes to read about. We barely even have a story.

"This is different than he usually is," Kara remarks , shuffling through the stack until she gets to the one that says, "It was because I loved you too much." She holds it up between two fingers, repeating the words quietly.

"That's what scares me," I admit. "That he's different. These notes—they're from a guy who would be easy to love. What if he's just really, really good at coming across this way on paper?"

"How's he been when he's walked you home?"

"The same, but still different. Better."

She nods and sets the note back with the others. She lines them all up, her forehead wrinkled as she thinks. "The thing is, he might be better and different, and he might be saying these things and feeling them, but what matters the most is that *you* have the same intentions. The last time you both wanted different things, and it didn't turn out well. You got hurt, and I don't want to see you hurt again—by him or anyone else."

I appreciate Kara for being so genuine and for not telling me what to do, even if she has her own set of opinions. She's on my side, no matter what, which is why I should have talked to her sooner.

"Kara?" I ask, nervously picking at the hem of my shorts.

"We won't tell Gabe," she replies, somehow reading my mind. "Eventually, we'll have to, but he'll just make things hard."

"Thank you," I say. "He's going to be mad."

"No," she says. "He could never be mad at you or me or anyone, really. Well, at Dad maybe. He just wants to see you happy, and it's hard for him to let you go and figure out things on your own." She bumps her shoulder against mine. "You're his favorite daughter."

She always says that, which is weird considering there's no one else in the selection pool for the designation of favorite; plus, I'm not even his kid. "He's my favorite dad."

She laughs, but quickly gets serious again. "Try to do me a favor? Play it close to the chest."

"I already am."

CHAPTER TWELVE

Boone

I take my sunglasses off as I survey the building Jason and I just toured with the realtor. It's red-bricked, has an apartment on the second floor I could use, and it's in the business district—down the street from the gas station Carter works at. The realtor took a chance on this one, knowing we'd like the price but not necessarily the inside. The place is outdated, considering it's been empty for about ten years and was built back when the town was founded. Of all things, it was a hardware store, which I think is fate or something kickstarting our asses. I even like the idea of making the place into a hardware store someday as an extra option for revenue. If we're already buying parts, why not buy in bulk? In the long run, that's cheaper.

"So, what are you thinkin', man? Is this Fell & Grant Company's HQ or what?" I ask Jason.

He's been keeping his thoughts to himself. I don't blame him; he's got the most to lose. Me, I don't have anything. The only thing I've ever owned is the keys to our trailer. Ironic, considering I'm the town repairman, and I haven't repaired the ripped screen door, forgoing the need for keys. It's a big jump going from owning nothing to having a store.

Jason clucks his tongue then looks back at his van as if his wife and kids were there with all the answers. "I'd better talk to Alex about it before sinking our money into it, but I'd like to go for it."

"Me, too," I agree. "It's a nice price. Outdated, yeah, but it's something we can deal with. Not like we need much."

"The location's good, too," he adds.

We tick off a few more bullet points we like about the place, as well as what could use some work. By the end of it, Jason seems on board, and I think he has enough to present to his wife to get her on board, as well.

Off in the distance, sirens start to blare. We take it as a sign to walk back to our cars. I've got just enough time to drive home, ditch my car, and then go for a run before I see Carter. Hopefully, she'll actually want to see me this time, not just ignore me.

"I've been telling all my clients about the company, and they're all into it—happy for me. There are a few who weren't okay with the slight price increase, but most of 'em are the ones who don't pay anyway," I explain.

"That's good to hear. I've talked to mine, and it's been the same thing."

I grin, glancing back at the brick building, which will hopefully be ours soon. This building is seriously going to be life-changing for me. It's going to set me up for a future, get me out of the damn trailer park, and put me on a path completely unlike my dad's. I never thought I was going to amount to much—but now ... who knows? This must be what hope feels like.

"Looks like someone's having a bad day," Jason says as not one, but two cop cars speed down the twenty-miles-per-hour street.

My gaze follows them. "Probably heading to the park."

You can't say it's a new day unless at least one cop has visited the trailer park.

"Sad they didn't stop and let you hitch a ride."

If there's one thing I can honestly say about myself with pride, it's that I've never, ever been in the back of a cop car or on the wrong side of the law. Sure, that probably means I'm too sneaky for my own good when I do bad shit, but it also means I don't have a record.

The car doesn't keep going as I expect. Instead, it swerves to a stop, nearly landing on the sidewalk.

Right in front of the gas station.

"Carter."

I barely manage to get her name out before I'm running. I'm in the best clothes I've got—khakis and a polo—and brown "dress" shoes I brought at a yard sale. None of it's good for doing anything fast or panicked, such as running as hard and as fast as I can. I hear someone else running, too. Probably Jason. I don't look to see.

I pass the cop cars, both empty. Their sirens are off, but the lights are on. That's got to mean something good, right? If it were serious, they'd have everything on, letting the world know something's happening. Plus, there'd be more than just police cruisers—there'd be an ambulance if people are hurt. If *Carter's* hurt.

My stomach broils at the thought. She's got to be okay. This can't be anything. I can't lose her in the process of trying to get her back.

I grope blindly at the door handle and yank it open. My vision is focused on getting to the cashier's counter— seeing she's okay.

I immediately run into a female cop who's shorter than me but built like a wall. "We ask that you stay outside until we're done here," she says, all formal. She looks sort of familiar, as most people in this town are, but I don't care to place her.

"Is Carter here?" I demand, which is probably a stupid

question because it's not like they've been here any longer than I have. "Carter Hart?"

"Sir," she warns.

"Carter!" I yell, trying to look around her. I can see the other cop's back, but nothing beyond that.

"Hey, man," Jason says.

His hand falls on my shoulder, and I shrug it off. I yell her name again, a concoction of terror, exhaustion, doom, and misery washing over me.

The other cop takes a step to the side, to check what's going on, and I see her. All the air leaves my system. She's pale and obviously shaken, but she looks okay. Safe. My relief is short-lived when I realize something bad had to have happened if the cops were called.

"He's okay," she says quietly. "He was here ... before."

The female cop nods to Jason. "And him?"

"He'll keep me quiet," I mutter, stepping around her.

"I'm obviously very good at it," Jason says.

The closer I get to Carter, the more frantic I feel. She doesn't just look shaken—she looks out of sorts and lost. Her normally expressive eyes are completely blank and shut down, her eyebrows stiff. There's a slight cut along the underside of her jaw, red and bleeding, that I didn't notice from far away but is all I can see now.

"What the hell happened here?" I demand, immediately moving to make my way behind the counter. Being close to her is the reassurance *I* need to make sure she's okay.

She flinches, automatically raising her hand to the side of her head. Her hair is a mess, falling out of her ponytail and down over her shoulders. Her lips start to tremble as if she were about to lose it.

"Carter, you're okay," I say, trying my best to soften my voice, even though all I really want to do is pulverize the whole damn place. "It's okay."

She shakes her head, looking from me, to Jason, to the officer, and back to me. Her hands are listlessly at her sides, squeezing shut and opening. *She's not okay. Shit. What happened?*

The officer clears his throat. "There was a man who came in here a few weeks ago—a junkie. Ms. Hart tells us you saw him, as well. Can you give us a description of him?"

I can't clean up the mess happening in my mind right now, but a clear picture of that junkie forms in my head. I made sure to memorize the jackass so if I ever saw him on the streets again, I could tell him a thing or two about how to treat a woman. Particularly, Carter.

"Thin, about my height, had a gray beard, bald with liver spots on his head, and enough track marks to pinpoint cities on a map," I recite. I don't miss the hint of recognition in the officer's eyes. I haven't seen the junkie before, which is weird because this is such a small town, but he's somebody. Maybe an out-of-towner who's caused enough issues to get on the cops' radar.

"That matches Ms. Hart's description," the officer—Taft, by his name nameplate—says.

" Why're you asking me this? What happened? Did he come back?" I look to Carter and, without being answered, I know he did. She looks like she did the day he first came in and freaked her out, only this time he roughed her up. "Carter, talk to me?"

"He-he …" She looks down at the ground. "He thinks I have money for him, and he was here to take it." She raises her hand back to her head—this time, her face contorting. "He grabbed me, and I slammed my head." My gaze drops to a cardboard display of candies, which is tilted over and spilled out. There's a red smattering on the thinner slat, and I'd take a guess that the edge caused her cut.

"Goddamn it," I mutter, sick to my stomach. *I wish I'd been here to keep her safe. I wish someone had—anyone.*

"You fought back," the officer tells her soothingly, like he's trying to reassure her. He looks at Jason and me. "She maced him, he ran, and she called 911."

"You maced him?" I ask, smiling despite myself. "You did good, Carter."

She smiles back weakly, but it doesn't quite reach anywhere else. I approach her slowly since she's so jumpy. This time she goes still but doesn't move away. Before I can think twice about it, or she can, I slip my hand down into hers. I lean into her and ask quietly, so neither of the officers or Jason can hear, "He didn't do anything else, right?"

She shakes her head.

I let out a long, relieved sigh. I must've been holding that in my whole life based on the size of it. I squeeze her hand and look at the officer. "Do you think you'll be able to find him?"

"We'll do our best to," the officer says. Most people might take his guarded expression as being honest, but I can sense a *but* to it. I've dealt with enough cops, thanks to my dad, to know when there's something more to be said.

"Good," I say, slow and steady. "Is she done here?"

"Yes, for now," he answers. "We've got contact information if we need to know more."

I look to Carter. "Is anyone coming to get you?"

She shakes her head. "I didn't get to call anybody."

"All right. Then how about I take you home?"

"Kara and Gabe ..."

"Will understand," I finish. I look to Jason, who's been slowly creeping closer. He's a good guy who cares about everyone. "Think you can take her out to my car?"

"Sure," he says.

"Aren't you coming?" Carter asks.

"Yeah," I say. "I just want to tell him some other things I remember about the guy."

An eyebrow raises as if she doesn't believe me, but she doesn't say anything about it. She'll either save it for later, or maybe it just doesn't matter. My wanting to talk more to the cops is nothing compared to what just happened. She probably faced enough reality for one day.

Jason follows closely behind her out the door, and I'm thankful for it. She obviously can take care of herself, but I'm happy he's there for an extra hand.

When I hear the bell *ding*, signaling they're gone, I turn back to Officer Taft.

"You don't expect to find him, do you?"

The female officer, Officer Lockson, walks up beside him, and they exchange glances. "Getting him won't be a problem," she says, "but keeping him might."

"They've got a camera, so there'll be footage of what happened," Taft explains. "But assault charges like these usually only end up with probation. If it does end in an arrest, it'll only be for a year."

"Shit," I mutter. I run a hand over my chin. This is why vigilantes are so popular. "And chances are, if this guy thinks she's got the money, he got the idea from somewhere, and there'll be more with the same goal."

"Let's hope that's not the case," Lockson says. "It's a good thing she's obviously feisty on her feet."

"Yeah," I agree, feeling pride wash all over me again. "She's somethin' damn special."

They both look unimpressed and as though they'd be ready to get a move on with things. They explain they're going to wait around for the owner to get there, and I thank them for taking the 911 call then go out to Carter. I need reassurance she's there, safe, and okay. This scared me out of my ever-loving mind.

I don't know what I would've done if something had happened to her.

#

Boone, 18
Declan, 18

"You broke her heart, you know," Declan says out of nowhere.
I grimace and drop down to the ground, leaning my back against

the wall of a giant fountain, which Declan's currently in. He asked me to go out tonight and help him "work." I should've known better. Declan's never worked a goddamn day in his entire life. What he really means is he wants to go around and scrounge up some cash.

We used to make fun of Tish for her desperate ways of making quick cash, and here he is doing the same thing. He's crossed over from the cheap stuff to the drugs that are an expensive lifestyle. I don't know why I didn't choose to see that until now. I don't know why I'm not stopping him, either.

The dude's going around and stealing people's wishes, and I'm letting him. We're the lowest of the low.

He's got his tattered jeans rolled up to his scrawny knees, slipping all the change he can find into a plastic bag he stole from a garbage can. I've got no doubt he could probably be a millionaire if he did this every day. Crazy, the amount of people who throw silver dollars away.

Every time he picks a coin out, I try to imagine what it's in there for. A wish for true love. A wish for a sick family member to get better. A wish for a promotion. A wish their significant other won't find out about the cheating.

"Can we not talk about this again?" I groan.

"Hey, you're not the one with the sister who's moping around like she's a puppy that just got kicked. Hell yes we're gonna talk about this and keep at it. You shouldn't have kissed her." This is the most sober I've seen him in years, which is probably why he's chomping at the bit to make some cash.

"You think I don't regret doing it?" I smack my hands against my knee for something to do. I'm lying through my teeth; I don't regret it. I would never trade getting to kiss her or show her the time of her life for anything. I do regret pushing her away, even if it was the right thing to do. "I may be a fucking idiot with impulse control, but that doesn't mean I don't—"

"If you say 'have feelings,' I'm going to drown you," Declan interrupts.

"Well, it's the truth." I narrow my eyes. "It's no better than what you did to her."

"No, what I did is somehow a lot better," he says. "You managed to make my shit seem like a walk in the park."

I glance over my shoulder at him. He has a focused look on his face as he pulls out a handful of coins. His lips move, counting them. He'd be a pretty good accountant if he tried to make something of himself. Imagine that on your resume: good with money and numbers due to many years as a drug addict.

"So, what's with your newfound sobriety?" I ask. *Consider that Band-Aid ripped off.*

He raises an eyebrow, which reminds me so much of Carter I feel sick to my stomach. "It's not a newfound sense of anythin'. Just ran out of cash. Plus, I'm tryin' to be there for Carter since you ain't able to, too."

"Not gonna last then?" I ask.

"No. Not for long."

Sometimes, when I let myself think about it too long, I blame myself for Declan. I've never been one for extracurricular activities, but drugs seemed like one I could get behind. They promised relaxation, a hideaway from the world, an escape. They seemed like the perfect solution to our messed up situations. For a while it was all good, and it worked—no harm, no foul. Then Declan wanted something stronger, and he wanted it more frequently. Then he was out of control.

"How much have you got?"

Declan drops his money into the bag. "Fifty bucks and twenty-two cents. They don't clean this that often, I guess. There's more to grab."

"Huh." Almost fifty dollars in wishes. In a small town, no less. Guess not everybody's lives are what they're cracked up to be.

Headlights appear down the road, and I tense. The fountain is in the middle of town, which makes it the worse place to be committing any crimes.

"The cops?" I wonder, squinting. The last thing I need is to run interference with the cops.

Declan shrugs and leans down to pick up more coins. He's been arrested twice already. The first time Kara helped pay bail, and the second time she refused. Carter had trouble digesting that, despite knowing tough love was best. It obviously didn't work.

The headlights blind me for a split second as they come toward us and then fall out of alignment with me. I blink to get the black spots out of my vision. It's not a cop—it's a plain, black car.

I sigh, relieved out of my mind. "Man, maybe it's time we give this thing up."

"Hey, I'm making money tonight. I don't give a shit what you do," Declan bites out, an edge to his voice that hasn't been there all night. He's been fine because he's working toward his fix. The last thing he wants is to leave.

A car door slams, and I jump. Shit. It had better not be a good Samaritan or an off duty cop.

"What are you two doing?"

Worse, it's Gabe.

I nearly fall over in my rush to stand up. Normally I'd have a quip or a comeback for anyone else, but Gabe terrifies me. He might not be Carter's dad, but he's in that role. He's not my buddy or my friend; he's my judge, jury, and executioner. He knows it, too.

He looks furious, as though he planned to tear me limb from limb. Guess that means Carter told him everything.

"Working," Declan answers. I'm not sure why he's even trying. It's preferable to just keep quiet in the face of imminent death.

"You're stealing," Gabe corrects icily.

He doesn't pay Declan any mind and comes straight for me. I'm taller and stronger than he is, but I'm no match for the fury in his eyes. I messed up, and he's not going to let me get away with it.

Gabe charges me, throwing a punch when he's close enough. I see it coming a mile away, and I could easily avoid it, but I deserve the hit. I take it. I relish in the pain because it's my penance for hurting Carter.

The reason for the punch—not the punch itself—is why I stumble back. I don't wipe at my face or try to brace my nose. I just let the blood ooze down my cheek, mouth, and chin.

There's clinking behind me, where Declan is still picking out change as though he could give a shit about me getting punched.

Gabe points at me. "You hurt her again and you'll pay."

I have nothing to say because I agree with him. If I do anything to upset Carter again, I should pay. Hell, I want to. Trouble is, I can't seem to shake my recklessness. No matter how hard I try, I'm still the same imbecile bred out of trailer trash and booze.

He spins and stalks off. Over his shoulder, he calls, "That goes for you, too, Declan."

#

Carter doesn't say a word the entire ride. I wish I were the reason for her silence; at least that's something I can fix. Right now it's as though I were back in high school Algebra, trying to solve for a variable.

When I first got into the car, she flinched. *Flinched. She's afraid of me,* all because of some random druggie who doesn't know his manners.

I glance at her as we pull into her driveway. She hasn't tried talking me out of coming home with her. I'm sure it's because Gabe's nowhere to be found—or at least his car is. Still, I think he'd take one look at her and forget all about me. She went from looking freaked out to like she's not here anymore. If she were crying or screaming, I think I'd know how to handle it. But this?

"You ready to go in?" I ask, quiet-like. I don't want to scare her.

She gives me a stiff nod. I can't see the side of her face from here, but I'm sure it's already bruising like mad.

We both get out of the car, and I walk around the front to wait on her. She walks in a slow slouch. Her body's got to be sore from getting smacked against the countertop. That sort of pain ricochets everywhere.

Before we're even to the front porch, the door opens, and Kara steps out. At first, she only sees Carter. "What are you doing home so early?" Then she sees me and then Carter's face. "Oh God, what happened?"

She practically runs to Carter, panicked. Kara reaches up to touch her face, to get a closer look at the damage, but Carter rears back, shaking. The jolt brings her out of that place she disappeared into, and now she looks like she's about to burst out in tears.

Kara looks as though she were about to go into hysterics or go postal, "What happened?"

"Somebody roughed her up at the gas station," I say through gritted teeth.

"No," Kara whispers, voice cracking. She covers her mouth, shaking her head. "No. Why—who—"

Something cracks in Carter. Maybe it's her heart—I'm not sure. All of a sudden her shoulders lift, and she starts to sob. As much as I hate seeing her cry, this is the reassurance I needed to know she's okay. She needs to feel what happened before she can heal. This time she doesn't freak out when Kara pulls her into a hug; instead she just hugs her back.

They don't stop hugging, even after we're inside the house. They take residence on the couch, and I realize they probably want to be alone together. I busy myself by going to find some ice for Carter's face. I remember the house pretty well, considering I used to have a space on the counter for my keys and everything. Many of times I raided their fridge and cabinets. I grab an icepack and a cloth towel, then head back into the living room.

Kara's touching Carter's face and wincing. They both look up when I get close, but it's Carter who reaches out her hand. "Thank you," she whispers. "For everything."

"Hey, you're where I'm supposed to be," I tell her hoarsely. I don't want her to see how close I am to losing it. "I just wish I'd been there."

"It wasn't time yet," she says simply.

"Can you get the first aid kit?" Kara asks me.

"Yeah. It doesn't look too deep, thank God," I say. "Be right back."

Back in the living room, Carter holds the pack to her face, and Kara wipes the blood from Carter's neck. "I wish you would've called me."

"The police came fast, and I was too freaked out … I don't know what I would've done if Boone and Jason didn't show up," Carter says, looking lost again. "I couldn't think straight."

"Of course you couldn't," Kara tells her. "I just feel like some mother spidey sense should have gone off."

"You're not a superhero," I say to Kara. "Unless you've got a lasso of truth or are from the planet Krypton, you ain't gonna be able to know that stuff."

Kara's phone starts ringing over on the arm of the couch. A picture of her, Carter, and Gabe pops up on the screen, along with Gabe's name. She holds it up. "I'd better take this. I texted him, and he's probably about to jump from a cliff over this." She holds the Band-Aid and the antiseptic out to me. "Can you take over?"

"Sure, yeah." I take them from her, then sit down in her place. I don't know if I imagine it because I've been Carter-free for so long, but I swear she shifts closer to me. Her elbow is almost on my thigh, and her hip is pressed into my knee.

"I can do this on my own with a mirror," she says.

"Yeah, but you want me to do it."

She closes her eyes. I think she's about to ignore me or go with some offhanded remark, but instead she says, "Yes."

I stare at her for a long second, waiting for her to change her mind. I've never really given her a choice when it comes to me, so if things are going to change I need to give her room to do that.

When enough time passes so I'm sure she's not going to tell me something different, I reach for her and run my thumb just below the still-bleeding cut. Her skin is hot, even though she's been holding ice on it. If that's any indication of the bruise she's going to have, it's going to be bad.

"You're beautiful even when you're hurt," I tell her.

Her eyes are surprisingly soft when she opens them. "That's not a very healthy comment."

"The fact that we're always patching each other up isn't healthy, either."

Her lips pull into a small smile. I should be finishing up what Kara started, but I feel as though I were finally finding my footing with Carter, as if we were both finally in the right headspace.

"I wasn't really mad, you know," she whispers.

"About what?"

"You kissing me. I wasn't mad—not really."

"I'm not sure if I believe that."

She brings her hands up to my cheeks. "Okay, I was mad. You're right. But I was also confused and scared."

"You're not now?"

"Not as much."

She leans into me and brushes her lips against mine. I stare at her, wide-eyed and stock still. What if this is post-traumatic stress or something like that? What if the same thing's going to happen where she regrets the kiss later? Here she's been guarding her heart, but maybe I should be doing the same, too.

Only I can't do that—not really. Where Carter is concerned, I'll give everything I've got.

So, I do exactly that. I kiss her back, trying to say everything that's gone unsaid or not-believed between us. Words might not convince her of the way I feel, but actions might. With just a kiss, I'm telling her I love her with my lips, promising to be around forever with the pressure, and cradling as a promise that I'm not going anywhere.

CHAPTER THIRTEEN

Carter

Kissing Boone is like finally coming home.

I don't want it to be the case, but it is. I can't help it. He's not just some drug I can't seem to quit—he's a lifestyle. Boone has and will always be my home.

He's the one who ends the kiss first, even though I'm not sure enough time passed to call it a kiss. I think it was really more of a peck. Still, it was enough to make a blush creep over my cheeks and leave me breathless.

I try to focus on the kiss and the way his lips felt against mine, instead of his fingers as they press the Band-Aid over my cut. I wish this all wasn't stemming from what that man did.

I squeeze my eyes shut. Back at the gas station was the most terrifying experience of my life. The guy somehow managed to seem scarier than he did the first time. He had obviously gone without drugs for too long, because he seemed desperate. I've always heard that of anything a person can be, desperate is the worst. It can make them aggressive and mean and horrible. Most of all, it makes them unpredictable.

This time, he didn't ask me for cigarettes, just demanded money. He wasn't even asking for the money in the cash register—he was asking for *my* money, as if I were to just carry it on hand. When I told him I didn't have it, he told me Tish said I do. I tried to barter with him—to tell them I could go to the bank and get some for him. He didn't like the idea, saying I would only get the cops involved (which I without a doubt would).

So instead he grabbed me by the hair and slammed my head into the counter and the candy display. As if violence would make the money materialize. He only ran because I sprayed him with the mace, which distracted him enough so I could dial 911. He didn't have any other option, unless he wanted to go to jail.

He could've hurt me worse or taken advantage of the situation, which makes everything so much more alarming. *Anything* could have happened. I did fine on my own, but what if he hadn't been scared off so easily?

"Carter, what's wrong? Was it the kiss? Or are you …" Boone trails off. I guess it clicks because he reaches for me and pulls me into him. I've been so scared since I left the gas station, and I didn't think I would want to be held— the thought of being touched made me feel sick—but I need him, like I needed Kara. I feel safer with his arms wrapped around me and like everything isn't falling apart. "He's not going to hurt you again. That ain't going to happen."

I want to believe him, but I can't. I'm worried if I do, the man will come back. It's like taking an umbrella when there's a chance of rain—you're being prepared because if you don't take it, that'll be the time it will rain. I thought the man would come back, but I didn't expect to come away bruised. If I was more prepared I might have.

Outside of Boone's breathing and his thumping heartbeat—and mine, too—I hear Kara come back into the room.

"Is she okay?" she asks softly.

Boone's head moves against the top of mine. I'm not sure what his answer is, but he'd be lying if he said I am.

The couch gets displaced beside me as she sits down. "Gabe is coming home."

"Is he ready to hunt this guy down?" Boone asks. "Good old fashioned search party through the town with pitchforks and fire?"

Boone's ever-present humor always comforts me just as much as it can annoy me. He knows how to make a situation better and diffuse it.

"Let's just say after he talked me down, I *tried* to talk him down," Kara answers.

I pull away from Boone. Kara's eyes roam over me, as though checking to make sure I was really there. Her gaze lingers on my face, which feels like it's the size of Texas and hot like the desert.

"Would you like some tea?" she asks, brushing my hair away from my face. "Or maybe to go lie down?"

"I think I just want to lay down," I say.

"Okay, but I don't want you to be alone." *Good, because I don't want to be alone, either.* "I need to talk to Gabe, though. Boone, can you sit with her?"

"Yeah," Boone says.

I'm surprised Kara's suggesting it, but this whole thing has forced an armistice. If she'd have seen the kiss, she'd know it's not even close to that.

#

Carter, 16

Dinner is awkward, as always. Dad is picking apart his salad—and me—while Deirdre has completely given up on small talk. Kara is clearly smiling through her pain, and Gabe looks as if he wanted to clock my dad. I'm sure I look as though I want to bury my head under the lettuce. One small, almost insignificant comment about how I've been having car issues and my dad launched into a

Declaration-of-Independence-sized rant about how he refuses to pay for something that's going to keep breaking down. Little does he know he hasn't put a cent into it. Even if he did, it sounds as if he'd prefer to just buy me a new car that won't break down because he prefers the hassle-free route, as always. If he loved me or was looking after my best interest, he'd know how much my beautiful, ratty, old car means to me.

I reach for a piece of bread and start to nibble on it. I can honestly understand why stress eating is a thing.

Kara stops her pretend-smiling and cocks her head, frowning. "Do you hear that?"

"What?" Gabe asks, looking around. If the house was on fire, we'd all rejoice.

"It sounds like someone's ... yelling?"

We all take a break from our drama and listen. Sure enough, I hear someone yelling—wailing. Gabe immediately stands up and heads to the front door. We all follow behind him, curious to see what's on the other side when he opens it up.

I'm not prepared for where the yelling is coming from—Tish. I'm surprised I even recognize her because I haven't seen her since Kara took over guardianship. Her hair color isn't the same (now a brassy red that almost looks purple), she's thinner the last I saw her, and she's dressed like an early-2000s throwback in a matching hoodie and sweats (which are pink but turning brown from wear). She's horrible looking compared to what I remember, which is scary because she's the thing of nightmares.

Still, I recognize her sort of like you recognize the symptoms of getting sick. You just somehow know it's there—that you're about to come down with a nasty flu. Every single wall and fence and mote I built as a kid to protect myself from her instinctively goes up.

She's in the neighbor's yard across the street. Her head is thrown back, and she's screaming something incomprehensible, with only the obscenities decipherable. The woman who lives in the house is outside in her pajamas, yelling back at her to leave, while the man is on the phone—no doubt calling the cops.

"What is she doing here?" I say, almost to myself. "Why is she here?"

"Who is that?" Deirdre asks, but it also sounds as though she already knew the answer. They've never met, and I'm sure she's wondering what was so good about my mom that my dad slept with her. I don't know, and I don't think I ever will. He probably won't, either.

"Tish," I answer, unable to call her anything else.

"How'd she find out where we live?" Gabe asks. "Have you talked to her, Carter?"

I shake my head.

"It's my fault," Kara admits. She looks at me apologetically. "I thought maybe she might get clean and want to be a part of your life, so I gave her our address when we first moved."

"You gave her your address?" our dad repeats incredulously. "What the hell were you thinking? She's not going to change."

For a split second, I want to argue with him. I agree with what he's saying about Tish, but I don't like the fact that he's telling Kara she's wrong when she was only trying to help. Kara believes in people, and she's the reason why I'm still hopeful. She shouldn't be told she's wrong for that.

But I can't do it, because that would mean I believe Tish can be better. If I'm being honest, I've missed Declan and Boone, even after what happened, but I've never missed Tish. The second I moved out, I gave up on her. I replaced her with better people—a new family. I haven't thought about her nor wanted to.

I don't have a choice tonight. I swallow, reigning in my courage, and then push passed Gabe and out the door. I hear him yell my name, but I trudge down the driveway toward Tish.

"Tish!" I call.

The woman in her pajamas looks up, surprised, which quickly fades into anger. My mom, on the other hand, only looks more agitated at the sound of my voice. She turns around and points a long, bony finger at me.

"You're comin' home with me."

I stop in my tracks. "What?"

"You heard me, girl."

The husband and wife start backing up, heading back to their house. I hear a mass of footsteps jog up behind me. I wish my family wouldn't have followed me. This isn't just embarrassing; it's sickening. I don't want them to know this was the sort of thing I dealt with every day.

Her vision focuses on something behind me, while the rest of her twitches and convulses. "You owe me more for her—she's my daughter."

Kara steps up beside me. "You should leave."

"I want more money," she says. "You owe me money."

She doesn't really care Kara took me away from her—she only cares that her cash flow is dry.

"I can't do that," Kara says calmly.

"Yes, you can," Tish screeches. "You think I don't know how loaded you are—your daddy threw money at me to fuck me. I know it's there. I want it."

"No," Gabe says, firmly.

"It's either the money or the girl."

The girl. Like she doesn't know me from any other brunette who could be her daughter. "You should leave," I say, keeping my voice level. "The cops are going to come."

She doesn't even look like she cares. She walks toward me, her hands outstretched and ready to grab me. "We're leaving."

I yank my arm away before she can grab it. "No, we're not. You are."

"You don't speak to me like that."

"Leave," I repeat.

"No."

My gaze is deadly, but she's unfazed. She doesn't care about anything except for her drugs—not even that the cops might show up or that this might all hurt me.

More footsteps. My dad appears, checkbook in hand. "How much do you want?"

#

"Hey kid, you wanna wake up?"

I stiffen, because Gabe hasn't woken me up like this in years. Did I sleep through Sunday breakfast? Or maybe

Dad's coming over tonight? I wrack my brain, trying to come up with the reason why Gabe is waking me up as if I were fourteen years old again.

I open my eyes and I'm met with Gabe's worried stare. That's enough to bring the last few hours back to me in a rush. My face starts throbbing in tempo with my heartbeat as I remember the junkie.

"How're you doing?" he asks, reaching out to touch my face.

I flinch, bringing my hand up to hide it. Hurt registers in his expression, and I instantly feel guilty. I did the same thing with Boone and Kara—I should know to just let it happen. They're all kind—they're not going to slam my head into a counter.

My gaze jumps around, looking for Boone. When we came in here, he walked over to the chair in the corner of my room and sat, telling me to sleep. I had the urge to ask him to crawl into bed with me and hold me—only that—but I figured Gabe's nerves would be too frayed to catch us like that.

Boone's still there with his hands clasped, forearms on his thighs. His forehead is wrinkled, and he looks ready to hold me in a second's notice.

Kara is just behind Gabe, holding a fresh ice pack and looking displaced.

"Talk to me, Carter," Gabe orders.

"I'm not doing okay," I say softly, sitting up and bringing my purple sheets up around me.

"That's all right, sweetie," Kara assures me, taking the spot next to him. She slowly sets her hand down on my blanketed leg, making sure I'm okay with it. "You're allowed to not be okay."

"*I'm* sure not okay," Gabe admits. "When Kara called me, I was scared out of my mind." He leans and says in a mock whisper, "You're sort of my pride and joy." His serious face shows back up as he eyes the gas station vest I'm still wearing. "Listen, I think maybe you shouldn't go back there."

"I have to," I sputter. "I can't quit."

Gabe narrows his eyes. "Yeah, you can and you should. What if he comes back again?"

"That's not fair," I say.

"But it's true."

It is.

Kara pats my leg. "Gabe's right. Maybe you can just find another job."

I don't think that it'll be easy to just find another job after this whole thing. I'm officially going to be the girl who got attacked and nobody is going to want to hire me because it might happen again. I don't blame them. I'm already the girl with the crazy mom. Bad mojo spreads like wildfire in a small town this small.

Over in the corner, Boone clears his throat. Gabe's been actively ignoring him since I woke up. Their coexistence is some sort of a miracle in need of documentation.

"I, uh, actually know of somethin'," Boone says, his accent exceptionally deep. "You'd have an office and chances are you wouldn't be alone. Pay would be good, too."

Pay doesn't really matter much, but the idea of an office and safety sound good. I loved getting a job because it felt as if I was on the road to something—as though I was being independent and doing well for myself. Growing up, I never knew anyone who worked. I thought people who did have jobs, like Kara and Gabe, were professionals. I wanted to be like them and having a job has always made me feel like I was.

I don't mind quitting the gas station or the ugly vest, so long as I don't have to quit my independence.

"What job is it?" Kara asks.

Gabe's jaw pops.

"A secretarial position," is all Boone answers.

Gabe turns. "Who's the boss?"

Boone points at himself. "And a friend."

Gabe shakes his head, "No," just as I say, "Yes."

We stare at each other, gazes warring. "Carter, you can't be serious," Gabe argues.

Too bad I am. I rub the palm of my hand into my eye, a tension headache brewing. We need to talk about Boone and what happened at the gas station and so much more, but I don't think I want to *right now*.

Kara senses this and says, "Why don't we talk about it later, all right? This is all …"

"Overwhelming," I finish with a half-smile.

Both Kara and Gabe stand, but Boone remains sitting. The expression on his face—panic—is pretty indicative he's not ready to leave me. I'm sure I have the same look; I'm not ready either. I don't want any of them to leave.

I sit up, but Kara waves me back down. "Stay," she commands.

"No, I'd like to be downstairs with you guys." I pull my lip in between my teeth, which is a bad idea. It makes the side of my face throb and a stinging start on the inside of my cheek. I must've bit there or something. "And I'd, um, like Boone to stay."

We all automatically look at Boone. His gaze doesn't waver, burning me a higher temperature than my cheek is. He somehow looks out of place in my room, but also as though he belonged there with us.

He's clearly shocked by my words, but a slow smile pulls at his lips. It's not egotistical or flirtatious—it's genuinely happy and relieved. He didn't see what happened as it was happening, but he saw the aftermath. No matter what's gone on between us, we have a history together, and I know this has got to be hard on him. We both know how easily events like today's can taint you forever.

CHAPTER FOURTEEN

Boone

I listen to the popcorn go *pop, pop, pop*—the bag growing with each passing second. We've been watching movies I haven't been paying attention to, which explains why I was the lucky soul elected to make a snack. That or Gabe's trying to vote me off the island as if it were *Survivor* or something. Now that he's calmed down, I'm sure he's back to imagining up ways to kill me.

This situation is strange as hell—I hoped but never expected to be able to spend time with all three of them. Their relationship has a pull that makes you want to study it. They're unbreakable when they're together.

"Watched pot never boils," Carter says, joining me in the kitchen.

I glance over my shoulder at her. I was probably staring a hole through the microwave, my eyes alone causing the heat.

"Good thing this is popcorn," I answer. "No pot necessary."

Carter's arms are wrapped tight around her middle, but she seems lighter than before, which makes me feel better.

I keep telling myself this all could've been worse, not that it helps.

I reach for her forearm and pull her toward me. She comes willingly—thankfully no flinching. "I thought you were engrossed in the movie," I say.

She smiles. "Do you even know what movie we were watching?"

I shake my head.

"I didn't think so." Slowly and definitely unsure, she puts her arms around my waist. I want to kiss her again, but I don't want things to go too quick for her. She has to be the one to make the first moves. "It was at the boring part."

"Gabe and Kara were okay with you following after their least favorite SOB?"

"Is it possible to have a favorite?"

"Yeah, sure. Everyone's got a guy they sort of love to hate."

"Do we really have a long enough list you could be our *least* favorite?"

Her face contorts as if she were deep in thought, and it makes me laugh. "My dad is our least favorite, for sure," she says finally. The popping behind me comes to a sudden stop and the microwave beeps. Neither of us moves. "Were you serious?"

"About not watching the movie?"

"No, about the job."

I nod. "Wouldn't have brought it up unless I was."

Her eyebrows pull together, and she fists her hand in my shirt at the base of my back. "Will you be wearing a shirt and shoes?"

"Ah, pretty girl, don't you like me naked?"

She blushes. "I like it when you abide by the rules."

I sigh as if it were this huge, horrible thing to do. "If it's a part of our terms and agreements, sure, I'll wear one."

"Okay. I'll take it."

"Seriously? That's it? What about Gabe?"

She pops up on her tiptoes and licks her lips. Then, in the time it takes me to blink, she gives me a quick kiss. "He's going to have to learn to deal with it."

I grin. "There's going to be a lot of that, I think."

"Hey, Carter? Everything okay?" Gabe calls. I'll bet his ears were itching with us talking about him.

#

"Thanks for letting me stay," I say to Kara as I'm getting ready to leave. She's the type of person you hate disappointing, and I wish she still trusted me the way she used to. She once pulled me aside and thanked me for being so good to Carter. Now she looks like she wants me to leave.

She smiles anyway because she's nice through and through. "You're welcome, Boone," she answers. "I hope I have a reason to do it again."

I glance at Carter standing next to me on the sidewalk. She said she'd walk me to my car, which would've pissed Gabe off had he been around for it. He disappeared a few minutes before the credits rolled on the last movie (or so I was told, because I still wasn't paying any attention) to talk to a cop friend on the phone. He must've once stitched him up and it made them buddies. Maybe next time I get hurt I'll go see Dr. Gabe Matthews and the same thing will happen.

Or hell will freeze, pigs will fly, and Pluto will become a fucking planet again.

Carter looks up at me, smiling shyly. Almost hopefully. If she can look at me this way, anything is possible and everything can be okay.

"Yeah, you know, me too," I say back to Kara. "This time I'm not gonna make a mess of things."

It's the wrong choice of words because Carter's smile falters. I know she's never going to be able to trust me again if she keeps getting reminded of why she shouldn't, but I also don't want her to go into this blind. Forgiving is okay, but forgetting isn't. That's how you survive.

Kara gives me one final wave before heading back into the house. Carter turns and walks toward my car wordlessly. I follow her. We weren't able to do much after the kiss in the kitchen—not even talk—so I'm not sure how this thing is going to end. It makes me nervous as hell. Basically everything I described about the June Carter Hart Syndrome is true. Every last one of the symptoms is ravaging my system.

It's so bad I mindlessly unlock my car, get in, then put the window down. I'm not leaving room for there to be some sort of an epic exit.

"Shit," I say. "What am I doing?"

"I don't know," Carter says back.

"I'm a lost cause when it comes to anything between us," I mutter. "I don't want to be—it's just I don't really know how to, uh, be with you."

"You already have been."

I swallow thickly. "No, not like that. I don't know how to date you, I guess, or whatever direction we're going in. I've been too focused on the chase and not so much what happens when I've caught you."

"You haven't caught me yet, Boone," she tells me quietly. "You're still chasing."

Doesn't help with the nerves, but I completely deserve it. "Probably a good thing, considering I've got a learning curve against me."

Her eyebrows move toward each other and raise—a sign she's about to say what's on her mind. She tucks her hair behind her ear and straightens. Yep, she's about to serve my ass on a platter.

"You said it wasn't that you didn't love me, but that you loved me too much. If that's really the case, you'll show me. Being nervous and awkward—that's what I want to see. Sometimes it feels like I'm just a character in whatever charade you're playing. You always lose ... you lose sight of our present and only see what we've had."

"I wish I could argue against that." I lean my head back against the seat and angle it to look out at her. "There's never been anyone else for me but you." I let out a shaky breath. I'm good at being confident and blunt, but I'm not good at ... I don't know, *emotions*. I'm especially bad with the ones that wear you down, which are all I've felt today. "I'll show you I love you."

She doesn't agree or say she hopes I will. She just nods. I never gave her any sort of validation, so I guess I don't deserve any either.

I turn my car on and put it into gear. Her hand drops to my window and grips my car.

"There's a ladder in the shed. If you come back in an hour, my window will be unlocked," she tells me in an urgent whisper.

I cover her hand with mine. "What are you saying?"

"We can talk some more," she answers.

I stare at her, wanting to tell her I'm pretty damn thankful for the opportunity, but I think she's already got the memo. This is her way of letting me in. Telling me about the ladder means she's making me work a little less for her.

How the hell am I going to do this? There's no way to quietly go about moving a ladder from a garage to a window. I'll alert the whole house—neighborhood, probably—then the cops will get called. I've honestly never been so scared in my entire life.

New territory has that effect on you.

#

Carter's given me an inch, but that inch could stretch for a mile in difficulty. She made getting the ladder in the shed sound easy. Who knows—maybe she thought it would be. But no one just leaves a ladder laying around in an unlocked shed *easy* to get to. That's like putting a sign out in the front yard that says, *Yard Sale for Robbers.*

"Well, this ain't happening," I grumble.

The ladder is visible at the back of the shed, but it's basically a Herculean trial to get to. A lawn mower, garden stuff, boxes of who-knows-what and a whole lot more are in the way. I'll either die getting to the back of the shed, or Gabe'll hear me, which is probably the worst of the two outcomes. I'm better off putting my hands through hell.

I shut the shed door and go to the back of the house. If I'm looking to gain everyone's trust, this is a horrible idea.

I move ahead anyway. Luckily I've gotten better at scaling the side of the house with minimal damage. As she promised, the window is unlocked. It makes me grin.

I push it up and then try to quietly maneuver inside the room. Carter's got it dark, and for a second I worry she's asleep. Maybe this isn't the best thing for her after what happened today. She had the scare of a lifetime, and the last thing she needs is me sneaking into her room.

"Hey," I hear.

I jump. This might be the last thing *I* need. My eyes adjust, and I see her sitting cross-legged on her bed. She's in a tank top and pajama pants, her hair on top of her head. She looks more as if she were ready for bed than ready to see me. Here I was hoping that this was some sort of a date or something.

"Hey."

I run my hand over my chin where my beard has grown to lengths, which surely puts me in lumberjack territory. This girl sees me for all the stupid shit I've done, and it unnerves me. I'm used to scaling walls and writing notes and trying to wield her heart like a courtroom, but this part is all new for me. Now my heart's in her hands, and I'm worried about my beard.

Maybe I need to talk to Jason. He's the one with the wife and the family, so he'd probably know a thing or two about keeping a girl once you've got her.

For now, I guess I've got to go with my strengths. I

reach into my pocket and pull out the note, this time without any flowers. "I, uh, wrote you again."

"You did?" Even in the dark, I can see her eyes light up. "Will you tell me what it says?"

I swallow. Writing them is one thing, but reading them out loud? "Don't you want to read it?"

She laughs softly. "It's dark."

"Yeah, that's a problem." I squeeze my eyes shut and let out a long, shaky breath, then take the few deliberate steps to her bed. I sit down beside her, so close her bare leg touches my jean-clad one. It's innocent, but enough to make me harder than glass. I unfold the paper as if I'd be able to read it or something. Good thing I've got it memorized. "'I started writing these notes because I wanted to protect the things that made you, you. I wanted you to know you're special and gorgeous and strong. I wanted you to know I loved you—that I still love you, Carter. You're perfect. You're beautiful. You're brave. You're safe.'"

I fold the note back up and grit my teeth. I didn't get the flowers because I was too busy trying to find the perfect thing to say. I needed to be raw because tonight matters. So I spent the last hour huddled up two streets down in my car, looking like a creeper, while I wrote and rewrote this so many times I ran out of paper. I ended up using a page out of my car owner's manual.

My heart thuds as Carter remains still. This is how it should've been all those years ago. I should've had my heart on my sleeve and been strong enough to favor love over fear. It guts me to think if I wasn't such a dumbass, we could've been together for years. Maybe even for as long as we've known each other—practically forever.

Her hand slowly moves up and over my thigh, searching for mine. When she finds it, she holds onto my wrist. She steals the note away with her other hand.

"I have a box," she tells me quietly. "I'm keeping them all."

I let out a ragged breath and twine our hands. I'm sure mine is clammy and gross. "I feel like a teenager."

She laughs breathlessly and lies her head on my shoulder. "Me too."

"At least we're making up for lost time."

"Too much lost time," she agrees.

We sit for a while in the quiet, me reveling in the fact I'm holding her hand and her staring down at the note she can't read in the dark. Then her head shifts on my shoulder and her lips press against the corner of my mouth.

I move to kiss her deeper, dropping her hand and cupping her chin. I half expect her to pull away or for another angry mom to yell at us, but nothing happens. Instead, she manages to set the note out of the way and maneuver onto my lap. It's as though we were made to be together like this. This part of our relationship is always effortless.

I slip my hands from her chin and down her back to press her into me. Her tongue flicks against mine as I stand, lifting her, then lay her down on the bed. I balance above her, knowing full well she can feel my cock straining against my jeans. I won't go any further tonight than this, but I want her to know how she makes me feel. She's literally the only one who can do this to me, dysfunctional as it makes my dick sound.

She moans, and I capture it with my mouth. When her hips buck against mine, my whole body goes rigid. I've got to keep myself in check. If I let this get out of control, I won't be able to contain myself and get caught for sure. Beyond that, I've got to make this about her and *only* her.

She wraps her legs around me and desperately gropes her hands at my back. She wants to be just as close as I do—just as badly. Fuck, I want her.

I cup her breast with my hand, thumb rubbing over her nipple. So much for control. I'm kidding myself to think there's even such thing as control around her. It would be so fucking easy to take off all of her clothes, kiss her and touch her and fuck her. I just ... can't. I won't do this heat-of-the-moment thing with her again, where I'm there and then gone.

I won't stop, but I won't go any further. I squeeze her nipple, now in a hard peak, and she arches against me. Someday, I'm going to see what her face looks like when I've got her feeling like this—I'm going to open my eyes when I kiss her. I'm completely enamored by her gorgeous face—her expressions. They say it's important to find your passion in life, and she's mine.

Her hips rise, and she presses into the bulge of my cock, grinding. I know she's close because she's not kissing me back anymore. She's just groping blindly at my back and moaning into my mouth. I slide my hand from her breast to her waist, guiding her hips. It doesn't take long before she starts shuddering, her cries muffled by my mouth, as she rides out an orgasm.

I kiss her through it and only pull away when she's gone limp. In the moonlight, I can see her smiling up at me, dazed. I fall onto my side and pull her against me, spooning her. We fall asleep like that.

CHAPTER FIFTEEN

Carter

When Boone picks me up the next day, he gives me a sheepish smile as he rubs the back of his neck. He only left my room a few hours ago, when the world was first waking up. I pretended not to hear him sneak out because I didn't want to ruin the magic of what happened last night. Kissing him and being with him ... I never dreamed it could be real. I'm afraid if I think about it too much, it won't be. There'll be some sort of a glamour showing me what I want to see instead of reality.

I heard him scribble something on a notebook before he left, so the second he was gone I was up and checking what he wrote. It wasn't romantic, as I hoped, but it was still a big deal. The note was an assurance this wasn't going to be just another moment between us. In it, he told me he'd pick me up at nine to visit where his future business is.

"Good morning," he says. "Sleep well?"

I blush. "Very well. You?"

"Better than I ever have," he admits. "But I've got some bad news."

My heart drops. Here it is. Oh, God, this is the magic getting ruined. "What's that?"

"Last night was great ... but it, uh, can't, you know, happen again." He pauses and works his jaw as he stops at a stop sign. "If I want to earn Gabe and Kara's respect, I can't do that with you under their roof. It ain't right or fair to them."

"What?"

He glances over at me. "You can't think last night was a good idea, Carter. That'll get me an execution notice if someone finds out."

"So you're saying last night was okay, just not in my house."

He nods slowly. "Exactly."

I fall back against my seat. "Oh, I thought—never mind."

"Wait, did you think I was telling you I don't want to see you anymore?" he asks. The car comes to a stop, and I worry he's decided to just stop in the middle of the road—he would be the one to do that—but instead he somehow parked us in front of a store without my noticing. "Is that what you thought?"

I try to come up with an excuse, but my mind goes blank.

"Carter."

"Yes, that's what I thought."

"Shit, I'm sorry," he murmurs. He reaches across the consul and lays his hand on my thigh. "I could've worded that better. See what I mean? I've got a learning curve here."

"Obviously I do, too."

"At least we're learning together, huh? Sort of like we're on an even playing field."

I guess that's good, although there's still that evil, vindictive side of me, which only comes out around Boone and wishes we weren't on level ground. I've always felt so behind and lost compared to him, so I wish this could be the one thing I'm good at.

"Is this the place?" I ask, successfully redirecting our conversation. I've passed this storefront a thousand times, but it's sort of a permanent fixture you forget about. I don't really remember a time when it's been in business, and it's one of those places that, even when it's owned, you don't expect it to be treated well. Hopefully it'll be different with Jason and Boone.

A grin spreads across Boone's face as he stares at the building. I don't think I've ever seen him beam like this. He's always been a kidder, trying to lighten up every situation, but this is different. He's ... proud. "Yep, this is it. Jason's meeting us. This venture is going to be really good for all of us."

"Is it going to be weird with us ... working together?"

"Not if we're together for the long haul. Even if we aren't, we'll make it work." He cups my chin and places a quick peck on my lips. "But *I'm* in it for the long haul."

It's hard for me *not* to yell, "Me too!" I want this to work also, but I'm not going to put myself in the position to lose ground by admitting it.

We both get out of the car and meet at the front. His fingers graze mine, then eventually tangling, faster than when he walked me home.

The door opens when we're close and Jason steps out. I asked Boone for his phone number so Kara and I could call him to thank him for being there yesterday. He barely even knows me, but he showed so much concern. Being business partners with him will be good for Boone. He hasn't had a lot of Jasons in his life. I need to keep reminding myself of that and remember there's a reason why Boone is the way he is. Fifty percent of it might be his own stupidity, but the other half is his upbringing.

"Hey, man," Boone says, giving him the ever so meaningful manly-chin-tilt greeting.

Jason, who doesn't really seem to care about looking cool, waves, then turns his attention to me. "How are you?"

"Better, thank you," I say. "Still a little shaken."

"Well, I'm glad Boone thought to offer you a job. You'll be a ton of help, *and* you'll be safer here.

Until the man finds out where I work now. Boone thinks this is going to be the magical cure-all, but I disagree. The man was desperate, and desperate people will do anything to get what they want. Even if Boone and Jason are here, it might not be enough to scare him off. Worse, there's also the chance neither of them will be here when he shows up again.

I smile at Jason, trying to make it seem as though I were agreeing, but my lips feel numb and forced.

Boone rests his hands on my lower back as he guides me inside. "How'd you get a hold of the keys?" he asks Jason.

"I talked with the realtor and told her we'd buy it, but we just want an extra look."

"How did Alex take the news."

Jason rubs his freckled arm. His cheeks turn a color which matches his hair. "She was kind of the one who persuaded me to say yes. You know I'm into the idea—I'm the one who brought it up—I'm just ... I don't know ..."

"Hey, you've got a family," Boone tells him. "You've got a whole hell of a lot more to lose if this goes south."

Do you want a family someday? I don't know why that pops into my head to ask. Would Boone be as worried about a business venture as Jason is if he had one? Does he want kids and a house and a dog and all of the other stuff I thought only happened on TV? He's been chasing me, but what if he doesn't know what he wants beyond that? What if he doesn't want the movie-esque life? Because I do. I want what I could've had if I'd been raised from the beginning by Kara and Gabe. I want to give my future children the life I never had.

I wander off because the weight of all those thoughts is too much. If I'm not careful, my sensor will temporarily short out, and I'll spill everything right in front of Jason. I'll want to be put down right then and there. We're not even to the naming-this-between-us step. I'm *way* too ahead of myself.

The good thing about the building is it was clearly a hardware store before, with what could be a general supply area and a back door leading to a small warehouse. Boone said they'd eventually like to make it a store in addition to the services they're going to offer. First thing's first is to make sure their venture is a successful one.

He told me about his plans last night, whispering excitedly as he held me. I felt just as excited because it was dark and I could let my guard down. Hearing him talk about the building and the business made me believe it could all happen. On top of it all, he sounded so mature, as though he really knew what he was doing and was prepared for it.

"So, that'll probably be your office."

I jump and turn around. Boone approaches me slowly with his hands up before he slips them to my hips. He's been extra careful about not scaring me, which is good. This morning I got up to go grab a drink and just running into Gabe nearly gave me a heart attack. Even when it's someone safe, I still feel out of control.

I hold my breath, then let it out. I need to focus on being relaxed. It's Boone and—while it's always an emotional roller coaster when it comes to him—he would never hurt me physically. I cover his hands with my own and let my back melt against his chest. I can feel his heartbeat, strong and steady, and it calms me. The warmth of him brings me back to the present.

"Sorry," he says.

"It's okay," I tell him. I hate how I've made both him and Gabe feel bad for doing something that normally wouldn't bother me. "It's nice and spacious here."

I didn't even realize it, but I'm standing in the doorway of an office-sized room at the very back of the store. This area must have been an addition because the wall with the door on it is brick like the outside of the building. I can visualize painting the white walls terracotta to accent the brick to make it warm and inviting. I never imagined having my own office.

"We'll get you a desk and some shelves and whatever else you want." He points to the two doors, which are on either side of mine. "We'll be in here, but probably not much until we hire some other service techs. We'll be too busy solving all of the world's issues."

"You've got to solve your own, first," I say, playfully nudging him with my shoulder then kissing the underside of his jaw. "So, what exactly will be in my job description?"

"Well, I was thinking you'll have to let me kiss you at least once every fifteen ..."

"Boone," I say.

"Well, pretty girl, that's my long-term goal for the rest of our lives. But as for here, I guess we'd like you to assume the role of our secretary for now. Schedule our appointments, keep us updated about what problems are coming our way, and maybe handle some of the bills. Eventually, maybe you could be the manager when we're up and running. That something you'd be interested in?"

"Bossing people around? Yes."

He laughs. "Be honest with me if that's not what you want."

"No, I do. The gas station wasn't enough for me, and I think that this will be fun—challenging. It'll give me a chance to do anything I want. Like maybe I can handle advertising or get a little creative for you guys."

"That would be great. Your bozo co-workers are about as creative as a rock with edges."

"Hey, I heard that!" Jason calls from the front of the store. "You should see the flowers I drew with my daughter yesterday. Pretty creative, if you ask me."

Boone squeezes me tighter and buries his face in my neck, muffling a laugh.

166

#

Carter, 17
Boone, 20

"So I don't know about you, but I hate this class," the girl whom I'm paired up with in Spanish class says. I think she's a grade below me, and I don't know what her real name is, only that she chose Cecilia as her Spanish name. Everyone in the class—probably the whole school—already knows she hates this class. She's been very vocal about it. "Don't you?"

I raise my eyebrows. "It doesn't really matter. We have to take it. It's a required class." I kind of hate every class, so why should I specify that, yes, I hate this class? That'd be like picking favorites. I think it'd be more original to ask me if I like a class.

She clucks her tongue disapprovingly. Obviously, she's officially decided I'm the worst partner ever. Hopefully she doesn't realize how bad I am at Spanish or else she'll hate me more than this class. I can't even pronounce the name I chose for myself right.

We're supposed to be matching up Spanish words with their definition, sort of like a puzzle. Most pairs are already almost finished. The incentive to win is a free pass from the next test, which I need. Kara's help is the reason why I've at least got a B-, and without the pass, we have a long night of studying ahead of us.

"Cecilia y Luciana, trabajen más rápido," our teacher says as he passes by our desk.

Cecelia gives him a blank stare, but I know what he's saying. He's told me to work faster so many times I'm to the point where it's next best phrase to "May I use the bathroom?"

I move around the cards just for effect. I hate being called out; it only brings attention to me. I've never really had many—well, any— friends at school, and I've found it's best to remain unnoticed.

The intercom makes a loud beep, signaling someone's about to speak. "Please send Carter Hart to the main office," the school secretary says, her nasal tone making the other students cringe.

"All right, she'll be down shortly," our teacher calls back.

I squint up at the ceiling. The only times I've ever gotten called through the intercom were when I forgot my lunch and when I had to leave early for a doctor's appointment. I don't know why I'm being called today, unless something came up at home. Hopefully Kara and Gabe are okay. Maybe I forgot something, or they thought I forgot something. Maybe they just want to save me from Spanish.

They're cool, but not that cool.

"Luciana, puedes irte," the teacher says.

That's a new phrase I definitely don't know. Still, I'll bet he's telling me to get a move on. At least I won't have to solve the puzzle or deal with Cecilia.

I quickly gather my things since I don't know how long this will take. Then I head out into the hallway and toward the front office. I immediately see Gabe standing at the front desk, watching for me. He's wearing the dress pants and tie he usually wears in when he's making rounds. There's something about his expressions that is sending off alarm bells in my head. He's not just pale and a little sweaty, but he's grimacing, and his normally bright eyes are clouded with concern.

Fear.

"Gabe? Where's Kara? Is she okay?" I ask when I'm inside the office.

"She's fine—she's going to meet us. She called me, and I was closer to you." He lets out a long breath, then steps closer to me. He puts his hands on my shoulders and bends down to my level. "It's Declan. He overdosed again."

I should be used to this by now. Only I'm not, and I don't think I ever will be, not when every time feels as though it were going to be the last. What if this is the time he dies? When was the last time I spoke to him—told him I loved him? What if I would've tried harder to get him to quit? Or maybe I shouldn't have been so hard on him. Maybe I should just learn to love him the way he is for as long as I can.

No, I can't do that. That would be like letting his addiction defeat me, too.

"Is he ..." I choke into a sob.

"He's alive."

#

I feel as though I were six years old as I clutch Gabe's hand and let him lead me down the hall they said Declan's room is in. Even though Gabe said he's okay, I can't really believe it until I see him.

"You know what we're about to walk in on," Gabe says to me quietly. "They've probably got him hooked up to just about everything, and he's probably on something to get him off the drugs."

No amount of drugs meant to curb his addiction will help. My brother will be clean while he's in the hospital, and the second he's out, he won't be able to refuse a fix.

I stop right before his door and try to prepare myself. Gabe squeezes my hand and then lets go. There's nothing to say, really. He can't tell me Declan will be okay. Even if he survives his overdose, he's never really going to be okay. All I can do is try to keep my emotions at bay—armor up for this never-ending battle.

When I'm ready, I walk in. There are tubes everywhere, including one to help him breathe. His skin is pale and looks like it's been beaten then stretched over his bones. He's not awake, but he's in restraints. He's always violent coming out of his overdoses.

Kara is sitting at his side, absently rubbing her hand up and down his arm, which is covered in scabs and sores. She looks up when I walk in and immediately stands, opens her arms, and comes toward me.

"Hey, sweetie," she says as she envelopes me in a hug that smells like strawberries. I hug her back, while Gabe's hand rubs at my back. "The doctor came by and said he doesn't expect Dec to wake up for a few days."

"That'll be good—at least he won't have to go through as much of the withdrawal," I say, even though it's not like it matters. "Where was he found?"

A throat clears from the corner of the room. Without checking, I know it's Boone. I know it by the way my body starts to tingle and how my heart feels about thirty thousand different emotions ranging from love to hate to pissed off to perfect. I pull away from Kara to look at him.

I haven't seen him since he told me our kiss meant nothing. I can honestly say time doesn't heal all wounds. He looks thinner, but more bulky in muscle mass, and his hair is long enough to pull back. He's wearing black athletic shorts and a T-shirt with grease stains all over it. I try to take in everything but his apologetic, wounded-dog eyes. I'm not ready to forgive him.

"I found him," he explains, his voice rough. "I hadn't seen him for a while, so I went to some of his haunts. I found him in an abandoned house—no one else was there. I don't know how long he was out of it."

"It's a good thing you went looking," Kara tells him.

A pang hits my chest. I should've been looking, too. I've just gotten so tired of all the worrying and fear when there's really nothing I can do. Tired or not, abandoning him hasn't taken away my guilt. From now on, I need to be better. Even if he doesn't care, I need to make the effort.

"He was alone?" I ask.

He nods. "Someone must've been there recently, but I'll guess they all scattered when they realized he overdosed. Didn't want to be there when the cops showed."

How strong does your addiction have to be to make you more worried about your own self-preservation than a person who is literally dying right in front of you? Has Declan been in a reversed-situation? Has someone died or almost died because he's cared more about himself?

I don't have time to process the thought before bile rises up in my throat and I make a mad dash for the bathroom. I hurl myself at the toilet bowl just in time. All of the contents of my stomach and my emotions rise up and topple out.

Footsteps follow behind me, groping for my hair and lifting it away from my neck. "It's okay, Carter. Let it all out," Kara says soothingly.

Someone else follows in behind her. There's enough room for everyone because it's a sizable hospital bathroom, meant for a nurse and patient to be able to move around in. I know it's Boone because he whispers, "Junebug," under his breath and takes post on my other side. He rubs small circles into my back. Elsewhere, I can hear Gabe calling out to a nurse asking for a bottled water and nausea medicine.

"He's not alone now," Kara continues. "He has all of us. We love him, and he needs a lot of love if he's going to get through this."

Hideous crocodile tears start rolling down my cheeks and plop into the bile-ridden toilet. "I'm sorry," I say.

Kara pulls me away from the toilet and into her arms. Boone flushes the toilet. We're all sitting on the tiled floor, huddled together. Boon is still massaging my back.

"Why are you sorry?" she asks.

"Because I'm s-so stupid—I'm m-making this about m-me," I manage.

Kara shakes her head. "You're allowed to feel this way, Carter. Honestly, it's better to get this out now rather than when he's awake. You want to be strong for him, don't you?"

I nod.

"Then you have to be weak right now." She leans back, presses a kiss against my head. I notice that she's crying, too. "We can all be weak together."

CHAPTER SIXTEEN

Boone

I don't remember ever being this happy. Hell, if happiness were a person, I'd put up a strong argument that I've never even met him/her. With Carter, a fledgling business, and some security in my future, I feel as though I were on top of the world. For once, I've actually got something good going for me.

Still, I can't help but wait for it all to just turn to shit. I've learned everything tends to take a turn for the worse when you're at your happiest.

"You promise you seriously like this color?" Carter asks me.

We're currently standing in front of a wall in her office. The room is filled with painter's tape and plastic. She painted a streak of rust-orange (which sounds like a horrible color to me—bad naming on the paint company's part) on the wall. After I took her home yesterday, Jason and I signed the papers for the place. When I told Carter, she started talking about oranges and all her plans. She sounded so damn excited I told her we'd get ankle-deep in her office renovation today.

"Yeah, sure, it's your office."

She rolls her eyes exaggeratedly and holds up her paint-covered roller. "I'm not asking if it's my office. I'm asking if you like the color."

"You're asking me if I *seriously* like the color," I say back, smirking. "I like it if you do. I'm not good at deciding on colors or whatever. I haven't picked a color for anything in my life."

"So you don't make a conscious decision about your clothes?" she asks.

"Not really," I mumble, looking down at myself. I only wear solid colors, and all my clothes are from Goodwill.

She huffs and crosses her arms, careful not to get any paint on her, even though she's wearing a shirt she doesn't mind getting paint on. "Any other time it's like you enjoy speaking your opinion. Why is it when I want you to, you won't?"

"I like to keep you on your toes?"

"No, you like being difficult." She turns to face me. Even though she should be pissed at me for being "difficult," she's got a grin stretching from ear to ear. The grin has me about three seconds away from losing my cool and kissing her silly. "One last time, you don't hate it?"

"I don't." I tilt my head and squint, trying hard not to glance down at her. Looking at her, touching her, doing anything that involves her—it's all a horrible idea when we're alone and in close quarters. "In fact, you can paint my office this color."

"Stop joking with me."

"I'm not. I'm sure Jason will want the same."

"Really?"

"Not even kidding a little bit, here, Carter. Straight face, see." I somehow manage to keep my expression blank when all I want to do is smile back at her. "I'm not about to fib about a damn color. I mean, let's be clear right here and now. I don't do red."

"What do you have against red?"

I shrug. "Just don't like it."

She laughs. "You're weird, you know that?"

"Hell yeah, I am. Wouldn't be me if I wasn't."

"No, you probably wouldn't." I watch her side profile as she bites her lip and squints at the color. "Thank you for this, Boone."

"Hey, you deserve it. You deserve more, but this is what I can give you."

This time, she turns and walks straight toward me, dropping the roller on the plastic-covered floor. She doesn't stop until her hands are fisted at my chest and her lips are on mine. I growl. Self-control is a waste of time.

I lift her by the ass, guiding her legs to link at my back. She follows my lead, as if she'd done this before a thousand times. Now's not the time to wonder if she has—if there's been other guys. If there were, I need to accept it, because I can't change the past. The only person to blame for it would be myself; I pushed her away and set all this in motion.

I kiss her—probably too roughly—trying to connect with her as much as I can. She fights right back, just as needy and as savagely, because we both want to be so close that we're merged. I walk her back toward the wall, not giving a shit about the wet paint. The wall can get another coat painted on it, and we can get washed. As long as she doesn't care, I can't bring myself to either.

She starts to pull at my shirt, lifting it so she can get her hands on my chest. I want her to initiate the steps we take, so if my shirt's going to be the first thing she wants gone, then so be it. I take it off, trying not to get it tangled around my head or drop her in the process. I wish I was one of those guys who could just whip it off, but I'm not exactly practiced. Luckily, she doesn't seem to care. The second my shirt is off, we're back to kissing, and she's running her hands over my chest.

Whenever I've kissed girls before, I thought it was boring. Too much thinking involved, you know? Tongue, no tongue? Do I start trying to run the bases? Do I even want to run the bases? I never really got mindless sex—how it just happens and how you can't stop it, sort of like an avalanche.

Now I do because I can't think, let alone focus. There's nothing boring about kissing Carter—there's nothing boring about her to begin with.

My hands roam up the length of her body to her breasts. My tongue darts against hers as I palm her breasts, tweaking her nipple. She writhes against me, and this time I let her moan as loud as she wants. Her pleasure sends me into a frenzy. My mouth travels from her lips to her neck and down her chest until it finds the peaks of her breasts through her shirt. Her chest rises, giving more access. What I wouldn't do to have complete and total access. The naked variety.

Somehow, the gods above hear me, because Carter blindly paws at her shirt, working it up. I help her the rest of the way, pulling it up and off. I'm immediately met with a plain white bra with little orange dots spread across it.

I can't help myself; I grin down at her, probably wolfishly. "I'm sensing a theme."

Her head falls back against the wall as she laughs. I love the look of her lips, swollen from kissing, and how her eyes close. I could stare at her for hours.

I love you. I've known those words to be true my entire life. But even though I've said and written them to Carter a million times already, I want to try to be more deliberate. This time I'll be slow and steady and make sure things are right with her. Still, I yell it from mountain tops and rooftops of my imagination. I mentally King Kong those words.

My attention goes back to Carter's breasts before I say anything out loud and screw this all up. I unclasp her at the back, and her laughter stops as her bra catches between us. I throw it away, hopefully in whatever direction our shirts are in. I kiss the tops of both her breasts, watching for anything in expression that tells me I should stop. There's nothing but want. *Desire.* I swirl my tongue over her nipple, relishing in the taste of it as it rises into a bead. She jolts when I use my teeth and grinds against me.

She moans something unintelligible, groping at my hair. I want to make her scream. I need to give her everything I have because she trusts me when we're intimate. Physically, she knows I can be what she needs.

"More," she demands.

With one hand now at her ass, I drop my other between us. I don't know what I'm doing until I'm unsnapping the button of her shorts, then tugging at the zipper. Maybe my lips are distracting her, or maybe she just doesn't care, but she doesn't stop me from slipping my hand inside her shorts, then slipping my finger inside her.

She does exactly what I want. She cries so loud my ears ring, but in the best fucking way. Never getting my hearing back would be considered a medal of honor.

I suck her breast and fuck her with my finger, slowly unraveling her until she's chanting my name and shuddering. The sight of her coming—feeling it—has my cock threatening to explode right along with her.

I love you.

#

Carter, 17
Boone, 20

"You're really bad at this, Boone," Declan says, watching as Carter tallies up our scores from the last deal of rummy. Carter's beating the both of us with a score already in the three hundreds, but Declan's close behind. I'm sucking at the bottom, close to dropping down into the negatives. I'm not a strategy guy. I miss possible matches and constantly set cards down I could've gotten points out of.

Declan's sitting upright in his bed, while Carter and I are sitting in chairs. We have a table between the three of us to play on.

Carter snorts as she writes down the final half of Declan's score. She's been talking to me more since we're both hell-bent on staying around as long as Declan's in recovery. Right now, he's a version of what he would've been if he hadn't gotten into the hard stuff. It's important not to miss one of the few times when he's high as a kite.

"Maybe I'm just the king of a good bluff," I mutter.

"Or maybe you're just really, really bad," Carter adds. The fact she's smiling gives me some sort of a glimmer of hope. There might be a chance to repair our relationship.

"That's more like it," Declan says. "Remind me not to go to Vegas with you."

"Bright side, you wouldn't get beaten up for card counting."

"You're right, probably just get roughed up for being a lousy player."

I roll my eyes and wait for him to shuffle the cards, but instead he scratches his jaw. "Hey, Carter, can you do me a favor and go give the nurse my dinner order?"

She blinks rapidly. "Uh, sure, okay." She glances over his shoulder at the clock; it's only three in the afternoon, too early for dinner. "I'll be right back."

When she's gone, Declan lies down and stares at the ceiling. "Think I was too blatant about wanting her gone?"

"Probably," I say. "What's up with that?"

Declan rubs his hand down his face, then lets it drop to the mattress. "I needed to talk to you about something."

"Without Carter?"

"Yeah."

I hold my hands up. "Man, if it has got to do with your dick or something …"

"Shut up," Declan says, cracking a smile. "It's just something I don't want her to know. Ever. But, I, uh, need to tell somebody, you know?"

He gets all nervous, and that makes me uneasy. We've never been serious with one another. If we were, he'd probably have stopped hanging around me after I broke Carter's heart and I'd have been honest about him screwing up his life.

"My liver—it's shot," he says.

My whole body tightens up. "What do you mean shot?"

"Let's just say there's no hope for it," he continues. "I'd probably have more time in me, but I contracted hepatitis a few years back."

I stare at my best friend who's actually a complete stranger. Here the drugs did more to him than just screw up his head, and I've never known. Haven't even guessed. He's a junkie, but I never thought he'd contract something. I never thought beyond the overdoses.

Guess I didn't want to see beyond them.

"Why didn't you tell me?"

He shrugs. His answer's already clear—he's not ready to quit doing the drugs. "I'm not going to be around for much longer. I feel like shit, and I know ... I'm not planning on staying around if I haven't got much longer."

"What's that supposed to mean?"

"It means I wish you hadn't found me."

"What the hell? What are you saying?"

He grimaces, and I notice he does look more sickly than usual. I thought it was just the overdose, but it's more than that. He has the look of a dying man. "You know what it means, so don't waste your time with it. I didn't tell you so you could bother me about it. I told you so you can make sure Carter's taken care of. I know that I haven't exactly done that myself, but it doesn't mean I didn't want to. You were always there and now you're not ... man, you've got to make things right."

"So, you're telling me your final business is for me to make up with your sister?"

"Pretty much." He closes his eyes and throws a scabbed arm over his face. "You love her, right?"

"Yeah."

"More than a sister or a friend."

I don't hesitate. "Yes."

"Then do somethin' about it."

"That's easier said than done."

"I know. We're cut from the same cloth. You're probably gonna screw up a lot more, but don't give up on her."

I scoot forward on my chair and hang my head. "I can't believe we're even having this conversation. Are you sure?"

"Yeah, I am."

"You shouldn't have to go out this way," I say. "It's not fair. You could've gotten clean—made it all right. Started a life."

He takes his arm away from his face and looks me dead in the eyes. "Don't. The end or not, I have no intention to quit."

"Even if you're clean right now?"

He doesn't have to answer. I can see his answer in his eyes. What sort of mindset is he in that he doesn't want to get clean? How can he prefer to live a life with a needle in his arm or toes than have something like what Gabe and Kara have? Doesn't he want that sort of normal?

"You can't tell Carter," he says, "or Gabe or Kara. No one knows but you, me, and my doctor."

"That's not fair, and you know it. How am I supposed to keep something like this from Carter? I can't exactly make up with her if I'm keeping shit this huge from her."

"It doesn't matter. You'll figure it out. It's what's best for Carter, and you know it. I know you'll do anything for her. Given her and the rest of the fucking world, you choose her. You always will. So fucking choose her."

#

Five hours, two coats of paint and two orgasms (for Carter) later, her office is finished. I definitely want mine painted the same color, and I honestly would like her to come a few times in there, too. Although I'm not good at this whole decorating thing, I can recognize Carter's got an eye for it. After lunch we walked down to the antique store and Carter was able to scrounge up some gems, like an eclectically-detailed vase she wants to put fake sunflowers in ("Because," her words, "she'd kill the real ones by just looking at them"). She also bought a god-awful lamp with cream feathers on it I can only hope will look better in its place. That might be the one thing I veto for my office. Jason and I are planning on just building those old kinds of desks that are both heavy and good quality. We'll be able to cross that necessity off the list.

"This looks great," I tell Carter. I put my arm over her shoulders and pull her into me. She automatically wraps her arms around my waist. We've got a coat of paint on us, too. It's impossible to hide my grin as I kiss the side of her head. "You're beautiful, you know that?"

"The *wall* is beautiful, Boone," she emphasizes.

I shake my head. "You're gonna have to learn to take a compliment, pretty girl. You're beautiful on the outside, for sure, but also on the inside. This room shows it."

Lord knows how much energy it takes for her *not* to argue with me, but she somehow manages. She buries her face in my side and squeezes me tighter. Kissing her and fooling around is all great, but this is what I've missed—holding her close.

"You can go back to calling me Junebug," she says.

"Huh? But you said you didn't like that." I pull back from her so I can see her face. "Carter, just because I did somethin' right doesn't mean you need to reward me. I'm not a puppy who's peed outside and gets a treat."

She snorts. "I know that. I actually sort of like it when you call me Junebug—I didn't think I did, but I do. I miss it."

"I'm not sure I believe you."

Her eyebrows furrow as she thinks. Great, I've unknowingly thrown down a challenge for her. She's gonna want to *make* me believe her.

"Do you remember when Tish was dating that one kind-of-okay guy with the Tom Selleck mustache?"

"Yeah, I think he was even named Tom, except he had blond hair," I say. He was one of the only ones who didn't give me the creeps when he looked Carter's way. He was also the only one whose main interest wasn't having sex and taking drugs with Tish. Now that I think about it, I don't know what the man was sticking around for.

"That's him," Carter says with a smile. "I don't think he liked it when I was there while he messed around with

181

Tish, so he always brought me things to go off and do. Hoola-hoops, games, puzzles. And then he stopped coming around."

"You obviously had an expensive taste."

"My point is, I acted like I hated the stuff he brought, but when it stopped, I was really sad. I actually liked it when he brought me things because we never had anything like that before, but I didn't want to give him the power for it to hurt me if he left. So I pretended. That's how I feel about the nickname."

"I thought that Junebugs were ugly and horrible and everything else you listed."

She blushes and looks away. I like it when she blushes, especially now because it hides what that man did to her. The bruises are lost in her red cheeks. I've been in a push-pull of emotions when it comes to looking at her. In one light, I think she's a fighter and the strongest person I've ever known, while in the other I'm blinded by what he did to her.

"You made them sound … interesting."

"Interesting?"

"I'm giving you whiplash, aren't I?"

"Maybe, but I like it. You're keeping me on my toes." I stand up on my toes for emphasis and lose my balance, falling toward her. So much for trying to be cool. At least it makes her laugh. "I get the whole Tom thing. I liked the stuff he brought, too. So, if you're all right with it, then, I'll go back to calling you Junebug."

"The other thing is, I was trying really hard not to like you before, but now I'm not trying as hard."

I grin at her. "Not trying *as* hard? You're still trying not to like me?"

She only shrugs.

I get it. I don't want to, but I do. "That's fine. You do what you need to do."

#

Carter, 17
Boone, 20

Carter and I leave Declan at the same time. Neither of us talks on the walk down the hall or on the elevator. There's no elevator music playing—only deafening silence, which makes things more awkward. Outside, the darkness gives me an excuse to walk her to her car.

"Can we talk?" I ask when we're close to where she's parked.

Her shoulders shrug forward, defeated-like, but she doesn't say anything as she puts her purse in the car. She walks around the back and leans against the bumper. I do the same, trying to get as close to her as I can without touching her. All I've wanted to do since Declan arrived at the hospital is comfort her. She's already reeling from Declan's overdose, but I know Declan's secret is going to tear her apart. I just want to pre-emptively help her.

That right there has been weighing on me. I don't know how he can keep such a huge secret to himself. It's his to tell, yeah, but she deserves to know. At least then she can get out what she needs to say, rather than having to hold it in. He's being unfair to her. Cruel.

"What do you want to talk about?" she asks.

"I—"

For a split second, I almost tell her everything about Declan; I consider breaking his trust. I'd do anything for her, and that includes screwing Declan over on a promise I made him. It's the right thing as far as Carter's concerned. She shouldn't be in the dark about this. If he wasn't dying, then she shouldn't be spending time with him. He's poison the way he is. Maybe she might look past the drug usage and spend time with him.

I can tell he's jonesing for drugs whenever we're not looking. When we came in today, he hung up the phone fast, meaning he was probably talking to his dealer.

Not telling Carter is really only good for him. He's the only one who benefits, since he wouldn't have to deal with her fussing and worrying over him. When he's gone, there's gonna be a whole lot of blame and guilt, and he's not going to experience a minute of it. He's gonna be at peace, while poor Carter is forced to suffer.

Still, I know she deserves to hear it from Declan. It'll cause a rift if she hears it from anyone else, especially me. But as a friend, I'll give him time to change his mind and his attitude. By time, I mean a few days, tops.

"I just want to know how you're holding up," I finally say.

"I'm okay—I guess." *She hugs herself. At least she's talking to me. I half expected her to go back to not talking to me once we left Declan.* "I'm used to the way this all works, but I'll never be used to the way it feels. I hate that he does this to himself. But I know it's not just him—it's the drugs and his upbringing and our genes ..."

She trails off, shaking her head. Her cheeks are pale, and it obviously bothers her to blame Declan for his addiction. Even though all of the other things are factors, it's hard to see beyond the fact he said, point-blank, he wasn't about to quit using anytime soon. He's making a choice about not even trying, sick or not.

"I get what you're saying, Junebug," I say. *I tilt my head back and look up at the night sky. Not a star out tonight.* "You don't need to feel guilty about it."

"I just hate that we're here—it's like we're in this pattern and it keeps getting worse. He looks worse, right? Or am I just imagining things?" *Before I can answer, she brings her hands up to rub her temples then up and over her eyebrows.* "Maybe I just keep thinking he's going to die, so I'm imagining it's happening."

She's closer to the truth than she knows. I want to tell her. Hell, I'd like to force her back up to the room, past the staff who shooed us out when visitor hours were over, and force Declan to tell Carter everything.

"He's not ... Carter. He's going to get out of here. He's going to go ..."

"Home? Do you mean the trailer or wherever it was you found him? How is that him surviving?" *She drops her hands to her sides.* "I'm sorry. I'm just tired."

"This is a lot to handle."

"Yeah."

She looks up at me, her expression sad. "I'm glad you're here, Boone. I'm glad you love him, too."

The thing of it is I love Carter more.

CHAPTER SEVENTEEN

Carter

Over the next few weeks, we get the business up and running. It's already become clear how much people trust them and genuinely want to throw business their way. I've spent so long in my own little Boone-hating bubble, that I failed to see how much people like him. I honestly thought when we were over, he went on a one-man heart-breaking spree, boldly going where only a wrecking ball can go. I thought I was the start to a string of girls—that he hurt everyone, betrayed everyone. I'm beginning to realize I was wrong about that and a lot of other things.

It's been different with him this time. He's devoted to a relationship between us. I can't help wishing we're going to experience the unstoppable, soul mate type of love I've witnessed between Gabe and Kara.

He holds my hand and kisses me out of nowhere, he makes me laugh and tells me I'm pretty, he leans on me for opinions and gives his own, and he tries to understand everything I say even when I don't understand it. He never questions why I won't commit to the whole *boyfriend* thing or why I can't tell him I love him. It's as if he knew I'm not ready and he's giving me the room to heal and learn to trust him again, giving me the chance to feel something entirely new toward Boone: respect.

I want Kara and Gabe to have respect for him also, so I invited them to visit our store so they can both see it and spend time with Boone. Kara saw it sometime last week, but it was still a disaster zone. After their tour, we're meeting Officer Taft down at the police station who to see if they've come any further with finding the addict. Boone is going with us, which will be interesting.

We're all frustrated there hasn't been any answers about the guy, which is why Gabe set up the meeting and took today off. I'm just so tired of being constantly feeling terrified and paranoid. I'm in a constant state of unrest, as if I don't move or change my mind, he'll show up again. He changed the way I see the world and the way I fear it.

I shake the thought away. The man managed to cause so much damage, despite being in my life for just a few minutes. I've been letting him torture my mind longer than he physically tortured me. I'm letting him win when I should be working toward feeling strong and safe again.

"Wait until you see it," Kara is gushing from the front seat. "Carter has done *amazing*. I think she might've found her calling. Hey, Carter, you should think about offering interior design advice. You would be good at it—like Joanna in *Fixer Upper*."

Kara's been talking non-stop since breakfast this morning, trying to lighten Gabe's mood and my apprehension. After years of forced dinners with our dad, you'd think we'd be pros at handling awkward situations, but no. We're as lost as ever.

I don't answer because I'm too busy texting Boone: *I hope you're wearing your lucky underwear and a suit of armor. We're turning into town and this is going to be fun,*

I immediately get a reply, *I'm not wearing either.*

Then another, *Actually, I'm going commando ;)*

Then, *This is all going to be fine, Junebug. Promise.*

When we get there, he's waiting for us in front of the store. I hold my breath as Gabe pulls into the spot directly in front of where he's standing. Since Gabe's a doctor, I'll try to pretend he isn't aiming for Boone. If Boone shares the same thought, he doesn't show it. Instead, he surprises us all by walking to Kara's door and opening it.

"Hey, Kara," he says. "Good to see you."

Kara smiles at him, looking a little relieved. I'm already halfway out of my seat, but Boone pulls my door open, too, and leans down to kiss my cheek. "I'm back to trying to impress. Am I doing good?"

I think about how he's sans underwear *and* holding doors open like a gentleman. "Yes. But again—"

"How am I going to know if I'm impressing people if I don't ask?" he points out, knowing exactly what I was about to say.

"I think the word we're missing here is also the lesson, Boone," I say, pulling back. "Humility. Practice it and maybe someone will like you."

He presses his hand over his heart. "Are you saying I'm disliked?"

I'm too much of a rotten liar to answer him.

Boone laughs and rubs his hands together conspiratorially. "My plan has finally been accomplished. Total and complete world domination through the power of my irresistibility."

I can't help but grin, even though Gabe is watching us like a hawk. Kara is clearly trying to talk him off his papa-bear sized cliff. Boone composes himself and walks up to Gabe, hand out. "Glad you could come by, Gabe."

Gabe takes his hand. "I wanted to see the place Carter's always talking about."

"I don't talk that much about it," I grumble.

Gabe cracks a smile. "You sort of do. Dusk till dawn and then some."

I shrug. "You're probably right."

"He is," Kara supplies.

Boone's hand slips into mine as we walk inside, which is something he always does. It's almost muscle memory now. It feels right, even in front of Boone's biggest critics.

"Jason's out," he says over his shoulder. "He took an extra job so I could go with y'all today."

Boone and Jason are pretty flexible with each other like that, especially since one of Jason's daughters had the flu and he had to watch her, leaving Boone with his workload. I've come to like Jason, Alex, and their daughters a lot. Boone and I even went out to a restaurant with them. It was my first ever double date, and I enjoyed it more than I thought I would. I loved getting to see Boone interact with people whom he's close with that are, well, *normal.*

"That's nice of him," Kara says. "Jason seems kind."

"Yeah, definitely. He's a real …" He pauses, searching for the right word, and when his lips pull into a grin, I want to face-palm myself. Cute or not, he's insufferable. "Swell."

"Have I met Jason before?" Gabe asks. Luckily, he seems more curious than a watchdog.

"No," I answer. "You wouldn't have had any reason to. He's Boone's age, but he was … and Boone wasn't—"

Boone chuckles. "Let's just sacrifice my dignity and be honest, here. Jason and I are pals, but we never ran in the same circles. Further clarification, he wasn't a stoner. Not that I was. Fine, I was for a time, but—"

"Boone," Kara says, walking up beside him. She puts her hand on his shoulder, and he stops in place. "We've always known about your past. We know you're not that person anymore. It's actions you're making up for, not your history."

Gabe makes a noise, which could probably be translated into: "She's wrong. We're judging you for everything. Past, present, future, and which foot you start off on. Literally."

"Thanks for saying that, Kara," Boone says.

"Well, we want to see the both of you happy." Kara

narrows her eyes. "But if you make her unhappy ..."

Boone lets loose of my hand to hold both of his up. "All right, all right. Loud and clear on that one. An angry Kara is not a friend I wanna meet."

"She isn't exactly classified as your friend," I tell him.

He rolls his eyes. "Yeah, well I wasn't about to piss her off by saying something that would get me on her bad side."

"Again, Boone," I say with a sigh. "You're not supposed to *tell* your motives."

He only shrugs. He's totally not understanding my point, and something tells me he never will.

I leave him and go to Gabe, looping my arm through his. Even if he's not happy in Boone's general vicinity, he still grins down at me. Sometimes it hits me that even though I look at him as a dad, he's not. He's just so *young*. You'd honestly think he's Boone's age. He should've been going wild and having fun, not raising me, but he acts as if this were the best job in the world for him.

I never thought I'd ever have anyone proud of me, yet it never fails that he and Kara always are.

He lets me drag him around the store, showing him all the would-be-could-bes—where the parts will go, where we'll put a cash register, how we'll section off aisles. He oohs and ahhs and adds his own suggestions. He surprises me by actually talking to Boone about a few things. They somehow manage to have a reasonable, even-keel conversation that doesn't push them further apart.

"Now for the best part," Gabe says as we approach my office. Boone carved my name into a piece of weathered wood and hung it on my door, then did the same to his and Jason's. I glued fake flowers to mine and small mechanical parts to theirs, like screws and bolts.

I pull my keys out of my pocket and unlock the door, then stand back so Gabe and Kara can pass.

"You've got a grin on that's both pretty and pretty big," Boone says as he leans against the door. My office is too small to fit him, me, Gabe, and Kara. I blush, then stand on my toes to kiss him. He runs his hand down the length of my cheek, which makes me shiver. He lowers his head and whispers in my ear, "You wanna come over later?"

I blink up at him, trying to clear my brain. At first I think he's inviting me to his trailer, but then I remember he's moved upstairs into the loft. By "moved" I mean he put a bed and his clothes up there but hasn't gotten around to doing anything else. He keeps saying he needs to get the rest of his things, and I always offer to help, but he refuses to let me come over to the trailer. I don't think he wants me around his dad, God-phase or not.

"Okay," I answer.

"Good," he says, his teeth catch the shell of my ear.

It takes all of my effort not to melt into him. He's definitely getting more and more good at this whole seduction-dating-everything-else thing. He's a fast learner and an A+ student, for sure.

He lets me go before I do something stupid such as climb him like a tree in front of Kara and Gabe. My cheeks feel hot, but I go inside my office anyway. Gabe and Kara are too busy looking at everything I've done to notice me. I've never had the opportunity to really be creative with my own space. I probably went too far and made what's supposed to be my "workplace" into my "home." Boone and Jason have my hand-crafted desk all set up in the middle of the room. I also have a small couch, a filing cabinet, and a bookshelf tucked into the room. On one wall I hung a painting I bought at a yard sale and on the other I have a plethora of frames filled with pictures of Kara, Gabe, Boone, and Declan. The office is windowless, so all I've got is the glow of my lamplight, which makes the orange room feel rustic and cozy.

"Doesn't it look great?" Kara asks cheerily while Gabe runs his hands over my desk appreciatively.

"Yeah. This is better than anything I've ever seen," Gabe says. "Carter, you've got something good going here."

"I think so," I agree.

"See, shouldn't she do some interior designing?" Kara asks loud enough so Boone can hear.

"That's definitely in the cards, Kara," Boone calls back. "No need to drop hints."

Kara grins. "Just making sure."

Gabe lets out a whistle when he sees my office phone and the number of messages on it. "Wow, someone's popular."

"I'd like to check through them before we leave and make sure there's no emergencies, but this is how it usually looks when I first get here." The three of us never fail to get excited when we see the number of calls we have, and it's even better when we hit an all-time high. We've even got a competition going to see who can guess the right number. "We're trying to get together a website, and we'll be able to take requests there. Hopefully then I won't be playing phone tag as often."

Gabe pats me on the back. "You seem like you've really got this under control."

"Thank you."

"We're really happy for you, Carter," Kara adds. "I think you've found your calling."

"Now maybe Dad will get off my back."

Kara's perpetual daddy-disappointment shows in her expression. "If he would come here …"

"He won't," I say. "He's never going to be happy with anything I do. Maybe Deirdre would like to see it?"

"Definitely!" Kara cheers. "I can bring Mom by one day and the three of us can do lunch."

I swallow, emotion suddenly flooding me. A lunch with Dierdre might be the tipping point for my happiness. It feels as though everything was finally coming together—as if my life were finally going right.

This is exactly how I felt before everything went kaput.

#

Carter, 18
Boone, 21

My hand is shaking as I knock on my old trailer home's front door. I really hope Tish doesn't answer, not that I think she would. I haven't seen her since my dad paid her to leave us alone. I thought for sure she'd show up again; I didn't believe it would just be a one-time cash deal. You don't just stop milking a cash cow.

I've wanted to visit Declan since he checked himself out of the hospital three months ago, but I haven't had the courage until today. It would be a different story if I was meeting him back at the picnic tables, Boone's, or somewhere else, but coming here is different. If I had a demon to face, stepping inside this trailer again would be it.

I take in a deep breath and reach for the doorknob. I'm the only person who ever locked the door. We never had anything valuable to lock away.

"Carter?"

I freeze, my hand in the middle of turning the knob.

"No one's there," Boone says as he walks across the yard toward me. "You could've called me. I would've told you he wasn't here."

I look at the door, sighing. I wish I wasn't so relieved to hear that.

Boone's been my main connection to Declan. We talk almost every day so I can keep tabs on Declan. I forgot how comfortable and safe Boone could always make me feel. I let our stupid kiss ruin everything, and not having our friendship has been worse than any heartbreak.

It's been easy to forgive him when he's the reason why my brother is still alive. A day doesn't go by where I don't blame myself for not being there for Declan. What sort of sister am I? Even now, after he OD'd, things haven't changed, and I don't know where he is. I'm letting the cycle happen all over again.

I can't meet Boone's eyes. "I know. I just thought—I don't know what I thought. I guess I wanted to see him is all."

"How about we go over to my place? My dad's not there—he's

out at Patty's Pub."

"Oh, I'm sorry," I say. "I thought he was back to God."

"Must've found him in the bottom of a bottle."

His joke falls flat—we just stand there awkwardly. Maybe I forgot what this part of my life was like because it feels even worse than it ever did, closer to a fictitious horror story than my past.

"Let's go," I finally decide. I follow him over to his trailer. He glares at the screen, which is in a worse state than I've ever seen it in. There's a piece of duct tape flapping in the breeze from an attempt to patch it up.

He gives me an "oh well" look then opens the door and steps inside.

The inside of his trailer is cleaner than it used to be. I try not to gawk at the empty sink and clear counter space. He walks over to the circa-1980s refrigerator and pulls out a pitcher of water. He pours it into two glasses, then hands one to me.

I stare at the glass, expecting to see floaters in the water. Nothing. Behind him, there's a filter on the faucet.

"He left last night. I think they've been staying with him. Tish's whereabouts are unknown, other than that she's been gone for who knows how long."

"She's probably got a new boyfriend," I say.

"That or a pimp."

"We definitely won the lottery, as far as families are concerned."

Boone raises his glass to that and takes a drink. "Amazing you and I aren't going down the same path. I guess you've had Kara and Gabe, and I've had ..."

"You've had what?"

"Well," he says, running his hand up his face and through his hair. "I've had you."

I set the cup on the counter with a little too much force. Water goes sloshing over the rim. "Don't do this to me again, Boone. We're finally in a good place."

"I know we are, and I'm so happy—you have no idea. I refuse to hurt you anymore—at least not on purpose. I'm done pulling all that shit and being a bastard. The way I see it is I've been so focused on all the ways I'm wrong for you, instead of all the ways I'm right for

you."

"*I don't understand.*" I'm somewhere between begging him to tell me more and wanting to wring his neck. "*What do you mean 'not on purpose'?*"

"*Carter, all I've ever wanted is for you to be happy,*" he replies as if what he'd try to say were hidden there.

I walk around the counter toward him. "*I am happy, though. I've always been happy. We didn't have the best upbringing, but that didn't ruin everything.*"

He rubs at his jaw. "*I'm what's been ruining everything.*"

"*I didn't say that.*"

"*You don't have to.*"

"*So make it right.*"

"*How?*"

I take a few more steps and close the distance between us. My hand trembles as I lift it to cover his. "*You'll figure it out.*"

His fingers lace through mine as we lean into each other. I'm not sure which one of us initiates the kiss, but I don't think it matters because we both continue it. This is levels above our first kiss. It's like our souls are trying to bond together.

I could also just want this to be something more—something permanent. I don't want him to give up on us again. Boone's not good with words, but he's good with my heart, and that'll make me give him everything and end up with nothing.

His tongue flicks against my lips, frantically basically for entrance. My knees nearly buckle when my lips part and his tongue darts inside, mingling with mine. So this is what it's supposed to feel like to be kissed. I thought that our first kiss was magic, but this ... this is more.

He lets go of my hands so his can travel down my back. I don't know what he's doing until my legs are hitched up around his hips and he's walking. He must be some sort of a magician because our kiss never ends. It only goes deeper and makes me weaker.

It doesn't take much brainpower—even during a kiss as earth-shattering as this one—to know he's going to his bedroom. They have two bedrooms since their trailer is newer and bigger compared to the one-bedroom brothel ours was.

He shuts the door behind us, locks it, and lays me back, finally breaking the kiss. The sheer emptiness which comes with not kissing him and being disconnected from him is jarring. He stares down at me, standing, while I lay on the bed, my head on a pillow.

"You're beautiful, Carter," he whispers, setting a knee on the bed. "I always dreamed of what it would be like to have you here with me."

"I've been here," I remind him. My voice is hoarse—sort of husky—and it's weird that it belongs to me. I sound as though I just ran a mile in my underwear: out of breath, embarrassed, but free. "Mama once brought home a man who yelled and threw things, so you brought me here and held me."

"All night," he finishes, fitting his body over mine. He somehow manages to keep his weight off me by balancing on his elbows. One of his legs nestles between mine. "You were twelve and it was just before Kara took you. I loved you so much back then, but in a different way."

"When did you ... when did you start dreaming of this?"

"I don't know. It happened slowly, I guess. I've never fallen for anyone before, so I didn't recognize it. I'd feel in small moments— when I'd kiss your cheeks or when you'd punch my arm. Then eventually it turned into more. When we kissed, my feelings for you turned to full blast. You were older—it didn't feel so wrong to like you as much as I did."

"I understand. For me, it was the same. You went from brother to friend to crush to something more." I pause, smiling to myself. "Can you imagine how grossed out we both would've been if we knew this is where we were heading?"

"You mean back in the time when boys and girls had cooties?" He lays his head into the crook of my neck. His muffled chuckle sends shivers down my back. "I'm just kidding, Carter. If you had cooties, I never saw a lick of them."

His tongue darts out to taste my skin. I'm immediately reminded of just how much of an adult I am as heat pools between my thighs. I fist my hands in his hair as I sigh. I don't know what I'm doing, but I don't care. I hope he doesn't either.

His thigh drops between my legs, pushing up against me, and I make a sound close to a whimper. That feels almost too good. My hips, of their own volition, press closer, electricity spreading over the surface of my skin. It feels so good I want, need, and will beg for more.

Slowly, he leads a trail of kisses from my shoulder and back to my lips. He lies down, half his weight on me and the rest on the bed, so his hand can rest on my stomach.

We kiss like that for a long time until I feel like I'm flying. I know enough about sex from being around Tish to know I'm getting close to an orgasm. She's always been way too open about that sort of thing, not only being loud enough for me to hear, but also talking about it afterward. I'm glad Kara and Gabe aren't like that.

When his hands touch my breasts, I finally find my release. I cry out, my hands reaching wildly for something to use to ground myself. Maybe this is why Tish was so loud. She just couldn't help herself.

Boone kisses me through it until I feel like a mass of nothing beneath him. I can feel him, hot and hard through our layers of clothes. With all the control in the world, he starts to shift off me, but I grab hold of his shirt. I don't know what I want or how to say it. I just stare at him, begging him to figure it out for himself.

If he's going to eventually change his mind again, then I want to have this memory of him. I want him to have every piece of me I can give.

He lowers his face to mine and kisses me deeply. When he breaks away, he stares at me with unwavering eye contact. "Are you sure?" he asks, his voice unsteady.

"Yes," I say back, just as nervous.

He lifts a hand to brush my hair away from my face. It's shaking, and for some reason that makes me more comfortable than anything.

"You're my first," I tell him. My cheeks feel hotter than the sun.

"I hoped so," he says back. "I wish you were mine, too. I wish I would've waited for you."

"Three years is evidently a big age gap," I tell him.

He laughs. "As far as this is concerned, yes." His hand moves to the buttons on my shirt. "This matters to me, Carter. This and that kiss both do."

I don't answer him, because I'm too busy watching him slowly reveal my skin. I've never been naked in front of anyone before—never even in just my underwear and panties. I know I have more curves than most girls, and I usually have to buy shirts in a larger size than I really am to compensate for my boobs. I hope I'm his type or else this is going to be a lot like unwrapping a Christmas present and finding coal.

Cold air tickles my skin as he helps me sit up to take my shirt off. When I lie back, he stares at me. He's as serious as I've ever seen him, with a slight glimmer to his eyes. He swallows, then his gaze finds mine.

"Perfect," he tells me hoarsely. He tries to takes his shirt off but gets it caught on his head. For some reason, it makes me relax and laugh. By the time he gets it off, he's laughing, too. He juts his thumb at his chest. "Not perfect."

From my point of view, he pretty much is. Yes, it's the abs and the chest and the general gorgeousness of him, but it's also how he's smiling down at me and how when he looks at me, the whole world sort of slows down and takes its time.

I answer him by craning my neck to kiss him. He kisses me back, letting me pull him in until we're skin to skin. He curls his hand behind my back, fumbling with my bra strap. It's cream and ugly, even though Kara always tells me to "have fun." I've never seen the point of having fun underwear until now, because I always said, "Why? Not like anyone's going to see it." I think Kara meant it would be a fun secret. I don't think she intended for this to be the very moment where I realized next time we go shopping, I will get the fun, colorful, probably uncomfortable underwear—the non-granny kind.

Boone doesn't seem to care if I dress like an eighty-year-old as he pulls my bra off and tosses it to the side. Here I am worrying about my body and what I'm wearing, and he just wants me for me.

His lips find their way to my nipple, where his tongue swirls against it, then he tugs on it with his teeth. My back bows as I press my breast further into his mouth. I can already feel a residual orgasm on its way.

Between us, he unbuttons and unzips his pants. He leaves me to

197

do the same with mine—giving me that option to back out of this if I want to. I don't. Still, I'm beyond nervous as I work my shorts down my legs, then my underwear.

He slides his hand down my stomach, and I tense. This is all so new and awkward and ...

"Hey, relax," he says. "Look at me." I hesitate, but then do as he says, despite the blush creeping over my cheeks. His eyes are wide, but kind and deep, the brown invitingly sweet. "I promise you'll love this. It'll just ... it'll be weird and hurt at first. I promise it'll all get better." He gently strokes the skin of my abdomen with his thumb. "I'm out of my mind with nerves, too."

I try to smile at him to let him know how much what he's saying means to me, but my lips are numb and trembling. Instead I reach between us and wrap my fingers around his wrist. Even if it's nothing, I just want a little control.

He swallows and leans back in for more kissing. Just as his tongue flicks against mine, he moves his hand over my folds, a finger slipping inside of me. I cry out into his mouth, blissfully happy. The more I react, the more insistent his fingers become, until he has me writhing beneath him, begging for more.

At that point, he rolls off me and disappears. He comes back with a sheepish look, then says, "I never keep anything on me ... I had to get protection from the bathroom." I don't know what it says if he doesn't always have protection, but I don't really want to ask. I'm too focused on how he's about to be inside of me—all of him. His fingers felt good, but more?

Before I can think too much, he's turning me into a mass of mindless and contented putty with his hands, fingers, and tongue. Somewhere in it all, he poises himself at my entrance and slowly slides in. I immediately go still. It feels as though he were stretching me— tearing me open. Maybe he's too big for me. Is it possible that sometimes people can't fit together?

"I love you," he whispers into my ear as he pushes deeper, faster. A sharp pain brings tears to my eyes, and Boone surprises me by kissing them away. He stays inside me, unmoving, as the pain dissipates and my body gets used to him. "Better?"

"Yes," I breathe.

He sighs and the small movement causes pleasure to shoot through all my nerve endings. My hips move, seeking something more. I need it. Crave it.

"Shit, pretty girl," he whispers. "I'm not gonna last with you."

Painstakingly slow, he pulls out of me, then pushes back in. I moan, groping at his back. I don't know if it's just him or if this feels this good for everyone, but I'm thinking it's him. This is his special power. I would've regretted letting him be my first, even without knowing how great it would feel.

His next thrust is faster and harder, and I lift my hips to meet his. This time he groans and buries his head in my neck. He lets out a string of curses, which are still audible, even muffled, as his lips move deliciously against my skin. I'm not sure who's more frenzied as we continue, but it becomes like a competition for who can feel the most and who can express it.

By the time I have the same existential feeling as before, I'm exhausted. My body hurts just as good as it feels. Boone follows shortly after me, moaning and cursing his way through a release.

As he holds me, our bodies still joined, I let myself believe that he does love me, even though at the end of the day it doesn't really matter. As long as I love him back, it'll never matter. I'll let him take anything I give him, because I want everything he'll give me in return. I want to try to get as close to everything with him as I can.

#

The four of us sit in the waiting room because Officer Taft is on a phone call. The police office is newly built, so it still has a cold, bland atmosphere to it. This is probably advantageous for the officers as far as perpetrators are involved, but it's unsettling for the everyday person.

I shift in my seat and tug at the hem of my shorts. It's something to do, since all I want to do is escape. I'm afraid if we don't speak with Officer Taft soon, I'm going to give up. Maybe it doesn't even matter if they find the guy or not—it's been a while since he attacked me, and he hasn't shown up since. Maybe I'm safe and it's best not to go poking around.

I open my mouth, ready to say exactly that, when Boone laces his hand with mine. He's already got one of his arms over the back of my chair, so he's basically caging me in and keeping me here.

This is what needs to be done. The addict can't just hurt me and get away with it.

"You know what I found when I was cleaning out my room at the trailer? A whole box of notes I never gave you. They're embarrassing as hell, but I thought you'd get a kick out of 'em. I wanted to save them for another time, but I think I might just go ahead and show them to you," Boone says.

He's either trying to distract himself or me, so I guess I'd better go along with it. "Why didn't you give them to me when you wrote them?"

"'Cause they're embarrassing as hell, like I said."

"And the other ones you wrote aren't?"

Boone shakes his head. "Hey, those were written out of love. These were … I don't know. I go on for a whole page about the color of my socks and how it reminds me of your eyes. I've never owned anything other than black and white socks in my life, so I don't know what the hell was happening there."

"You were probably high," I say.

He shrugs. "It was written during that time frame."

"How is that embarrassing, though?"

"Because you were basically a kid still."

"You were, too," Kara interjects, leaning around me to see Boone. "From my point of view, you were basically a tween."

"Tween? What's a tween?" Gabe and Boone ask at almost the same time. It makes Gabe glower and Boone grin.

"It's like a kid that's between being a child and a teenager," I explain.

"Basically, it's a phase where the kids are ready to grow

up, but the parents aren't," Kara clarifies.

"Well, tween sounds like a horrible stage," Boone says. "I can't even remember anything from my *tween* stage, if that's any indicator. So, yeah, my kid's ain't gonna have the opportunity to have one of those. They're gonna be as straight-laced and boring as they come."

I gape at him. *Kids? Straight-laced and boring?* I never considered Boone might have aspirations to be a dad. I always assumed his upbringing ruined any of those sorts of dreams. If I hadn't moved in with Kara and Gabe, I don't think I would've wanted kids. It's hard to want to bring children into a world you know is dangerous.

Before I can try to get more out of him about it, Officer Taft walks into the waiting area. "Good afternoon," he says and shakes all of our hands, saying our names individually. "You all can follow me. I've got some extra chairs set up."

Officer Taft leads us into a room that is filled with desks. Most of them are empty, but clearly used. Only three other people are currently in, one of which is sleeping. Officer Taft goes to a desk in the corner of the room, which has four chairs cramped together. My sister and Gabe immediately take the chairs on either side of me. I expect Boone to put up a fight, but he walks behind me and stands instead. He puts his hands on my shoulders.

"Have you found him?" Gabe asks before Officer Taft can sit down.

Officer Taft takes his seat and leans back in his chair. "Yes—he was admitted to a hospital four counties over. He was hit by a car."

"Oh," Kara says, putting her hand over her mouth.

Gabe doesn't make any noise. As a doctor, I know he probably wouldn't wish any ill on anyone, but in this case, who knows.

"Well, that's good news," Boone says.

I want to disagree—the man is in the hospital in lord knows what condition—but I can't.

"He's stable," Taft continues. "We'll need him in better shape before you can identify him, Carter. The problem is we quickly learned from a few of his *friends* that it's not just him who's interested in you. Evidently your mom has been telling people her debts are transferable to you. She thinks you'll pay them for her."

"Why would she think that?" I ask. Boone begins massaging my shoulders, which saves me from the tiny panic attack brewing.

"Because of Dad," Kara answers quietly.

"Paying people off is his specialty," Gabe finishes. He leans forward and sets an elbow on Taft's desk. "Their dad gave Tish money over the years to get her to disappear. We're her own personal bank."

"I don't think she ever realized Dad only paid her when it inconvenienced him," I explain. "What happened to me doesn't inconvenience him."

"It should," Gabe and Boone say. They're sharing a lot of the same thoughts today. At least they have something to bond over—my crappy father is their common enemy.

Taft frowns. I've got to give him credit for taking the time to be thorough with us. He's been kind and understanding, even though chances are nothing is going to come from this. "There's really not much we can do. We can only keep a close eye on Carter's safety. I wish there were more, but ..." He trails off. "There's also no clear sight on where Tish is."

I don't know how to react. *Does that mean she's probably dead?* is the main thing I want to ask, but I know I'll sound more like I'm asking for an update about the weather. Even if Officer Taft is getting a front-row seat to my crazy family drama, I don't want him to know it's not just that I don't love my mom, it's that I've *never* loved her.

"Chances are she's holed up somewhere," he continues, "but she could also be deceased. We don't know."

We all just sort of stare at him. What does it say about us if we don't care?

"O-kay, then," Taft says, "that's all we've got to update you about."

"So let me get this straight," Boone says from behind me, and I only now notice his hands have gone still. "Carter's on her own, while Tish is out sending people after her for money?"

"Well, no—"

"That's shit." Boone's voice is sharp, and it makes me flinch. "You're basically saying if something happens, you'll help her after the fact."

"Boone," I say softly, turning around to face him. His expression is hard, and his eyes are full of emotion, a tsunami brewing inside them. "They can't exactly see the future."

His gaze falls to me and his face softens. "Sorry," he says. "I'm just frustrated. Don't want to see you get hurt again. Ever."

"I know," I tell him. I put my hand on his. "Nothing has happened, and it's been a month. Maybe nothing is going to happen at all. He might've just been desperate."

"I hope you're right, Carter," he says.

"Me too," Gabe agrees. "I don't like this any more than you do, Boone."

"Me, either," Kara adds.

"Neither do we," Taft says. "Which is why we do want to stay involved in this. Like you said, he could've been desperate, but so might the other people Tish has promised money to. Until enough time has passed, we'd like to be alerted about anything out of the ordinary. If anything alarming starts happening, we want to do what we can to step in before it escalates."

"Thank you," I say.

He smiles at me, then stands. We all take turns shaking his hand before he shows us outside. When we're in the car, it's Boone who talks first. Of course.

"I just don't like it," he says. "Think we can make a pit stop? Carter needs a taser."

#

"We're not going to practice using that thing, if that's why you keep playing with it," Boone says as he cleans the dishes from the dinner he made us. He caused my heart hurt in a good way when he told me he was going to make it for us, then proceeded to order me to "sit my pretty ass in a chair" while he did. He said the same thing when it came time to clean everything up. I didn't know he could cook food other than the microwavable stuff and ramen. Evidently he can, and he's good at it.

I set the taser back down on the table and push it to the middle. Far away from me. "I'm trying to figure out where I'm going to put it. I can't see my attacker waiting for me to find my purse *then* find my taser in said purse."

"Little faith in the politeness of humanity, huh?"

"Absolutely none," I say. The man who attacked me sure wasn't interested in *pleases* and *thank yous*. I doubt he ever even learned them.

"That's probably for the best. What's humanity ever done for us?" He turns to face me as he dries off our wine glasses. We didn't actually drink wine. Instead we had some Sprite to create the—his words—"fizz effect," which I guess is important when drinking out of a wine glass. Who knows. It shouldn't surprise me Boone's not a drinker. "I'm sorry again for my shitty reaction back at the police station."

I grab the taser up and point it at him. "If you apologize one more time, I am going to get some practice with this."

He laughs. "Fine, then. I'm done."

I gently set it back down in its place. Don't want to make it angry. "I think Gabe felt the same way."

"I wish we had something else in common, but for now it'll have to do." He turns back around and puts the wine glasses up in a cabinet. He refinished his bottom cabinets, but not the ones on the wall, so everything is mismatched. While he's made some progress on his loft, most of it is still under construction. Getting the downstairs has had a priority for him.

From the way he's been talking, this is actually better for his relationship with his dad. I guess they get along better now that they're not forced to be in each other's business. Boone's actually been going over to visit him, and they managed to have a conversation, which didn't revolve around religion.

"You'll get there eventually. Gabe just ..."

"Blames me for everything wrong that's ever happened to you?" He folds up the towel neatly and places it on its rung. "He should. And I guess I probably shouldn't be rushing for him to approve of me since that's the case."

"You're not the reason why *everything* bad has happened to me."

"Fine, it's pretty damn close to it." He shakes his head and looks down at his feet. He rubs his palm into his face hard enough to leave a red mark behind. "When you think about it, I'm the reason why Declan got into drugs, you know that? I'm the one who introduced him to the thugs we hung with, talked him into trying that shit. If I wouldn't have done that, he might still be here."

"Boone, that's not your fault. I wanted to blame you—I won't lie. But no matter what, it was in Declan's DNA to have a problem with addiction. He made the active decision to try the harder drugs. He gave up on himself. No one—not you, me, or Tish—were involved in any of that. It was him. Declan." By the time I'm done talking, I'm on the verge of tears. I'm actually shaking. I clench my hands on my lap, trying to hold it all in. "You're not the reason for everything that's wrong in my life or in the world. You're giving yourself too much credit if you think that."

I blink to clear my vision. He walks toward the island I'm sitting at, pushes the taser away, leans into me, and cups my cheeks.

"How is it you know everything I need to hear?" he asks. "I've been carrying that guilt around with me for what feels like forever, then you magically take it away."

I lift my hands up to cover his. "I think I've been putting pressure on you to carry that guilt. I've made you feel horrible."

"Because I've *been* horrible."

"You've been human," I correct.

He closes the distance between us to kiss me. The kiss is there and gone, leaving me wanting more. *As always.* I wonder if Boone and I were together for the rest of time, if there would always be this all-consuming, underlying passion or if it would eventually fade. Something tells me I could be old, wrinkled, forgetful, and cranky, and I would still love him just as much as I do today. I would still see him the same way, too.

"You're too understanding," he tells me.

I roll my eyes. "You didn't think that when you were bugging me to be friends with you. I probably wasn't understanding enough then."

"I thought you were. I just didn't verbalize it," he explains. "Besides, how can I be sure you get the best if I'm not the one giving it?"

"Your ego is so sporadic. I've got a kink in my neck."

"Look at us being sexual without even meaning to," he says. "Giving you the best and a kink. Pretty girl, it's not kink, it's *crick*."

"No, it's kink."

"Crick," he says, grinning an insufferably sexy grin as he presses closer to me, then nuzzles his nose against my neck. "There's a difference between a crick and a kink. I'll show you sometime if you want."

I blush. "Are we seriously arguing about this?"

"If you're asking that, then you clearly see I'm right and don't want to admit it." His lips brush against the sensitive spot behind my ear. I shudder and grip his forearms. "Tell me I'm right."

"You're wrong."

He chuckles. "It's a damn shame you're cute when you argue with me or else I'd keep this going longer."

My knees nearly buckle when his thigh parts my legs. "My cuteness has never stopped you from arguing before."

"Yeah, but now I've got a reason to stop."

"What's that?"

He answers me by pressing his hips against me so I can feel how hard he is. *Ah. That.* The sudden need rampaging throughout my body is definitely a good reason to give up on the argument.

And talking.

And thinking.

Our lips slant together in a hungry, lusty kiss that's more about bonding souls than bodies. It's almost scary how everything around us disappears when we're together like this. The only thing I can focus on is us and how I want more. Need more. Talk about drugs.

He grips my hips, but he doesn't lift me as he usually does. For some reason he has a thing about lifting me or carrying me. I agree it's a lot easier because the last thing I want to do is fall and break a hip in the middle of the best kiss of my life (they all are the best kisses of my life). That would be an embarrassing call to make to Kara and Gabe or anyone for that matter.

He turns us away from the counter and starts walking me backward. Somehow my legs work, even if they have the composition of Jell-O. Maybe the feel of his lips, his hands and his tongue twined with mine are so euphoric it's causing me to have an out of body experience—then again, maybe I'm not giving myself enough credit. Maybe I'm good at this.

Ha, yeah, right.

He stops everything just outside of his bedroom door. When he pulls away, I make an embarrassing mewling sound. My whole body becomes hyper-aware when he only stares at me, eyes churning with raw emotion. He's tense, a hand on my back and the other tangled in my hair, but other than that he's barely even touching me now. It's as if he were trying to be as far away from me as he can without actually being away from me.

"We're goin' in there," he says cryptically.

I try to keep my face blank, even though I'm confused as all get out. I don't want to give him any reason to freak out. "Yes."

He swallows. "That's my bedroom, Carter. Once we're in there ..."

I bring my hands up to his face. I force him to look into my eyes by pulling him to my level. "I don't want to stop, Boone."

"We let this happen the last time and you regretted it," he says slowly. He looks worried and as though he were poised for disappointment. "I don't want that to happen again."

Guilt pummels low in my stomach. All this time I've placed so much blame on him and resented him, but I never once thought about how *I* hurt *him*. After the kiss, I was so mad at him because he changed his mind, but I changed mine after we made love. Even if it was for a good reason, it still had to hurt him. I always thought I was the one who went into his room and lost the most, but maybe it was him.

"I didn't regret anything with you—*ever*," I tell him, just like I did with the kiss. "It's the after I regret."

"We're pretty damn good with the during, but we're bad at those afters," he says. "Let's make it different this time, all right?"

"What do you mean?"

"I'm in it for the long haul," he tells me, not for the first time. "Forever. This is going to be another beginning."

Has he always been this way? I think he has. He's shown versions of himself to me, but never this complete view of him. He's risking a lot—everything—by being so personal. He's basically giving me and showing me his vulnerable, beating heart, fully knowing it could be easily broken.

"I am, too," I promise him. I step back beyond the door frame and start pulling at my clothes. He watches me as I slip my shirt off, then my shorts, until I'm only in my underwear. I sit down on the bed, willing my body not to miss and break my tail bone.

I'm not this bold. Ever. I'm all talk. That's clear in the way I was constantly trying to push Boone away but letting him in. If this is going to be different, I have to show the both of us I'm willing to try harder, too. I've been relying on him to be better, but I have room to improve also. I can be what the both of us need, just like I expect him to be.

He blinks, as if he were trying to get everything in check in his mind. "Did that just happen?"

I nod.

"We'll have to see if we can do a rewind of it later," he says. "You know, to make sure I wasn't just imagining things." He's not laughing or smiling, which means he's totally serious.

He saunters toward me the same way I walked away—losing his pants and shirt. This time he's actually wearing a pair of boxes, which I only laugh about on the inside. I sort of want to mark it down on the calendar. Today Boone Fell wore *all* of the clothes he was supposed to like a good little boy. Although, he's getting naked and defeating the purpose. Here I was yelling at him about it, and now I'm enabling him.

"You think a lot," he says as he cages his warm body over mine. We measure up in all the right, delicious places. "And you even think in snark, too."

"How do you know that?"

He traces my eyebrow with his thumb, making me shiver. "These tell me all your secrets."

"You're too obsessed with my eyebrows."

He grins and kisses where his fingers have just touched. "Not possible."

I huff, but it turns into a sigh as he massages his hands down my body. We've been in this position more times than I can count over the last month, though it hasn't gone further. You'd think I'd be used to it or immune to his touch, but I'm not. I'm not sure I ever will be.

We kiss, my bra disappearing, then my undies, then his as he works me toward the edge of an orgasm. As it roils through my body, it takes everything in me to stay on this planet. Somehow I manage, and when I open my eyes, he's still above me, not moving any further. He's just staring at me. Studying me.

He wants me to make the move. I slide my hand between us, until he's hot and heavy in my hand. The times I've tried to touch him, he's warded me off, always telling me it would lead us farther than we're ready for. This time he lets me. I slowly run my fingers down the length of him, then back up. He shudders, and his muscles tense as he tries to stay poised above me. I like the power this gives me over him. I like how I'm giving him pleasure for once.

I apply pressure with my whole hand this time, moving in a way I hope is making him feel good. I try to judge how to work him over by his grunts and moans, but I don't know if they're an indicator that he likes it or if I'm hurting him. When his hips jolt and he starts moving with me, I decide it's got to be the first.

"You need to stop," he says raggedly, tracing his teeth down my neck.

He says it with such desperation, that I do as he says. He draws in a heavy, hard breath, his eyes squeezed shut, then he moves off me and over to the nightstand. I watch him as he pulls out a still-sealed box, struggles to open in, then finally manages to take out a packet. He makes short work of it, retrieving the condom, sliding it on, then putting the wrapper in a trash can.

My heart is pounding as he comes back to the bed and

crawls back on top of me. He pushes my hair away from my face and traces his hand down along the curve of my cheek. "Last chance to back out," he says in a hoarse voice.

I put my palm against his cheek. Warmth spreads beneath my hand. It's a reaction as simple as that which makes me ready for anything with him. It's not loud or noticeable, somehow more meaningful than any grand gesture.

"Never," I say back. "It's your chance, too, you know."

His answer is to kiss me.

This is exactly where we both want to be.

He snakes his hand down mine and hooks my leg around his as he lifts himself and slowly slides inside of me. Unlike the last time, the movement is automatically delicious. There's no pain or tears, just something like a strangled cry from me and a grunt from him as he continues deeper.

Loving him has been trying, but *this* is so easy. So perfect. I honestly can't help wondering if I've just had an aneurysm and am now in heaven. No, I've gone beyond heaven and into the stars, floating and going *somewhere,* destination unknown.

I'm not sure who moves first, but suddenly we're both racing toward a higher greater than any drug. He buries his face in my neck, going faster, harder. There's nothing happening and everything happening all at the same time. There are almost too many sensations to handle. His hands, his thrusts, his breath against my skin. His muscular back against my fingertips, the feel of him inside me, our heartbeats merging as one. Maybe it's all just *us.*

From the second he entered me, I must've been in a perpetual orgasm because it was like I was just building, building, building toward it, but not working toward one. Then my head is spinning, my heart is soaring, and I can't see, hear, or know anything other than that this is perfection.

Boone follows shortly after me, suddenly still and

holding me tighter than ever. I slowly come down off the high, realizing I'm crying again for an entirely different reason.

Because that was *love*.

Eventually he rolls us onto our sides and holds me, and in that moment I can see the feeling reflected in his eyes. We're always going to wind up here—together and in love.

From the very beginning, we were destined to be together forever.

CHAPTER EIGHTEEN

Boone

Boone, 21
Carter, 18

I wake up and roll over, expecting Carter to still be in bed with
me. One night and I already want to wake up to her every morning.
I've always thought of myself as belonging to her, so it's no wonder I'd
slip right into thinking she belongs to me, too.

She's not here, though. Her side is warm, and the sheets are
distressed. I lie still for a second, listening for her. Maybe she's
looking for water or food, or she went to the bathroom. She wouldn't
just leave, would she?

That's enough to get me up and off my ass. I'm still naked as the
day I was born because after Carter and I made love, we sort of
passed out. I slept better than I ever have because she was in my
arms. Normally I'm constantly worrying about my dad and Declan
and Carter, but last night I wasn't. I guess at the end of the day,
she's really the only thing that matters.

After I throw on a pair of boxers, I look around for any evidence
to prove she was even here. Her clothes are gone, but that doesn't
mean anything. Carter's got more self-preservation than I do and

actually wears clothes. I dig around on the counter in the kitchen for the shitty cell phone I bought at a dollar store.

"Fuck," I mutter when I see it's dead.

God, she can't leave me. I can't let this happen again. Letting her go about killed me the first time. I can't do it again—not when I'm out to make this thing work. Plus she needs me for when Declan … shit.

I immediately start for the door. Just as I'm about to open it, I see her shoes lined up against the wall. She's still here. Now I almost wish she wasn't.

It's not that I don't trust her with Declan … well, I'm lying. I don't trust her with him at all. If he can't tell her the truth, then he shouldn't be around her. He's probably doing God knows how much drugs now that he knows he's gonna die. Another reason why she needs to stay clear of him.

I step out through the broken door and jog on over to Tish's place. The door is open, leaving no doubt Carter's here. Hopefully he didn't come home. Maybe she's just having a look around.

"Carter?" I call as I walk in.

Silence.

The whole trailer is dark and grungy, with decayed trash and used plastic plates everywhere. The place looks as if it came straight out of an impound lot or a junkyard. It's always given me the creeps, which is why I always hated the idea of Carter being alone here. Still do.

"Carter?" I yell again.

I walk back toward Tish's bedroom, doubting Carter would be there. I don't know where else she'd go. I guess she could've gone back to the picnic area, but I can't see her going too far without her shoes.

I freeze the second I step inside Tish's room and see Carter collapsed on the floor oddly. At first, the only thing that registers is she's crying because that's the worst sort of torture for my soul. I resent the damn tears streaking down her cheeks and vehemently hate whatever has her looking like she's having trouble breathing. All I want to do is comfort her.

"Carter?"

She doesn't look up at me. Instead she stays focused on …

The Carter fog I always get around her disappears, and I realize she's holding Declan in her arms. She's rubbing his head, brushing his greasy, matted hair away from his face. He's ashen, his eyes are completely blank, and there's something crusted around his mouth.

I blink, my view widening. Next to him is a syringe, and in his toe is a needle. There's a bottle of pills open on the ground, empty.

The fucker—he did it.

My hands tighten at my sides as I witness the love of my life holding her dead brother in her arms.

"Did you know?" she asks in a strangely calm voice.

"Know what?" I ask. Did she somehow figure out he was dying—how he killed himself because of it?

She looks up at me, tears pouring from her eyes and splattering angrily on the floor. "Did you know he was dead?"

"What? No—I would never—"

"You stopped me from coming in here ... you distracted me from it ... you said he wasn't here." Her sobs make her words barely decipherable. "We had ... while he was ..."

"Carter, no, I didn't know. I promise. I thought he was gone. I thought—"

"You stopped me, Boone. We could have helped him ... saved him ..."

I swallow thickly. Maybe I deserve this for not biting the bullet and just telling her the truth about Declan. But how could she think I would take advantage of her if Declan was dead? He's like family to me.

She looks down at Declan's limp body and starts rubbing his head, patting it almost. It's like she's trying to wake him up.

"I hate you for this," she says. I don't know if she's talking to me or Declan. She falls against him, hysteric and clinging to his lifeless body. I start forward, but think better of it. She needs basically anything except for me right now. Instead, I rush outside, puke my guts out, and call Kara.

#

I breathe in Carter, pulling her closer to me. Holding

her feels too good and it's going to be hard to let her leave my loft. If I had it my way, she'd spend every night here instead of at Kara's. We haven't been dating long, but I've known and loved her for enough time to know I want her to live with me. Hell, I'd marry her today if I could.

Her face is buried in my side, her head resting on my arm. My other arm is draped over her waist—well, over the covers that are on her waist. She fell asleep about an hour ago and just woke up, complaining about not wanting to leave. I didn't say anything, because the devil is on my shoulder begging me to ask her to stay. Not the best way to gain Kara and Gabe's respect, but I can't help it.

I run my hand through her hair, which is tangled but still soft and smooth. I love that with how close she is, our hair is blended together, blond and brown. How her skin is so pale and soft compared to my scarred and sun-tanned skin. I'm mostly just in love with the way she fits against me—a perfect match.

"I need to admit somethin' to you," I say.

Carter doesn't reply, and for a split second I think she's fallen back asleep. Then she stirs, and I can tell I've worried her. I should've tried to say it differently—better. "What's that?" she asks softly.

"I just, uh, want you to know there hasn't been anyone since you. Barely anyone before that, either."

She sets her chin on my chest to see me. "Are you talking about dating or sex?"

"Both."

Her eyes go wide, and she draws in a quick, surprised breath. I guess she never expected that out of me, though I've never chased anyone's tail except hers. Sure, there were a few girls from back when I wouldn't let myself have Carter, but I wasn't interested in any of them. I guess I thought I could exorcise any thoughts of Carter with other girls, but the second I realized that wouldn't help, I gave up on wanting anyone except for her.

"So you haven't ..."

"I haven't done anything with anyone other than myself since you, Carter. Before that it was pretty damn limited. There's not many women who want a guy who's waiting around for another woman."

She tilts her head. "You waited for me?" There's a certain awe to her voice. I would die for if it meant hearing again. I like when I've done something that wows her.

"Well, we both know I didn't ... "

"You know what I mean."

"Then, yeah. I, uh, told myself if I love you as much as I do, then I've got to be devoted to you. Gotta practice being the man I want to be before I can be him, you know?"

Her eyes shine as she smiles at me. "Sometimes you say the right things."

"I like how you say *sometimes*."

"Well, *sometimes* I worry you might've gotten things from a fortune cookie."

I smirk at her. "Once or twice, maybe."

She reaches up and runs her hand down my shadowed jaw. "There hasn't been anyone for me either—ever. Just you."

"Not even Luke?" I try to sound like I'm joking. I know how she operates and that she'd probably take things slow with Luke since she doesn't know him. They didn't have enough time to get beyond starting anything up. But, hey, guys can be insecure, too.

"I haven't talked to Luke since we caught you in my window. I think he probably realized my heart wasn't in it." She pulls her lip in between her teeth, then lets it out with a pop. Normally I'd find it sexy as hell, but right now I think it means she's unsure. "So there's really been no one?"

"No one," I confirm." I move my chin more into her hand. Her fingers feel too good against my rough skin. "If I'd had it my way, it'd only ever have been you for me." I rub her hip with my hand. "You're the only girl I've ever wanted or thought about. It's been that way my whole life—like no one else exists for me but you."

"I wish I would've known that sooner," she admits in a whisper. "When we were younger, I thought you saw me as a sister. Then when we were older, I thought you just felt sorry for me. I never thought ..."

"I never lead you to believe any differently."

She closes her eyes. "That day we made love, you did."

"That was the best day of my life until recently," I tell her. "I was finally getting everything I ever wanted. It was as if I was able to realize why I was put on this earth and that maybe there was something out there worth living for."

She buries her face back in my side, but not before I see the tears gathering in her eyes. "You didn't know about Declan, did you?" she asks.

I'm glad she can't see my face. I didn't know he was dead, but I did know he would be. Someday. I was waiting and so was she, just for different reasons. "No."

"I'm so sorry I blamed you," she says. "I—I didn't know. I just needed someone to blame. Losing him—you two were all I had for so long. I couldn't face it—"

"You shouldn't have been the one to find him, and I should've done more than just call Kara." I wrap my arms more around her and hug her to me. "I promise I didn't know he was in there or else I would've gone in myself. I honestly thought he left. He must've come back when I wasn't payin' attention. It's been one of the hardest things I've had to live with—knowing he was dying or dead and no one was there."

"He never let us be," she says and starts to cry heavy, hard sobs. I don't know what I'm doing until I'm burying my face in her hair and whispering a mixture of *I'm sorry* and *I love you* into her ear, crying, too.

I've lived with dad's depression for so long I started overlooking it—started forgetting he was broken because he'd lost my mom. If I had a kid, I like to think I'd be stronger. But here I am, with Carter alive and well, and I'm bawling like a baby. This could be what love's supposed to look like.

You cry as much as you laugh, because you do it together. When you don't have each other, it's like there's nothing left in the world. So you live it up for however long you're honored to.

CHAPTER NINETEEN

Carter

There's a letter sitting for me on Boone's table when I let myself into his apartment. Since Boone cooks a lot for me, I want to return the favor. I plan on having a delicious dinner on the table by the time he gets home from work, thanks to a recipe Kara lent me. If I don't burn it, that is.

Hey, beautiful.

Sorry again I can't help out. I'll tell Mrs. Kripke to avoid flooding her basement on our date night. Just know I'm wishing I was there with you, and I'll back by seven. (If not, send out a search party because Mrs. Kripke has a thing for my ass and I do not trust her—eighty years old or not, she might steal me and never give me back. Be a damn shame, wouldn't it?)

I love you,
Boone

I fold his letter and neatly put it inside my pocket. When I get home, I'll put it with all the others.

Mrs. Kripke made an emergency call this afternoon. Boone had to take it since Jason was working on something else. I was kind of hoping he'd be here to chaperone me, seeing as the last time I tried to cook, there was a small fire.

I try to get acquainted with Boone's kitchen, only to realize that he's got a lot more cooking utensils than I would've guessed. I should've known better after learning he's Jesus in the kitchen.

Later, as I'm putting the ricotta-cheese stuffed shells into the oven, I take a quick picture of it. I send it to Boone and text, *This is what you have to look forward to so fight for your life if she offers you candy or asks you to find her puppy.* I also text Kara the picture along with, *What do you think?*

Little dots immediately pop up on my screen, then the next thing I know, she's calling me.

"I'm proud of you," she says. "It looks so good. You're feeding Gabe and I, too, right?"

I snort. "If you think a double date is safe, sure."

She giggles. "Not a good idea. But they're getting better. I think Gabe's actually starting to hate Boone a little less."

"That's a big step in the right direction," I say. I walk over to the oven and preheat it. The one thing I forgot, of course. I lean on the cabinet. "Maybe someday he might sort-of, kind-of, maybe-less-than like him."

Her laughter is muffled on the other side of the phone. We've been talking more and more about Boone and what he means to me—that I love him. We've been trying to get Gabe used to the idea, but he's not close to being on board yet.

As embarrassing as it is, they know I lost my virginity to Boone the day Declan died. Kara and Gabe scheduled family meetings with a counselor and when she asked about Boone, the truth came rushing to the surface. I didn't know how I was going to recover from Declan's death and Boone's betrayal. I don't believe Gabe was ever mad at Boone because of the sex, no matter how disappointed he probably was; I think the sole reason he's hated Boone is because *I've* hated him. I blamed Boone for Declan's death, so Gabe did also. Except Gabe's been blaming him with the fury of a father-figure.

"When are you expecting him home?" Kara asks.

"Not until later. I wanted to give this time to cook so I can make up crescent rolls, but now I'm thinking I gave myself too much time."

"You're just excited to do this for him."

"I am," I admit. "It's stupid because it's just a meal, but …"

Kara makes a sound as if she were agreeing with me. "I remember how nervous I was to cook for you for the first time. It was right after I bought the house and I'd never made a meal on my own before. It was terrible, but you grinned through it."

"It was good."

"Don't flatter me."

"It was first the meal I'd had that didn't come out of a box."

"That's true. What I'm trying to say is—it's your first step toward a life together. It's domesticity. It's exciting and nerve-wrecking."

We continue talking until I hear Gabe's voice in the background, signaling he's home from work. I tell them both I love them and let them go enjoy their evening together.

I busy myself by putting the shells in the oven and readying the rolls to go in next, then I just stare at the floor. What am I supposed to do now? Boone has a TV set up, but I don't really want to watch it—that'll put me to sleep for sure. He has a lot of books, but I'm also too keyed up to sit down and read.

The letters.

I grin as I think about Boone telling me he kept the notes he wrote but never sent. We haven't gotten around to reading them yet. I'm sure he wouldn't mind if I read them now, considering I've read all the other ones without

223

him.

I check the places where I would expect him to store things—in his closet, under his bed, by his desk—but I don't find anything. Well, other than that, Boone has developed definite qualities of a neat freak. Everything is very minimalistic and bare, only the in-use items out now that his place is finished.

Where did we always hide the important things—social security cards, birth certificates? Tish always left them lying around to get muddied by the dust and general grossness of our trailer, but then Boone gathered everything up to store it in the freezer as a result of my trip to the hospital after the fair.

"You put all of the important things in here to keep them safe," he'd said as he reached down to tickle my cheek. "Think I should put you in there?"

The memory makes me smile. I walk over to his freezer and move his frozen meats and vegetables around until I see a brown box. I lift it out, passing it between my hands because it's cold. I set it on the table and pull the lid-flaps open.

Sure enough, the letters are neatly stacked inside. I lift them out, set the stack in front of me on the counter, and read each one carefully. The first ones are more recent so they mostly talk about how he wants to get back into my life. The farther into the stack I get, the less he talks about winning me back and the more he apologizes for what happened between us. Almost every letter has a, "I love you," that effectively makes my heart a professional gymnast. If I had read these sooner, would we have been together sooner?

I keep going until I get to the bottom one. There's nothing on the page except for my name then, *I'd trade places with him in an instant if it made you happy. I didn't know about him being in there, because if I had, I would've died rather than let you go in.*

My heart starts to hurt, and my eyes well up with tears.

I shouldn't have ever thought he could know Declan was dead and not tell me. Boone's always been the most honest person I know, and he wouldn't lie to me about this.

I was so stupid.

I shake my head as I set the letter back. Things between us were all twisted and wrong, when they shouldn't have been. It's a combination of both our faults, but our last fight was all on me.

Another note catches my eye, tucked and forgotten at the base of the box, just barely visible beneath one of the taped flaps. I give it a hearty tug because it's wedged.

That last one should've been the very beginning. Is this one from earlier? What would he have had to say then? I flip the box over and tear the tape off to get it out. The wrinkled paper is a mess of words. He always puts time and effort into it, but this one looks more as though it was all racing out of him.

Carter,

You deserve to hear this in person and you deserve to hear it from Declan. The only reason why I know anything is because he wanted me to take care of you. Guess he doesn't know that taking care of you means telling the truth.

I'm a coward for not being able to tell this to your face. I just don't want to break my word to Declan and I don't want to break your heart. I keep trying to tell you, but nothing will come out. Never thought there would be a day when I'd be speechless, but I am. Writing stuff down has always been easier, especially when it comes to my feelings and you.

Declan—he's dying. Hepatitis and liver failure. Worse, he wants to die. He's going to take it into his own hands—his overdose was on purpose. He told me afterward. Made me promise not to say anything. I just don't think I can keep something like this from you. You need to know—you should have whatever time you can with him.

I can't give you much, but I can give you that. I love you more, so I'm choosing you. Maybe I'm choosing him, too. Maybe this is best for everyone.

Just don't blame him. Don't try to talk him into things. Don't try to make him better. Show him you needed to know and how you finding out was worth it. Show him life is worth living.

Boone

CHAPTER TWENTY

Boone

The drive back to my loft feels as though I were Rocky fighting Apollo Creed. There are two opinions in my mind's boxing ring, with one wanting to enjoy the evening as Carter planned and the other wanted to drag Carter to bed. Surprisingly, it's not for sex. It's for sleep.

Mrs. Kripke kept me longer than I thought and, while she's as sweet as can be, she drained all the energy out of me. She talked non-stop and half the time I couldn't even follow where we were in the conversation. I'd ask her something about her washing machine and the next thing I know she'd be talking about her niece's cousin's ex-boyfriend's uncle.

Still, tonight's important to Carter. I know she worked hard making us dinner, and I can't wait to tell her how much I appreciate it. There's something good about knowing someone's waiting for you at home.

I park and head up to my apartment. The door is ajar, which makes my stomach churn. She should know better than to just leave doors open—especially with the stuff that's been going down lately. Except when I step inside, there's no Carter.

Maybe she's playing some weird game—hiding. It's a stupid thought, but it's better than the alternative of being terrified out of my mind.

"Is this some sort of a surprise, Carter?" I call out.

Nothing.

I set my keys on the end table and close the door behind me. I check the time on my phone. It's close to eight, so maybe she got fed up and left. I'd told her seven, and if I were her, I'd be pissed.

I did warn her, though. I texted her at seven to let her know I was finishing up, but that it was going to take longer than expected. She didn't answer me, but I thought it was just one of those texts that don't need answering. Unless something happened?

I find her contact and dial, heading into the kitchen to check for any trace of her. The line rings, echoing through my ear, as I notice our charred dinner sitting on the countertop. What she made is burnt to an unrecognizable crisp.

Mid-ring, the line goes to voice mail. She ignored my call. "This is Carter. You must have—"

I stuff my phone in my pocket when I notice a letter partially beneath a dirty pan. I immediately recognize my handwriting, which looks like total and complete shit because of when it was written. I don't have to read it to know which letter it is. It's the one I kept meaning to burn so she wouldn't find it when I showed her the others. The one I carried around in my wallet for months following Declan's first overdose. The one I couldn't bring myself to give her because I thought Declan would get smart and tell her himself.

It was a true test of honesty, and I failed her.

#

I've never been arrested, but tonight could change

things. I realize it as I speed through town to Carter's place. I'm definitely going more than the recommended speed limit, and if anyone tries to stop me, there'll be a fight on their hands. I'm not looking to slow down for anything until I'm in Carter's driveway—hell, until I'm able to explain things to her.

I haphazardly pull into the driveway, and get out, leaving the door open and the car running, propelled by a grimness eating away at my stomach like cancer. I don't have much space in my mind to think about anything other than getting to Carter. Even if this messes up my future with her, I need to make sure she's okay.

My hand slams against the door somewhere between a knock and me breaking down the door. My other one rings the doorbell. I'm one step away from going full Marlon Brando on this place and yelling out Carter's name.

I'm so keyed up, I'm not prepared for Gabe to answer the door and *not* look like he wants to kill me. Instead he just looks annoyed in his T-shirt and sweats.

"What are you doing here?" he asks.

I push past him. The inside of the house is dark, except for the TV flickering in the living room. Kara is sitting on the couch in her pajamas, gaping at me. "Boone?"

"Where's Carter? I need to talk to her," I say.

Kara's eyebrows furrow, making her look so much like Carter a pit in my chest threatens to open up and swallow me from the inside out, whole. "She was supposed to be with you. When we talked, she was at your apartment."

"You mean she didn't come home? She's not here?"

"No, why would she be?"

"Are you saying you don't know where she is?" Gabe demands.

"No. She—I guess she got pissed at me—and left. She was gone when I got home, so I came straight here." I look around, dread eating me up. "She's not here?" She always comes back to Gabe and Kara. They're her safety net. They literally know everything about her. If she didn't come here, then something's gotta be wrong.

The look on Gabe's face tells me he knows it, too. "Kara, I need you to put a call out to the cops."

"Gabe, please tell me you—"

"Kara, everything could be fine, but we've got to be sure," he says carefully. "I'm gonna take care of all this. Call the cops, call your mom. I'm going to go with Boone."

"I want to go with you," Kara says. "I can do all that from the car."

"Kara—"

"No, Gabe," Kara says, standing up. "I'm coming."

I start toward the door before they can keep their argument going. My anvil-sized anxiety is telling me we can't afford to wait around. They follow after me, Kara talking into her phone. Gabe takes the passenger seat, and before he's got his door shut, I'm driving.

CHAPTER TWENTY-ONE

Carter

Carter, 14
Declan, 17

There's a knock at my bedroom door and I immediately pull my blankets up over myself. Even though I've lived with Kara for some time now, I haven't gotten out of the habit of always being on edge. At Tish's, nobody knocked. They'd just open the door and walk straight on back to her room. Even if they didn't do that, nothing would happen because I could just go find Boone. But Boone's not here ...

No. I'm fine. I'm safe. I have Kara and Gabe now. Plus, I do still have Boone—he's just not my neighbor anymore.

"Hey, it's me."

I relax at the sound of my brother's voice. Tonight is the first time he took up Kara's invitation to stay the night. He's never even been here before or really spent any time with Kara and Gabe. Whenever I've tried to set anything up, he always bails on us.

"You can come in," I call.

Declan opens the door, doing his best not to blind me with the light from the hallway, and then closes it behind him. He walks over *to my bed and sits down. "Hey."*

"Hey," I say back.

He shifts until he's lying beside me, on top of the covers. He's wearing a pair of Gabe's sweatpants and one of his shirts. They're huge on Declan, literally hanging off of his bony frame. Declan's become so thin, so unhealthy.

"It's quiet," he tells me, as if that were to explain something.

"I'm sorry?"

His raspy laugh sounds as if it needs to be oiled. "I was layin' in bed and it was so quiet. Couldn't hear anything. I'm used to—well, the sounds of a trailer park. You don't hear that here."

"No," I say. "It's nice. It took me some getting used to, but it wasn't hard." It was easy, actually. I fell right into a perfect sleeping pattern without the dogs barking, the slamming doors, the revving engines, the talking, the sex noises.

"Maybe for you," he says, almost sadly. He tucks his arms behind his head. "This place is actually pretty awesome, you know?"

"Isn't it?" I close my eyes, trying to hide the pride swelling up in my heart. I don't want to make Declan feel as though he doesn't have enough or as if he didn't give me enough. I'm just glad to hear him sound like he's happy I'm here. Sometimes I feel selfish for having my new life.

"Yeah, Carter. I wish I had a sister to come swoop in and save me."

"Kara wants to save you, too, Declan. She's said she'll let you stay here and everything. She might not be your sister, but she wants to be."

"Doesn't happen like that, Carter."

"Boone's like your brother."

"But that doesn't make him your brother, right? I know how you feel about him, Carter." He lets out a long sigh. "My point is, sometimes things don't work out so simply. I'm probably not meant to have a place like this or a chance like this."

"So you're just not going—"

"The place is nice, all right," he says. "I was just tryin' to say I'm glad you're good here. I don't want to get into a discussion about my own life. That's for me to worry about."

"I'm sorry," I automatically say. *I don't want to scare him away. He's always only half-existed in my life. I don't need to give a reason to permanently go away.*

"It's okay. I'm sorry, too." He moves one arm from beneath him and takes my hand in his. *"It's just that ... you're the only thing good in my life. I remember how I used to crawl into your crib with you. I was so scared something would happen to you or I'd miss something, so I refused to leave you alone. I guess I didn't want to be alone, either. I'd never had anything special in my life until you came along. I loved when I didn't really know what love felt like. You were my baby sister, and I wanted to be a big brother to you."*

"You're still my big brother," I remind him softly.

"Yeah, but I don't get to crawl into your crib anymore, do I? I don't have to worry about you leaving me alone as much as I need to worry about me disappearing." He squeezes my hand. *"I've been a shitty brother, and I don't know how to stop it. I'm sorry for what I said to you. I shouldn't have—you need to be somewhere where you can start a life. A real one with fences and dogs and a family and all that other shit. I can't give that to you, and it was wrong of me to resent you for moving out. I might be your big brother, but I guess your big sister's better fit to take care of you."*

"You took care of me just fine, Dec."

"Thanks for sayin' that, Carter. You've always known what to say to me and when to make me feel better, even if it's a lie. This time, though, that's not the case. Boone's always taken better care of you than I have. Everybody takes better care of you than me. You even take better care of yourself than I do."

"I don't mind."

"I know you don't. But I do." He swallows, and I can almost hear the emotion he's forcing down. *"I love you, kid."*

"Well, I love you more."

"Sometimes that's what I'm afraid of," he says.

\#

My cheek is cold and burning, wet and achy. The rest of my body feels numb and immovable. *Where am I? Why do I feel like this?* My mind can't seem to function; it's just acting on a series of garbled questions.

Ringing suddenly fills my ears, and I try to move my hands to grope at my head—to make the noise go away, but I can't. I have to listen to it, praying it won't shatter my eardrums or my brain or make me go crazy.

"This bitch better do what you say she will."

The deep, slurred voice echoes through my head, ricocheting with the ringing. *I'm not alone? There's someone here? Why aren't they helping me?* I try to force words out, something close to "help me," only nothing comes out except for a moan.

"She's awake," the voice says. "Try again."

A figure moves in front of me then bows down for me to see. Through my blurry vision, I recognize her. *Tish.* Her hair is messy and cut in what looks like a homemade bob. She's aged decades since I've last seen her, but there's no missing those eyes. They're the same eyes I've spent my whole life searching for love in.

"Try again," the voice commands. "Get the money from her so we can leave."

"She ain't got it in her wallet," Tish hisses. "I told you her daddy's where it's at."

"Yeah, well, you led us to *her,* so she's gotta give it."

Their conversation allows my mind to clear enough to remind me what happened after I left Boone's place. It wasn't dark yet—although it's dark now—and I thought I would be fine if I walked to the cemetery. After reading Boone's letter, I wanted to see Declan. I just needed to feel him with me again. But right now, the only thing I feel is my face pressed up against Declan's gravestone.

I was talking to Declan when I heard them walking up behind me, arguing. Then he was yelling *at me* about how he wanted the money Tish owes him. I kept trying to explain I didn't have any money, and I finally realized my only option was to run, and then …

Bang.

My shoulder throbs. He shot me.

"Get it *now,* Tish, before she bleeds to death and we're in jail for murder."

"If she does, it'll be on you, Ronnie."

"And you'll be the accessory," Ronnie reminds Tish.

Tish squeezes her fist, her unkempt, jagged nails digging into her skin. "Your daddy promised me money and he ain't paid up. It's time for me to collect, so I can pay *my* collectors," she sneers at me.

"I-I—" I swallow, the pain so intense bile rises in my throat. "I don't ha-have anything."

She shakes her head and points at me with her finger. "Yeah, you do. You hafta. Your daddy's loaded—trust me, I know. So you're gonna pay me, or Ronnie here's not gonna be happy with either of us."

"I don't have hi-his money," I stutter. "He-he doesn't p-pay me."

"She's lying," Ronnie says. "I swear to God, Tish, if you don't fucking—"

"Shut up, Ronnie."

There's a click, then, "You don't tell me to shut up."

I don't want to look at Ronnie. He's not the guy from the gas station—he's not even on the same level. This guy sounds big and angry and serious. The fact that he's on something only makes that worse. When he walks into my line of vision, I have no choice but to see him. He's wearing a pair of jeans and no shirt, with a huge, heavy flannel coat. His head is shaved, and he's wearing a knit cap. His eyes are black, probably the same shade as his soul, and he's baring his rotted teeth.

His aim moves from Tish to me. I don't know what the point of this is. If I don't have the money, threats won't help. It's not going to make Tish do anything, either. She doesn't love me. I don't even really think trying to appeal to her as my mother would help. The only motherly thing she's ever done for me is carrying me for nine months and giving birth to me. She used to yell at me for even calling her mom or mama.

I'm Tish, you little bitch! Tish!

"We found a checkbook in your purse and a twenty. You wanna tell us how much else you got?" Tish asks.

Fifteen-thousand. I haven't spent a penny of the money I've saved since I started working. All of the money my dad "gave" me for college is with Kara. That fifteen-thousand could go a long way for Tish and Ronnie if they knew how to stretch it, but they don't want to stretch anything. They want to use it all, and they want to use it fast. If I offer them what I have, they'll want more.

Why did Declan have to be the one to die?

It's the first time I let myself think the thought. I felt so guilty when it first crossed my mind. I didn't want to wish death on Tish. But now? Maybe I do wish she'd been the one to overdose instead of Declan. The world is worse because she exists. She only takes up space and air and leaves destruction in her path.

Despite all of Declan's faults, at least he could love people.

"How much?" Ronnie demands.

"F-Fifteen," I manage to say.

"Shit," Ronnie says. "Still lyin' to us, bitch?"

He kneels down. The gun is shaking in his hand, but he's focused on me. His body might be failing him, but his mind's not. He will kill me.

God, what if I die here? Maybe he won't shoot me, but what if I bleed out? I don't even know if Declan's spirit is really here. Maybe I'll just be alone. And, oh God, what about when Boone, Kara, and Gabe find me …

No, this can't happen.

"Give us something else, something better."

I wrack my brain for something. Anything. If I do die, I want to go down fighting. I want to be brave again, as I was with the mace. But I don't have my mace. I barely even have myself. I feel as if I were on the fringe of reality.

"W-Wallet—secret—"

CHAPTER TWENTY-TWO

Boone

Police lights are flashing as my truck comes skidding to a halt in the middle of the road. Cops are stationed in front of my building and farther down by the parking lot.

"Shit," I mutter, stomach sinking. How the hell did I not think to look for her car? I just assumed if she wasn't here then her car wouldn't be either. I thought she'd be gone. If I had just looked down the fucking street, this wouldn't be happening. She might already be safe ...

Kara gropes my hand, then squeezes. She glances between Gabe and me, that fearlessness she'd had before gone. I have to look away from her because she looks too much like Carter right now. Hell, she could not even be related to Carter and I'd find something similar in them.

She has to be okay. I have to make things right. That letter ... we can't end this way.

Someone turns in the distance, looks our way, and starts walking toward us. My attention zeros in on him like a camera finding focus. Find Carter now, worry later.

I drop Kara's hand and head for Officer Taft. He's holding a notebook in his hand, ready to get down to business. "Her car was locked; no sign of her," he explains. He taps the notebook with his pen. "Tell me everything you know."

I recount the whole night, ignoring Kara's gasp when I talk about the letter and Declan. I go all the way up until the point where we got into the car to drive here. We all show him our cell phones so he can see our last conversations with her and when they were.

By the time we're at a point where there's nothing left to say, I'm on edge—ready to jostle everyone and anyone in my path until I find her. Why are we standing around talking about this? We should be looking for her.

"Do you think it was one of Tish's people?" Gabe asks.

Officer Taft remains deliberately calm. "We can't be sure. It sounds like there was quite a conflict about to brew with Boone here, so who knows what she could've done because of—"

"Don't—she wouldn't do this to any of us," I interrupt. "There's something wrong."

He gives me a complacent look. "We will take character into account, but often in situations like—"

"Got something!"

The proclamation feels as if the heavens had opened up and angels had swooped down to the rescue. I'm not much of a religious man, but this might just make me into one. We all jog over to where an officer is standing on the sidewalk ways down from her car. He's got a crinkled paper in his gloved hand. The letters on it are written in neat, cursive handwriting.

"Do any of you recognize this?" Officer Taft asks.

Kara nods beside me. She brings a hand up to her mouth. "It's my handwriting—it's the recipe I gave her."

"It's hers, then. She must've been going in this direction. Any idea where she'd go from here? And on foot?"

My mind feels too foggy to place where we're even at, let alone where she'd go. All I can focus on is my fear of losing her—I've already lost her once and I can't survive it again.

"Declan," Gabe says. "His grave. She goes there whenever something's wrong."

My mind might be lost, but my body's not. I take off running.

#

By the time I get to the cemetery, the police sirens are getting louder—closer. I never thought I'd be so happy to hear sirens in my life. Hopefully we all get here and find her hanging out with Declan. God, I hope she's here and not somewhere else. *She didn't mean to worry anyone; she just wanted to escape.*

I've got the path to Declan's grave memorized. Whenever I run, I usually run through the cemetery to check in on him. Any other time, I've got time to follow the path out of respect for the dead. Right now I don't. I run across the lawn, feet pounding on graves. Hopefully they'll understand.

It's too dark to see now, but I don't hear any voices or anything suspicious. I came here with her about a week ago and she talked to him out loud, as I sometimes do. If she's here, then I'd be able to hear her speaking to him. All I want is to hear her voice.

Unless she's not here but somewhere else. *God, please, let her be here.*

I charge up a hill and nearly collapse when I hit the top and see her.

She's here, only not in the way I hoped to find her. She's lying in a little lump on the ground with her face pressed against Declan's grave. In the moonlight, she's pale and glistening with sweat. What looks like the contents of her purse are all around her, littering the ground.

"Carter?" I say, approaching her slowly. I don't know why I'm going slow now when all I want to do is grab her

239

and hold her.

A series of flashbacks involving finding Declan after his overdose and then when he was dead bombard me. I thought that moment was the worst moment of my life. But this is paralyzing to my mind, body, and soul. This feels as though I were meeting my end. "Carter?"

I kneel down in front of her and press my hand against her cheek. Cold. There aren't any marks on her face. I slowly move my hand down the length of her body, assessing what I can see. I don't want to move her.

My fingers slide into something warm and wet at her collarbone. Blood. It's hard to see against her dark shirt, but it's there. I pull her shirt back to see the damage I already expect—a bullet wound.

I can't see straight, and my heart is dead. I wish I had taken the shot for her. I wish I was the one out cold and bleeding. That I was—

"Boone."

Her voice is a whisper, but it's loud in the silence of the cemetery, even with the sirens approaching. Her eyes are closed, making me wonder if I just imagined it—if it was something I only wanted to hear—but then her lips move to form my name again, this time nothing coming out.

"Hey, Junebug," I say, emotion wrecking me. "Hey."

I should be saying how it'll be all right, but I don't know if I can. I can't lie to her again when I feel as though the whole world just fell off its axis and now we're hurtling toward the sun.

CHAPTER TWENTY-THREE

Carter

Declan, 20
Carter, 17

"Doesn't it scare you? Doesn't death scare you?"

"No, Carter, it doesn't. Not really. I've made it so there's nothing else left for me to do but die. I don't have my whole life ahead of me like you do."

"You can't say that—you can have a life—"

"Not like you can. So live it, all right? Find whatever I've been missing out on."

#

The *MASH* theme song is playing quietly, but no one's whistling. *Where's Gabe?* He always whistles along with it, no matter how many times he's heard it. It's his favorite show—a show he would probably pick to watch until the end of time if he had to. It's the show that made him decide to want to be a doctor and also the show that talked him out of being an army doctor.

241

"Gabe?" I whisper. My throat feels as if it were full of gravel—the sharp rocks suffocating me.

I feel movement somewhere beside me, but I can't open my eyes. They feel as if they were glued shut. "Carter—Gabe, I think she's awake."

Kara? This time my voice won't work. *Where am I? What's wrong with me?* I try to see, try to think, but nothing. Just bleak, black, darkness. *Why do I feel like this?* Waking up to *MASH* is a thing from my childhood. For a while after I moved in, I would wake up worrying about Tish, Declan, and Boone, or afraid someone would sneak into my room, so I'd go downstairs, curl up beside Gabe, and fall asleep while he watched TV. I stopped doing that a long time ago, and I usually leave him when he turns on *MASH*, so I can get some sleep before work.

"Honey, it's okay," Kara says, running her fingers over my face. "You're fine. Gabe, I think she's confused. She's panicking."

A hand squeezes my own, and then I feel lips press against my forehead before a deep voice, rumbling and rolling, whispers into my ear. "Pretty girl, open your eyes for me. You're safe, but you're in the hospital. C'mon, look at me. See you're safe." *Boone.*

His commanding voice forces me to open my eyes and look at him. At first, my vision is blurred, almost foggy, but then it clears. The first person I see is Boone, looking ragged and unshaven. He's obviously exhausted, and his eyes are wet, as if he'd been crying. He's sitting in a chair, his back bent and his neck craned uncomfortably so he can be close to me. Kara is on my other side with Gabe; they look just as terrified as Boone.

"You were shot, Carter. Do you remember that?" Boone asks.

Shot? I shake my head. I want to ask what happened and how and why, but I can't seem to.

Gabe clears his throat, somehow hearing my thoughts. "It was Tish and her dealer. They were looking for quick cash. They're both in custody now for this and other charges."

Kara grimaces. "Hopefully they're locked up for a long, long time. I don't understand how she could ... she's so disgusting ..."

I cover her hand with my own when she trails off on the verge of tears. It's sort of coming back to me, but not really. What I do know is Tish will do anything and everything for drugs, but not for me. The fact that Kara doesn't understand that shows she cares about me more than my mom ever could.

"You did some quick thinking, Carter. Saved your own life before anyone else could. You gave them your black card, knowing it would be traceable," Boone finishes.

Suddenly, it comes back to me. The whole night, along with why my shoulder is throbbing. I remember bleeding out on Declan's grave, worrying about Gabe, Kara, and Boone, and praying Tish would grow a heart.

It wasn't brave that I gave him the limitless card my dad gave me. It was just my last-ditch effort to survive. In a way, I was giving up by giving in to his demands. Kara forced our dad to give it to me when I was fourteen, telling him, "You've never given her anything, so it's time to give her everything." Dad verbally beat into me that it was to be used only for emergencies, but from his tone there was a definite *but not even then.* Putting his money in jeopardy was the only way for her to punish him for abandoning me. I hid it away in my wallet in a little slit you probably wouldn't even notice, trying to put it as far out of my mind as possible. I kept it for Kara, but I never planned to use it.

I gave it to Tish and her dealer, hoping it would give them what they wanted so they'd either kill me or leave. Honestly, I never considered the police could track the card. Even if they didn't know to do so, Dad would have definitely caught onto it being used. He wouldn't care because of me, but because someone was spending his money.

"They were going to buy and pawn stuff for cash," Gabe explains. "Thank God you thought to give them that after … How's your shoulder?"

On cue, my whole arms pulses with a sharp, hot pang. It's almost searing, like fire diving through my veins. *Holy heck, I was shot.*

Gabe stands, his chair skidding across the floor. He looks as if he can barely contain his emotions. "I'll go get the doctor so he can check you over, then they can give you something for the pain."

He leaves on his mission. Boone leans in and lays his head on my legs. I don't realize until Kara reaches down to rub his back that he's crying. Sobbing. That's all it takes for my eyes to liquefy into tears.

CHAPTER TWENTY-FOUR

Boone

I try not to wince as the nurse removes Carter's bandage, revealing her stitches. For the rest of her life, she's going to wear a battle scar, and I'll be proud of her for it—always wishing I could've fought the battle for her.

I knew Tish was the worst fucking creature on this planet, but I didn't realize she could sink to leaving her own daughter to die. I had the urge to hunt down the first junkie who hurt Carter, but the urge is even worse with Tish. I want to torture that woman and leave her to die so she knows exactly what she put Carter through.

Carter smiles up at the nurse. Even though she has to be in excruciating pain, she's trying to reassure someone else to make them feel better. She's the model example of a good person, and I want to be more like her.

The nurse tries to smile back, but it doesn't quite meet her eyes. Everyone here pretty much knows what happened—you can see it in their expressions. They just don't know what to say or how to handle her, and Carter's too embarrassed to do anything on her end.

Eventually the nurse finishes and leaves us, closing the

door behind her. This is the first time it's been just the two of us. Gabe and Kara are downstairs eating lunch with Kara's parents. They showed up a couple of hours ago. I like Kara's mom fine, but I'm glad their dad's gone. I didn't think I could hate the man more than I already do. He was almost inconvenienced to visit his own daughter. It says something when you're own wife, the woman who you cheated on, cares more about your out-of-wedlock-kid than you do.

I take my seat beside Carter's bed. I haven't moved since she was first admitted except to let the nurses and doctors in. The thought of leaving her is terrifying. Like something will happen again, only this time it'll leave her in permanent ruin. I guess I'm also afraid if I leave, she won't let me come back.

We haven't had the chance to talk about the letter. I'm not even sure if she remembers it. If she doesn't, I know I'll have to tell her. I'd rather wait until she's out of the hospital and comfortable, but this can't wait.

"Carter, we need to talk," I say slowly.

"I know," she says.

"So you remember the letter?"

"Yes," she admits.

I don't know what to say next. I want to tell her I love her, but what's that gonna do? It'll come across as in-genuine, as if I were just using the phrase as a way to make her see me in a better light. I just want her to know that even if she stops loving me after all this, I won't stop loving her.

"I already knew," she tells me so softly I can barely make out the words. "I knew Declan was dying. He told me a week or so before he passed away. Just showed up on our front porch and told me. I just didn't know ... I didn't know he wanted to commit suicide or that you knew." She runs her hands over the hospital blanket on top of her, smoothing it out, distracting herself from her wavering words. "I didn't tell you about it because I didn't want to hurt you."

"It was the same thing here." I lean onto her bed, trying to get her to look at me. "I should've told you; then we could've been on the same page. I should've also told you he was suicidal. I just thought I had it under control. I was checking in on him and tracking where he went, and I tricked myself into thinking I could get a handle on him. But then … I was just so damn wrong. I guess I didn't want you to know he *chose* to die. I didn't want you to see him differently or as a coward, and I didn't want you feeling guilty. There's nothing anyone could've done to change his mind."

"But you did—didn't you? You saw him differently and thought you could change his mind?"

I swallow, trying to shove all of my rising emotions down. "Yeah."

She stares at me, determination in her eyes. "You couldn't have either. There was only so much we could've done—stopping him would've been impossible. All he wanted to do was say good-bye. He even asked me to take care of you when he was gone."

I can't help but chuckle. Of course he would. I need more taking care of than she does, the shooting aside. But even then, she handled herself. "He was more honest with me, but he asked me to take care of you, too." I bring my hand up to her face, running my thumb across the pretty curve of her cheek. "So what are you thinking? What about us?"

Her eyebrows furrow and her lips move as she fights to figure out what she wants to say and how to say it. "I was so mad at you for not telling me. I still am in a lot of ways."

"You're sure not showin' it."

"That's because I love you more than I could ever be angry with you. You might've not told me, but it's haunted you. You were *going* to tell me the truth, or at least someday you might have, but it was always going to be too late. And I can't really say anything because I was keeping his secret, too."

"Yeah, but it's nothing compared to knowing he was suicidal."

"He was *dying*, Boone. Suicide or OD or organ failure, he was dying. There was nothing we could do. We couldn't save him. I love you, Boone," she whispers.

I squeeze my eyes shut. I won't start crying like an idiot again. "If I hadn't been shot, I would've told you so that night. By the time I got to Declan's grave, I was already planning to come back to you. I had already forgiven you."

I open my eyes, not even bothering with narcissistic concerns. There are tears falling from her eyes also, and she's got a kind, angelic smile.

"I don't know what I'd have done if I'd lost you," I say. I don't know if I'm talking about the shooting or if she refused to forgive me.

I'm not sure she knows either. "You weren't going to lose me."

I grew up witnessing people cling to things that only made them desperate and half a person. After my mom passed, my dad found escape and solace in God and alcohol. Tish and Declan, because of their environment, clung to drugs as if they were predisposed and didn't have an option. They were all using infections to try to heal their wounds. I tried to do the same, but I ended up embracing and clinging to Carter instead.

She makes everything better. Tragedy, life, *me*. She *is* everything.

#

Two Years Later

"This a little macabre, isn't it? Given the date?" Gabe asks from the passenger seat of my car.

"Just go along with me please?" I ask.

I don't need to see the man to know I get an eyeroll.

He's managed to go from *hate* to *somewhat dislike* in his view of me—at least, according to Carter. It's taken more than a few double dates, some serious groveling and making Carter as happy as ever to bridge the divide between us. I've had to work harder to change Gabe's feelings than I've had to work on anything in my life, including my relationship with Carter. He does not forgive easily, that's for sure.

Kara, on the other hand, treats me like I'm already her brother-in-law (or son-in-law, depending on how you look at it). I'm at every family dinner, function and event. Things are even scheduled around my calendar. It's nice to have a family.

"Boone, I don't mean to ruin your plans, but is this really necessary?" she asks from the middle of the backseat.

"Yes," I tell her. "You'll understand in a minute."

I get their apprehension. Two years ago today was the day Carter was shot, and we're heading into the very place where we found her. Honestly, I'm light-headed just thinking about revisiting Declan's grave. I have nightmares where she's on it, bleeding out, barely living—and I'm sure it'll be much worse in person.

But this is for a good cause. I want to make a happy memory here, because there's just so much bad. I only wish I could include Carter in our visit, too. But there's a point to my madness, and she can't be here.

She's been taking classes at a local university, hoping to eventually earn a business degree. She's all about bettering her business, which I'm all for. Especially if it means she's gone a couple of nights a week, giving me the perfect opportunity to whisk Gabe and Kara away in secret.

I drive through cemetery and park next to Declan's grave. Gabe and Kara paid to have a new headstone put in, just because the other one always seemed to have a blood-tint to it. No one else except for us could see it, but I think it would've been as spick-and-span as Mr. Clean's head and we'd see the discoloring.

The three of us get out and head toward the grave. They have to already know what's up. I'm wearing khakis and a button-down for goodness sake. Plus, I bought a bouquet of sunflowers for Kara and a gift card to a coffee house for Gabe.

I'm not going to say I'm trying to buy my way into their family … but I am.

Kara lays a sunflower on Declan's grave and then faces me expectantly. Gabe puts his hands in his pockets.

"I brought you here because I want to … I want to ask the two of you, with Declan here also, for your permission to marry Carter." To say I'm suddenly nervous is an understatement. I've gone over this a thousand times, but this is the first time I've legitimately considered that they might say they don't give me their permission. I fumble in my pocket for the box with ring in it. I took all kinds of "What's her style?" surveys and drug Jason's wife shopping to finally find the perfect ring for my girl. I open the case.

Kara gasps. "Yes!"

I stare at her. Gabe does, too. "You're not the one marrying him, Kara, but you sound like it."

Kara covers her mouth and laughs. "I do, don't I? I just mean, yes, of course you have my permission. We love you and want you to be a permanent part of our family."

"You do?"

"Of course. You've loved her and cared for her more than anyone else has. Well, other than Gabe and I."

I can't help but smile. I've made a career out of loving Carter. I mean, I even went as far as to name her section of our store "Hart's Home." Not just because she's become a sought-after admin and designer, but because I want her to be everywhere. I'd rename the town and planet, maybe even change language system, if it could all center around Carter Hart.

"Gabe?" I ask.

Gabe stares at me, then the ring. After a minute he

finally nods. "Yeah. I say yeah."

"Really?" I ask. Even if I'm at *somewhat dislike*, I'm still baffled.

"It was hard for me to like you because you were just another man in her life who was disappointing her. Between her dad and Declan, all I wanted was for her to find a man who would stand by her and love her the way she deserves. I had a picture in my mind of what that was, admittedly. Luke, mostly."

I snort, because Gabe petitioned hard-core for Carter to date Luke after she was shot, but she refused. Thankfully, he accepted it and gave up. Gabe must be mentoring him because occasionally he mentions him. Carter's made a couple of friends who she'll say *would be great for Luke*. I'm sure he's a great guy, but I'm glad he wasn't the right guy for Carter.

"I wanted Carter to be with someone who loved her more than himself, who could challenge her and accept being challenged, and who would recognize what a beautiful gift she is. Most of all, I wanted someone to give her the best life possible," he continues. "Took me longer than it should've to realize you've got that checklist covered." He motions around us. "You brought us here, for God's sakes. If that's not a show of love, I don't know what is."

"Do you think he'd be okay with it, too?" I ask.

"Why're you asking that? Of course, Declan would want you to marry Carter," Kara assures me. "There's no doubt in my mind that this is the life he would've wanted for you both."

"Thank you," I say.

"Now, give me a hug and let me touch that ring."

#

I should've expected it, but Kara and Gabe's "yes" comes with a demand: in order to have their official permission, they have to be here when I ask Carter.

Kara said, to be exact, "I'll even hide in the bushes if you need me to."

Of course, I wasn't about to make Kara and Gabe hide in the damn bushes. Instead, I tell them to hide behind the jungle gym until I've asked Carter.

I decided to be less bleak and not include Declan in this part. Instead, I want it to be somewhere where I feel like Carter and I's relationship is immortalized—the park. Even if the swings down represent our best moments, it's a place where I've felt my love for her has burned the strongest.

Outside of the bedroom, of course, but that doesn't need to be known by Kara and Gabe.

Carter doesn't seem to think anything is out of the ordinary. She's just her usual fun, witty self. We went to dinner before we came here, so she's dressed in a pretty romper, with her hair curled and wearing lipstick that makes her lips look delicious.

Right now she's swinging, talking about something I'm not listening to. I can't hear her over my heart banging in my ears. When she goes up past me, I take the chance to sit up and get down on one knee.

As soon as she swings backward and sees me, she stops talking and her mouth opens wide. She sails past me a few times, looking completely dumbfounded. Eventually she shoves a sandaled toe into the ground and comes to a halt. "Boone Fell, are you doing what I think you're doing?"

"I'm asking you to marry me, Junebug. I'm asking you to become Carter Fell and spend the rest of your life with me. The past two years have been the best of my life. For the first time, I'm proud of myself and I'm excited for the future. That's all thanks to you. You've helped me to become a better friend, boyfriend and, hopefully soon, husband. So, June Carter Hart, will you marry me?"

Unlike her sister, Carter doesn't blurt out an answer. Instead she covers her mouth with her hand and starts crying, nodding her head fervently.

"You can't ever be done with me if you do," I remind her. "You and me always."

"I want that," she manages and then launches toward me for a hug. I have to fight to stay upright.

From their hidey-hole, Gabe and Kara cheer. Carter, almost strangling me with love at this point, moves to see them. "You're here?" she asks.

"Of course!" Kara says as they walk toward us. She and Gabe are both crying because that's what they do. "I'm not going to miss one of my kid's happiest moments."

"Me either," Gabe says. "Plus, I wanted to make sure he did this thing right."

"Did I?" I ask.

Carter waves him off and then moves my face toward hers. She kisses me deeply. It's the best kind of yes.

#

Four Years Later

"So, how're you holding up?" Jason asks, slapping my back.

"I'm still trying to wrap my mind around being married to the love of my life," I answer, tearing my gaze away from my now-wife. She's talking with some of Gabe's doctor friends. Gabe has his arm around her waist, playing the role of the proud father.

Jason chuckles. "You never will. Trust me."

I believe him. When I proposed to her, I was still trying to get used to the idea that Carter would want to *date* me. After I got a ring on her finger, it turned into wondering why she'd want to *marry* me. Now she wants to spend the rest of her life with me, and all I can really say is I'm the luckiest guy in the universe. No one else gets to grow up with Carter, become best friends with her, fall in love with her, and marry her. She's mine, and I'm hers.

Forever.

I clench my teeth, fighting back a world of tears. Carter's stayed strong through this whole thing, but I've been a blubbering fool. I thought I'd only cry when I first saw Carter, but it's been that and more, starting with last night.

While Carter was spending the night with Gabe and Kara, I went to visit Declan. I've been bad about seeing him because I still envision Carter bleeding out on his grave. But I wanted to tell him that no matter how many seats we filled, there was always going to be one person missing. Hell, he would've been my best man. Might've walked Carter down the aisle with Gabe.

After that, I just gave up on steeling away emotions and all that shit. One look at Carter in her wedding gown and I'm lost to everything. The memory of her walking down that aisle toward me is on replay in my mind, even when I'm not looking at her.

"You're holding up stronger than I did," Jason says.

"Yeah, well, the thing about this family is they're all sympathetic criers. If one of 'em starts crying, they all do."

"Even Gabe?"

I snort. "Even Gabe." I didn't think I'd ever see eye-to-eye with the man, but we managed to become something like friends. Somewhere along the line, he realized we both want what's best for Carter, and we've only moved forward from there. "Speaking of which, I guess I'd better go get my socialization on."

"Of everything from my wedding, that's the one thing I hated."

"Yeah, well, I plan on blocking the experience out of my mind the second I get the chance." It's my turn to slap him on the back now. "Thanks for playing best man today. And for letting me borrow your kids."

"They stole the show. Cutest flower girls I've ever seen."

"I'll ignore your first comment and agree with the second."

I leave him and walk across Gabe and Kara's backyard to where Carter is talking. We decided to do the backyard wedding because our best memories are outside, a lot of them being where the trellis used to be (Gabe took it down after he caught me in Carter's room once, but the purpose was defeated because Carter moved in with me soon after).

Carter doesn't notice me heading toward her, giving me the time I need to prepare myself. I can charm her pants off, but the whole love thing still leaves me stuttering. I don't think I'll ever get used to it.

She's breathtaking. Her hair is pinned back with her veil tucked in it. Her dress is huge and what you'd picture in a fairytale, catching the light and sparkling. Better than anything is the gold band on her finger that matches mine. I can almost feel them pulling us together like magnets, reminding us we have forever to look forward to.

I sneak up and wrap my arms around her from behind, then nuzzle my face in her neck, not caring who I'm interrupting. She laughs and kisses my cheek. Her hands cover mine, holding me where I am.

"Hey, wife," I murmur, pressing my lips against her skin. I can feel a blush brew from her collarbone toward her face. "I love you."

"I love you, too, husband," she whispers back.

"Gabe, we're going to get to the cake before it disappears," one of the men she was talking to says. I look up and see the same guy whom I met a few years ago in this very backyard: Luke. Even though that wasn't under the best of terms, he gives me a nod now before they all walk off. As if I needed any more of a reminder about what I already know: I'm lucky Carter decided to give me her heart.

When all of the doctors are gone, Gabe mutters something under his breath, then, "What are you doing, Kara?"

I can't help thinking the same thing when I notice Kara. She's coming toward us with her mom and dad in tow. I can count the times I've met Ray on one hand and the number of times he's talked to me ... shit, he's *never* talked to me. Probably because I went off on him once when he tried to dig into Carter.

"Carter, you look absolutely stunning," Deirdre gushes. "You're radiant."

Carter untangles from me to hug her. Their relationship is strange to me, but there's a whole lot of strange to the way we both grew up, so I guess I shouldn't question it. The only thing I can guess is Deirdre stopped looking at Carter like the product of an affair and more like a granddaughter. She even helped plan the wedding.

The same can't be said for Ray, of course, who doesn't look at Carter as anything. Good thing she doesn't look at him as anything either.

"Isn't she?" Kara says, nearly bouncing up and down. She's beaming. You'd think she's wearing the wedding dress instead of her maroon maid-of-honor dress. "I'm just so proud." She looks up from Carter and grabs my hand. "Of them both."

Kara's always reminded me of those videos or stories where an animal starts mothering all these other species because they don't have a mom. Even though I'm only a few years younger than her, she's taken me on as if I'm her family. The only thing I'm excluded from—which I think is just out of mercy—is the monthly dinners. Guess that won't be the case now that I've officially married into the family.

Deirdre clears her throat, giving Ray a look. Ray glares at her, then reaches into his suit coat. He pulls out a card with our names on it in decorative handwriting—clearly Deirdre's. "Here," he says, holding it out. I take the card, eyeing it like a poisonous snake.

"Tell them why you're giving it to them," Deirdre prompts.

"It's a gift from us."

"Because ..."

"Because Carter is my daughter."

"And ..."

"And I did the same thing for Kara and Gabe."

I hand the card to Carter to open. She does so carefully, and after she's read the front and opened it, she gasps. I nearly choke. There's a check inside written for an obscene amount of money.

"Wow," Carter says, out of breath. "That's ... wow. Thank you."

Her dad doesn't say anything. Deirdre grins. One guess can tell you how this check came to be.

Kara reaches for the card. "Why don't I put this somewhere safe? That way we can be *sure* it gets to the bank."

Her dad grunts. "We should be going."

"No, we're staying," Deirdre says. "We still have to eat cake, *and* I'm dancing with Carter and Kara later."

She drags him off toward the direction of the cake. "Well, that was a wedding miracle if I've ever saw one," I say with a grunt.

Gabe laughs. "Welcome to the family. They're included. Luckily, I know how to hide."

"Ugh, Gabe!" Kara says.

I grin. "Teach me your ways." We all laugh but stop when I notice someone else we need to talk to hanging out at one of the tables. I lace my hand through Carter's. "How about we get all of the parents out of the way at once?"

We hug Kara and Gabe, then head over to him. He's been dry for two and a half years now, thanks to a woman he met at church. She wasn't able to make it today, so I'm was surprised he would still come. He's dressed in a button-down I didn't know he owned and a pair of slacks. With his gray hair combed back and his face not as gaunt, he's nearly unrecognizable. We aren't on the best of terms, but we're on better terms than we've been. I don't think we'll ever be in a place where my entire childhood is erased.

"Hi, Dad."

He looks up from the table and gives me a shaky smile. "Son."

"Thanks for coming," Carter says in a rush. "It means a lot to us."

"Good. Good." He stands up and starts fishing around in his pocket. "Listen, I, uh, know I wasn't the best father, and this whole thing has made me realize that, uh, we ..." He trails off when he finds a black box. He doesn't finish what he was saying, which is probably as much of an amends or an apology as I'm ever going to get. He opens the box up and pulls out a ring. "This was Boone's mother's wedding ring and I'd like you to have it, Carter."

I blink.

"That was mom's?"

"Yeah."

Carter takes it and holds it out to me. I look at it in her palm. I've never seen anything of my mom's, and this ring has almost got me in a trance. I reach out and touch it, imagining I'll feel her or hear her.

"This means a lot to us," Carter tells my dad. "We'll treasure it."

"Well," he says and looks away. "Sorry." He doesn't say anything else, and I don't know what he's sorry for—his actions, not having words to say, everything. Before I can ask, he leaves. I'm not sure that I want to know.

"Now that was a miracle," Carter says with awe. "Do you want it for yourself? I'm not sure what we could do, but we could have the diamond reset ..."

"No." I close her hand over the ring, looking up at her. "I want you to wear it." I try to keep my hand steady as I pull back. My hands have been working against me all day—going berserk when I shook Gabe's hand during the ceremony, when I slipped Carter's wedding band on her finger, and now. "I've been thinking lately about how ... I haven't had anyone who fills in the gaps for me like you do. Maybe when my mom passed, she guided me to you. It might be weird or stupid …"

She manages to slip the ring on then cups her warm hands over my cheeks. She wobbles in her heels as she stands up on her toes. "It's *not*. I love you for thinking that way, because I believe you're right."

"Thank you." I press my lips against hers. "I want you to keep it because of that."

"If that's what you want."

"I do." I back away from her but twine my hand with hers. "Speaking of what I want, I'd like to give you something."

She gives me a curious smile. "Okay."

"We, uh, have to go inside the house."

Her smile falters. "Lead the way, husband."

I chuckle, loving the way that sounds. Luckily, no one questions us for leaving. I'm sure it means they're only taking the opportunity to *silently* judge us. All I can say is that we're a married couple and we're allowed to disappear as much as we want. I just want a minute alone with my wife.

"I think we should save this part for the honeymoon, Mr. Fell," she teases.

"Is that what you really want, Mrs. Fell?" I joke back as I push open her old bedroom door. She follows me in, not noticing anything out of the ordinary. For a split second, I can't even remember why I brought her here. All I can hear is the *Mr. and Mrs. Fell* part of things.

I reach for her, ignoring the massive amount of fabric surrounding her. I'd gladly die of suffocation if it meant getting to kiss her. She immediately moves her hands toward my tie, pushing it aside to find the buttons of my shirt. I lost my suit coat somewhere between the pictures and cutting the cake. I'm glad for it. Fewer clothes we have to remove and find later.

Our mouths ravish each other, fighting to be closer. Whatever magnetism it is between the rings—or us—it feels as if it were at full force. It could just even be the pure magic of knowing she and I belong together now. We're not only facing the world together, but we're now facing a future. Loving her was the best decision I've ever made in my life, but letting her love me was the turning point.

The backs of my knees hit her bed and we topple. Her mass of a dress weighs us down, somehow managing to cocoon us. Or kill us.

"If you're trying to murder me for the life insurance money ..." I trail off, grinning up at her.

She falls into a fit of laughter, struggling to get up off me and the bed to right herself. When she's up, she pats down at the dress, red in the face. When she looks up, her fit of giggles cuts off.

"What is that?"

My grin grows. "My gift."

Her eyes are wide and her eyebrows are nearly touching her hairline. This is an expression I hope I remember forever. "You did that for me?"

"Yep. With the help of your sister and Alex."

I track her as she passes the bed and heads straight for what I've spent the last two months stressing over. I had Jason sneak it up here, with the help of Gabe, when we had some downtime today. I'm just glad they got it up here without damaging the thing.

It's a huge collage of all of the notes I've ever written her, including the bad ones. I had Alex and Kara do the gluing because that part made me nervous as hell. I might be handy, but I'm not artsy. The one thing I did attempt to do that turned out well was welded some metal together to make little flowers. The girls spent time adding plastic gems and glitter to them to make them stand out. There's only a few so not to distract for the notes, but Kara said it would make the creation stand out. She was right.

Carter runs her fingers along the notes, focusing the longest on the ones that are my favorite. When she lands on *Because I loved you too much,* she turns to look at me with tears in her eyes.

"This is gorgeous, Boone."

I walk toward her and wrap my arms around her. "You like it."

"I love it. It means everything to me that you made this. You're the best man in the entire world. I love *you,* Boone. So much."

I kiss her head, squeezing my eyes shut. "We've got a whole history, Carter. It's longer than any road map can show, and I just wanted it to be a part of our new beginning."

This time, when we kiss, I think of how I don't have to leave her notes anymore because I can tell her everything. She's my best friend, my wife, and the woman whom I used to write to in search of a future. The truth is, she is my future, just like she is my past and present.

My *everything.*

ACKNOWLEDGEMENTS

This book started in my senior capstone course at Northern Kentucky University. The first few pages were probably terrible, but the love and support of my amazing classmates and professor, Kelly Moffett, helped me continue forward and turn this into a full-length novel (and not just leave it an electronically-dusty file on my laptop). The first half would be impossible to read without (fantastic friend, genius poet, and future Ph.D.) Brittany Smart, thanks to her edits and critique. The entirety of *Sort of Normal* wouldn't be what it is now without my editor, Yezanira E. Venecia, who's keen eye and kindness shaped it even further. Thank you to everyone who has been involved in every step of this process!

I am also unbelievably, indescribably thankful to Melissa Keir and Inkspell Publishing. You made my dreams come true by bringing my writing to life!

And, of course, I wouldn't be here without the most important people in my life: my boyfriend, mom and dad. Nathan, your love helped me look at this novel with fresh eyes and your devotion to music inspires me to keep writing. Mom and Dad, you've always supported and loved me no matter what—whether I'm an elementary schooler writing crappy books or a published author. You've molded me into the woman I am and no amount of dedications, awknowledgements or Facebook shout-outs can put that into words.

CHECK OUT...ANOTHER BOOKS BY LIZ ASHLEE

Step One: We admitted we were powerless over alcohol-that our lives had become unmanageable.

There are twelve steps in Alcoholics Anonymous and Silas Manning knows all of them by heart. He's been living them since a drunk driving accident resulted in the destruction of three lives. When he meets Rooney Oliver, he quickly realizes you can be addicted to things other than alcohol—you can be addicted to people, too.

Rooney's mother is dying and Rooney feels like she's dying with her. It's not until Silas comes into their lives that any of them start feeling hope—but Silas isn't ready to let go of the past or open himself up to a future.

Sometimes the only person who you want to lose is yourself.

AVAILABLE IN EBOOK AND PRINT
AT ALL MAJOR BOOK RETAILERS

Beaches, boyfriends and danger...summer is certainly hot! Grab a hold tight as these eight authors wow you with stories from sweet to sizzling! After all, every day can have some summer fun!

Breaking Girl Code by Brooke Moss

Aubrey is having the perfect evening out, with the perfect guy, on a perfect summer night. The problem is... Preston's not her date. His real date is her B.F.F., and she's passed out in the backseat.

Wishing on Water by Liz Ashlee

After watching everyone's else's lives hit huge milestones, all Hope wants is to escape to her boring, unchanging, single life. So, where's the one logical place to escape to? *A retirement home.*

Art with a Pulse by Clara Winter

Artist Alice finds herself rescuing a seal on the sands of Laguna Beach with screenwriter Elijah. Can Alice put her past behind her and give Elijah the chance he deserves?

A Natural Passion by Tammy Mannersly

How will marine biologist, Dylan O'Day, solve the illegal poaching problem threatening the ecosystem he loves and protects when the gorgeous, new intern, Kyra Shine, is occupying his every thought?

You Had Me at Aloha by Sarah Vance Tompkins

Social media guru Vivienne Parker's dream trip to Hawaii turns into a nightmare when her roommate in the luxurious surf shack is the hot Olympic athlete who just got her fired.

More Than Puppy Love by Kitsy Clare

Fireworks spark when Arianna, a city girl with an elite pet portrait business is in a wreck and asks Dave a country auto mechanic for help, but can these two beagle owners from different worlds see eye to eye?

Stealing Haven by Mark Love

Sand, sun, romance and a mystery to solve. Sounds like a perfect vacation for Jamie.

Harmony in the Key of Murder by Melissa Kay Clarke

Summer in the South can mean a different type of heat when a newly appointed investigator and a mechanical genius cross paths leading to murder and love.

AVAILABLE IN EBOOK AND PRINT AT ALL MAJOR BOOK RETAILERS.

ABOUT THE AUTHOR

Liz Ashlee is a romance novelist who is known for *Step Toward You* and "Wishing in on Water" in the *Once Upon a Summer* collection. She has her Bachelors in Library Informatics and English from Northern Kentucky University. She lives in Independence, KY with her parents, their three cats, and her dog, Hero. Her pride and joy is getting to be a dog-mother, friend, and daughter to those in her life.

Facebook:
https://www.facebook.com/LizAshleeAuthor/?ref=book marks
Twitter: https://twitter.com/LizAshleeAuthor
Instagram:

https://www.instagram.com/lizashleeauthor/?hl=en